Praise for the Thicke

"With careful attention to detail, emotion, and scene-setting, C. J. Darlington scores with her debut effort."
JERRY B. JENKINS, *New York Times* best-selling author and owner of the Christian Writers Guild, on *Thicker than Blood*

"Darlington's setting in the fascinating world of antiquarian bookselling is clever . . ."
Publishers Weekly, on *Thicker than Blood*

"Great job! You kept me turning the pages."
FRANCINE RIVERS, *New York Times* best-selling author, on *Bound by Guilt*

"C. J. is a wonderful, talented writer . . . extraordinary. . . ."
BODIE THOENE, best-selling author of the Jerusalem Chronicles series, A.D. Chronicles series, and more.

"A true page-turner, this tale uses the mystery and suspense to keep readers entertained. But it's the characters who will enthrall."
Crosswalk.com on *Bound by Guilt*

". . . a fresh tale . . . every reader will find a part of his or her own life within these covers."
TOSCA LEE, best-selling author of *Iscariot*, *Havah*, and the Book of Mortals series with Ted Dekker, on *Bound by Guilt*

"a tension filled, heartfelt book.. . . . This is a book that will touch your heart, mind, and emotions.
The Suspense Zone on *Bound by Guilt*

"Darlington's stellar storytelling rivals that of any seasoned pro!"
RT Book Reviews, on *Bound by Guilt*

". . . [A] delightful inspirational story. *Ties that Bind* is a winner!
Fresh Fiction

"C. J.'s characters remain real, honest and incredibly powerful."
LORI TWICHELL, RadiantLit.com, on *Ties that Bind*

FOR Julie —

RUNNING ON EMPTY

Thank you for your
support!

In Him,

Also by C. J. Darlington

Thicker than Blood
Bound by Guilt
Ties that Bind
Jupiter Winds

RUNNING
ON
EMPTY

C. J. DARLINGTON

Mountainview Books, LLC

ACKNOWLEDGMENTS

As an author, I get my name on the cover of any book I write, but readers sometimes don't realize there are many people who have worked behind the scenes and deserve just as much credit. A network of support is vital for writers, and I am blessed to be able to call my family mine. I don't know what I'd do without my mom's skilled editing skills. She always catches things I miss and makes any book I write stronger and deeper. My sister Tracy is a never-ending encouragement and a faithful first reader. When she laughs at something I tried to make funny or asks me about a character as if they are real, it brings me great joy. I love you guys so much! While I often write of dysfunctional families, I am thankfully not writing about my own.

Several others had a part in this story, including:

James Scott Bell—your kindness has meant a great deal to me over the years. I've learned so much from you, including the importance of having a positive attitude in this ever changing publishing world.

Janice Cantore—you pushed me to strengthen the ending of this book, and because of your suggestion, I dug deeper. I'm so glad I did.

Deena Peterson—for beta reading and offering encouragement. You are a true blessing to authors.

Special thanks to the real-life Ron Mangini (who is very much alive!) for lending me the use of your family's name. It's an honor, "Uncle" Ron.

Finally, a huge thank you to everyone who's read the Thicker than Blood series. I hope you enjoy this one.

1

Elk Valley, Colorado

Del Mangini recounted the wrinkled bills in her wallet as if the act could multiply them. Nineteen dollars. That had to be enough.

She approached the shortest of the checkout lines behind a tanned, fortyish woman in pink running gear. Del eyed the mountain of fresh vegetables, bags of fruit, and huge pack of T-bones the woman loaded onto the conveyer belt.

Her stomach growled, and by the woman's surreptitious glance she knew she wasn't the only one who heard it. Del stared down at her Goodwill-bought sneakers with the knot-repaired laces, embarrassment rising up her neck. She'd skipped breakfast and lunch to put three gallons in her ancient Chevy Malibu.

Plunk!

A bag of raw, organic almonds landed on Del's foot. She slowly picked it up.

"Excuse me, but those are mine." The woman snatched the nuts from her and tossed them on the belt.

Del tried to pretend she didn't care, but it had been months since she'd eaten anything that didn't come out of a can or box, and the proof lay in her grocery basket: loaf of Wonder bread, two boxes of spaghetti, quart of 2% milk, store-brand cornflakes, crunchy peanut butter, and her one splurge—a jar of pesto marinara sauce. If she added a little water, she could stretch it to last a week.

The teenage checker's scanner beeped like a pulse monitor, and when it was finally Del's turn, she lifted her basket onto the belt and watched as each price flashed on the screen.

"Total's twenty three seventeen." The checker popped her gum.

"But . . . I thought the pasta was on sale."

"Ended yesterday."

"Are you sure?"

"I can check." The teen reached for the phone receiver beside the register.

Del glanced at the fidgeting line behind her, clearly imagining their unvoiced thoughts about the sorry-looking young woman quibbling about a fifty-cent savings. She shook her head and pushed the marinara sauce to the side. "It's okay. I'll just come back for this later."

The clerk shrugged, and with a punch of a few buttons brought the total down. Del handed over her bills and escaped from the grocery store knowing she wouldn't be back. Couldn't be, actually. She headed across the parking lot. A flash of pink caught her eye, and she spotted the woman in the running suit loading her groceries into a shiny Escalade. Her back was turned, her cart unattended. One quick sprint and Del knew she could grab one of those bags before the woman would catch her.

She walked closer.

The woman swung around, and Del spun on her heels. What was she *doing*? She should be mapping out the next business to ask for a job, not thinking about stealing someone's groceries.

But how was she going to get through the month on nineteen dollars' worth of food?

She climbed into her rusted car. If she sold it she might get a couple hundred to keep her floating, but then where would she be? She couldn't walk everywhere.

Closing her eyes, desperation built in her chest as it had every day she watched her meager cash supply dwindle and every job opportunity slip through her fingers. She should've just slept with Eric.

Del blew air through her lips in frustration. It had been three months since she caught him swiping cash from the bank deposit at It's Only Natural Foods where they both worked. He swore he'd tell the owner, who happened to be his grandmother, that it was Del if she didn't give him what he really wanted. She refused, and the next day she was fired. Del tried to tell her side of the story and convince the owner she'd done nothing wrong, but she didn't believe Del.

In a town the size of Elk Valley, word spread like the wildfires that swept up the west slope of the Spanish Peaks last year, and no one in town would hire her. But even without her tarnished reputation, she didn't have much chance anyway. Her resume consisted of random fast food jobs and a stint helping a now-dead old cowboy break mustangs.

As she reached to start the engine, the Chevy's passenger door opened and a man climbed into her car, sat down, and slammed the door shut.

"Hey!" She pulled back her fist to punch him with all she had.

He raised his hands. "I'm sorry! I'm sorry! I should've knocked."

"Get out of my car!"

The man kept his hands up as if in surrender. He wore dark jeans, a red Rockies T-shirt, and a ball cap with a bill so frayed she could see the cardboard along its edge.

1

"I said get out!"

"Please just listen to me."

Did he have a gun? Was this a carjacking? She should get out and run. But something about him made her pause. If he wanted the car, wouldn't he have demanded that already?

"I'm going to reach into my shirt pocket," he said, pulling out a business card then slowly lowering his hand. "Are you Del Mangini?"

She stared at the man. With a ruddy complexion and graying stubble on his chin he looked like he was probably pushing fifty. "Who are you?"

"So I was right."

"You've got ten seconds to tell me what this is about before you're going to regret you set foot in my car."

He gave her a hesitant smile. "Right. I'm David Kirsch. A PI."

"What?"

"Private investigator."

"I know what PI—"

"I've been trying to find you for a month."

Great. Like she didn't have enough on her plate. She gripped her door handle hard. This guy was probably packing, but would he dare threaten her during business hours at a grocery store? Maybe, maybe not. Daylight hadn't stopped those thugs the cops picked up in Walsenburg a few months ago when they'd shot and nearly killed a woman for her purse.

"You've been trying to find *me*?"

"Not the easiest thing."

Maybe she should run after all.

"Why?" Del asked, scanning the parking lot. The lady in pink was gone. A guy her age was gathering up the shopping carts and pushing a huge line of them toward the entrance. If she screamed he would hear.

"I need to find your mother."

Del swung toward this strange man who'd violated her privacy. Kirsch tried to hand her the business card. She didn't take it.

"My mother?"

"Yes."

She laughed. "You're kidding, right?"

Kirsch's head tilted ever so slightly, and his expression remained serious. Okay, so he wasn't kidding.

"And why do you need to find her?" Del asked.

"Can't say."

"Who hired you?"

"That's confidential."

"I think you got your wires a little mixed up."

A faint smile played on Kirsch's lips again. "I'm good at what I do."

Yet it took him a month to find her. Somehow she found satisfaction in that. She had intended to drop off the radar from her old life in Pennsylvania, and apparently it worked.

"Not *that* good, because I'm your dead end." Del fingered her keys. Her stomach still gnawed for food.

Kirsch leaned forward, trying to catch her eye again. "Come on."

"Okay, you got me. I'll tell you where she is."

The PI stared at her, like he was trying to figure out if she was bluffing. "I'd appreciate it."

"Pennsylvania."

Kirsch blinked. She wondered if his ego was crushed for being so far off.

"At a place called Green Meadows," Del said.

Kirsch pulled out a smartphone and started tapping notes into it. "Thank you."

"Cemetery," Del said.

He looked up.

"I meant a literal dead end. My mother's buried there."

Clearing his throat, Kirsch paused with his finger hovering over the phone. "I'm sorry, but—"

"Time to leave, Sherlock. Now."

"But—"

"I obviously can't help you."

"Your *biological* mother."

It was Del's turn to stare.

"I know your adoptive parents passed away." Kirsch's expression was sympathetic. "Apologies for not being clear on that, but I'm trying to find your birth mother."

"My birth mother is buried in that cemetery."

"Are you sure?"

"What do you mean am I sure?"

"What was her name?"

"Listen, I don't know what game you're—"

"They didn't tell you, did they?"

The air in the car suddenly seemed to thin, and Del felt like she was on the summit of Mount Everest struggling for oxygen. She knew what he was implying, but she didn't want to entertain it. Her parents loved her, meant the world to her, and had died heroes.

Kirsch tapped again on his phone then turned it toward her. A woman's photo stared back, and Del had to do a double-take. The woman's dark blonde hair was wilder than her own, which she kept at shoulder length, but even she couldn't deny the resemblance.

"Her name's Natalie," Kirsch said.

"You're pulling my leg, right?"

"I think you know I'm not."

Del paged through memory after memory of her parents, a cognitive slideshow. Had they ever mentioned something, anything, to mean they weren't her real parents? She came up empty. So she didn't look like them. That was no big deal, right? She'd always assumed she took after some distant relative to explain why she'd ended up five foot two with parents who both played basketball in college. Or why two Mediterranean beauties had ended up with a towhead child.

Kirsch set his business card on the console between them. Embossed with silver lettering, probably on purpose to make himself look more legit. But any lug could buy cards online. This could bee one big con. But what would be the purpose in that?

"Are you sure you have the right girl?" Del asked.

He slipped his phone into his shirt pocket. "Like I said, I'm good."

"Get out of my car."

Kirsch gave one nod, as if he knew their conversation really was over, and exited as quickly as he entered. She watched him walk across the parking lot and climb into a black pickup. He touched the bill of his cap then drove away.

She flipped the locks and sat frozen in her seat.

2

Main Street
Elk Valley, Colorado

Del cringed when she pulled into her driveway. Situated on one of the last streets in town that didn't abut the golf course, the house was owned by a husband and wife who rented out the small apartment above their garage.

Del thought she hit the lottery when she found it. The online ad called it clean and tidy with a bedroom, bath, kitchenette, and living room. All she needed at a price she could just manage. But that was before her wages were cut and before she lost her job entirely.

She was behind three months' rent now. And both her landlords were home.

Grabbing her grocery bag, Del pretended she didn't notice the curtain part in the front window and took quick strides to the steps leading up to her apartment. The encounter with the PI still had her shaken up. Careful to keep her steps light on the stairs, she made it inside before she heard footsteps coming up behind her.

She locked her deadbolt and thought about locking herself in the bathroom. But she couldn't run away forever.

The knocks pounded at the flimsy, fiberboard apartment door.

Del set her bag on the threadbare loveseat she'd picked up at a garage sale. It faced the wall where the TV used to sit before she pawned it.

Another pound on the door. "I know you're in there."

She couldn't avoid this. They had a key and weren't afraid to use it. "I'm coming."

Del flung the door open and stared at her landlady, Tiffany Lopez. As short as Del but with a good fifty pound advantage, Lopez glared with her hands on ample hips.

"You can't hide from me, girl."

"I know," Del said.

"Three months." Tiffany scanned the room as if searching for the big purchase Del bought instead of paying her rent. "We've been patient."

That wasn't exactly true. The week after she'd missed her first payment, Tiffany and her husband Benny burst into her apartment unannounced when she was still asleep and demanded she pay them on the spot.

She was out of excuses. "I don't have the money."

Tiffany's eyes seemed to grow smaller. She smelled like the cigarettes she consumed outside on the porch every morning. "You think we're pushovers?"

"No, I—"

"I don't want to involve the cops . . ." Tiffany Lopez leaned forward. "But I will."

Nineteen dollars was all she had, and now that was gone. There was nothing left to sell. She barely had a suitcase full of clothes, and most of them were old and worn anyway. She'd applied for welfare last month, but she hadn't heard back from anyone, despite numerous phone calls trying to figure out where she'd gone wrong with her paperwork.

"I could do some odd jobs for you. Work it off." She

hated the desperation in her voice. She'd made the suggestion before to Benny, but he'd taken it as a jab to his manhood.

Tiffany didn't like the idea any better. She looked at Del like she'd just suggested she write her into their will.

"If you can't pay up in five days, you're gonna have to leave."

"I've been trying to find a job, Mrs. Lopez, I really have."

"Good for you."

"But no one's hiring."

"Not so good."

"If you'll just give me a little more time, I'm sure I can—"

Tiffany abruptly raised her hand to silence her. "No. No more excuses."

"I'm not a deadbeat. I just didn't expect to lose my job."

With a snort, Tiffany rolled her eyes. "This is a small town, girl."

Which meant she knew every lie Eric had spread. Del moved to shut the door an inch, but Tiffany pushed her bulk closer, the cigarette smoke now mixed with some weird, flowery perfume. Del could see clearly Tiffany's penciled eyebrows and how one was lower than the other.

"I just need a little more time."

"You've had plenty." Tiffany pointed a finger, complete with dark purple nail polish, in Del's face. "You take advantage, and it's going to stop."

Del waved at the living room. "I don't have anything anymore. Where will I go?"

"That's not my problem."

"I know it's not, but you have to understand I'm not trying to—"

"Excuses!" Tiffany shook her head. "That's all you have."

She was right, and desperation clutched at Del. She would have to sell the car. Could she even get five hundred for it?

"I need a little more time," Del almost whispered. "Please."

Tiffany's hand slapped against the doorframe, and Del flinched.

"We can get good money for this apartment! I got a call today from someone who wants to move in next week. What should I say to him?" Tiffany sighed, lowering her arm. "I'm sorry, but it's been too long."

Turning on her heels, she climbed back down the stairs and onto her porch. Del heard the scratchy complaint of the porch swing giving in to the woman's weight, and in a moment a puff of smoke wafted through the air and straight to Del's nose.

She didn't care if she made noise anymore and slammed her door, giving it a kick with the toe of her shoe for good measure. It left a light dent in the wood.

3

Outskirts of Elk Valley, Colorado

S olace could be found outside of town. Way outside.
Del eased the Malibu down the dirt road, each rut sending
the vehicle rocking from side to side. She wiped her eyes with
the back of her hand even as her stomach ached for the meal
she couldn't afford. She couldn't waste gas either, but sitting
alone in her apartment waiting for another Lopez ambush
wasn't an option. In a way, she didn't blame the couple. To
them she was a deadbeat who refused to pay her rent. But what
they didn't know was that she hated it as much as they did.
She'd tried every day for the past month to get hired by someone. She was even willing to scrub toilets at the Presbyterian
church, but they already had a custodian.

Soon she reached the end of the road and parked the car.
She'd have to hike from here to reach her destination. Would
they even be there?

Del hoped so. She needed their comfort.

At the barbed wire fence she carefully spread the wires

apart and stepped through. The aspen grove was her first sign she was near. Through the grass and fallen branches she hiked, glad for the exertion.

When the aspens thinned, she sucked in a breath at the view of the bucolic, golden pasture. She didn't know who this land belonged to, but whoever they were, she envied them. Del breathed in the scent of dried leaves and pine needles, the tension in her body dissipating.

She passed the last trees and walked out into the pasture, shielding her eyes from the sinking sun. Where were they?

Scanning the field, she finally spotted what she'd come for. The herd of twenty horses raised their heads as she approached, instantly wary with ears pricked forward. She recognized the lead mare, a black-and-white Paint whose mane flowed down her neck as pretty as a model's locks.

Prettier, Del decided.

"Hey there, guys," she said. "Haven't seen you in a while."

The herd slowly ambled toward her. She'd discovered them, maybe the ranch's string of work horses, when she'd first moved to Elk Valley. Back then, she'd done a lot of driving around admiring the mountains and came across the dirt access road by chance. Curious, she'd followed it and ended up out here.

Over the months she'd gained the horses' trust, sometimes bringing a carrot or two to share. Today she had nothing to give, but they had something she needed.

Del approached the animals as if they were long lost family. She could talk to them and know they wouldn't lie to her. Or spread rumors. They wouldn't pressure her to do things she swore she'd never do.

The lead mare she affectionately called Queen was the first to reach her. Pressing her nose into Del's outstretched hand, the mare snuffled her whiskers against her fingers checking for a food offering.

"Sorry, girl. I don't even have enough for myself."

Tail swooshing, Queen lowered her head to the grass at Del's feet as if signaling to the others she was okay. The second to approach her was a big gray gelding she called Knight because he stuck to Queen like a medieval knight would. She'd watched him chase others away from the mare if they got too close.

"Keeping out of trouble?" Del didn't hesitate to rub Knight's neck where he loved best, right under his mane. He leaned into her pressure instantly, turning his head in pleasure.

Surrounded now by the horses, Del felt no fear. These weren't wild mustangs, but she knew every horse's first instinct was caution mixed with insane curiosity. Although they were prey animals, they couldn't help themselves.

A nose poked her in the back, and she laughed when she saw it was Jester, the smallest of the bunch. He was pony sized—probably some kid's retired 4-H project—and thought he was in charge. By the nicks and scars on his rump and neck, apparently he had pushed his luck and needed to be reminded of his lowly herd status frequently.

"I *know* you haven't," Del said. She rested her hand on Jester's forehead, scratching the white star intermingled with his speckled coat. Little white hairs shed from the motion, and Del made sure they didn't land in his eyes. Flies gathered at the corners, irritation enough.

The horses calmed her. They were the only thing that could.

"What am I gonna do?" She spotted Ghost, the black mare who was skittish enough to spook at her own tail. She always hung to the outside of the herd like she had to constantly be on watch. Del had yet to touch her. "If I could run like you, I would," she said. "Just get away from everything."

But then what? Without money, she wouldn't last long.

"I can't believe Mom and Dad lied to me," she said to the

next horse, a bay mare she'd dubbed Lady. "I have a biological mother out there somewhere."

Del sighed, stroking Lady's neck, and the mare returned the gesture with a sigh of her own. But should she really be taking the word of some strange private investigator as if it were gospel? How did she know he was telling her the truth?

Suddenly every horse's head snapped up.

Del jumped away from Lady, searching for what startled the herd.

She saw him seconds later. On horseback, the cowboy loped his mount in her direction, yelling something she couldn't understand.

His voice boomed. He held a rifle in his right hand.

Could she escape into the aspens before he arrived?

Not a chance.

He brought his horse to an abrupt sliding stop. The horse's mouth opened from the pressure of his reins.

"What do you think you're doing?"

Del backed away. "I wasn't . . ."

If this man's eyes could kill, she'd be dead. Even with his felt hat pulled low, there was no mistaking the fire.

"This is private property!"

He looked old enough to be her father with the weathered face of a man who'd probably been a cowboy his whole life.

"I . . . didn't know."

"What are you doing?"

"The horses. I was just talking to them."

The cowboy rested the rifle on his chap-covered thigh. "Were you now?"

She was stepping away as fast as she could. "I didn't hurt them. I promise."

"Better not have."

"I didn't."

He took in the herd with a glance. "Get out of here."

She took the cue. When she made it back into the woods, she broke into a jog until she got back to the fence. This time she wasn't so lucky and a barb sliced across her arm, tearing her sleeve.

4

Twenty years ago
Boston, Massachusetts

The waiting was killing her. Natalie gripped the steering wheel with her gloved hands and forced herself to breathe in and out as deeply as she could. Her arms felt like taffy.

They'd been in there too long.

She pressed a button on her watch to light up the time. Sixty-two minutes. Why had she let them talk her into being the lookout? She should be in there ripping down paintings herself. At least then her flowing adrenaline would have an outlet. Out here all she could think about was every way this could go horribly wrong.

"What is taking—"

Then she saw the metallic side door open, and Adam quickly waved her over. Natalie fired up the van's engine and pulled up to the side entrance of the Elizabeth Dutton Stockton Museum. She jumped out, but Adam had gone back in.

Natalie stared at the door where her friends had knocked an hour ago claiming to be police officers responding to a disturbance. She'd watched with her binoculars as they demanded entrance and were allowed inside.

If things had gone as they'd rehearsed, Javier would've told the guard at the security desk he looked familiar and that there was a warrant out for his arrest. It was a ploy to lure the guard out from behind the desk where the museum's only panic alarm was located. The rest was a piece of cake.

At least that's how it went in their best-case scenario.

Natalie wiped sweat from her forehead and scanned the alley. No alarms. No real cops. Nothing. She would've heard something if they'd been caught, right?

The door burst open.

Javier and Adam rushed out, arms loaded with rolled-up canvases. Adam clutched what looked like a Chinese vase.

"Nat, get the door!"

She flung the van's sliding door open, and they carefully laid their prizes on the floor.

"We gotta make another trip," Javier whispered. "There's more."

"Hurry," she said.

Adam barely muffled his laugh. "I was gonna stop for a cup of coffee."

Then they were gone again, and Natalie was left standing by the van with a pile of art worth millions.

5

Present
Elk Valley, Colorado

Darkness had settled by the time Del got back to her apartment. She snuck in and hoped Tiffany and Benny were too busy watching *Jeopardy!* to notice.

Her groceries were right where she'd left them on the couch.

Del scooped up the bag. She had one medium pot she'd managed to hang on to and filled it with water. Once it boiled, she placed a fourth of one of the spaghetti boxes into the water. A pat of butter would have to do for her sauce.

Five minutes later she sat down on the sofa with her pasta and a piece of Wonder bread. She ate the noodles straight from the pot, trying to savor them.

Someone knocked at the door.

She closed her eyes and took another bite of the hot pasta. They just wouldn't leave her alone.

"I get it, okay?" She swung the door open, expecting Tiffany's scowling face.

Instead she faced Eric Borland.

Del tried to shut the door, but he shoved his foot in the way.

"I don't want to talk to you," she said.

"I want to talk to you."

She thought about slamming the door, but it would probably break before he did.

"Then talk," she said.

"It wasn't like you thought," Eric said. He'd buzzed off most of his hair since she'd seen him last and looked like a boot camp inductee. The tanned face and disarming grin would make some girls swoon, and she had a feeling that's what had bugged him the most about her—she was the exception.

"Tell that to your grandma."

"I was mad," he said, trying to push his way in.

Del didn't budge. "That's what I'm going to be if you don't leave me alone."

He laughed in a way that could've put her at ease if she didn't know what kind of guy he really was.

Eric smirked, looking her up and down.

"Listen, I'm not a bad guy," he said. "I thought you felt the same way about me as I felt about you."

"I never led you on."

He shrugged. "I'm a guy. I misread the signals."

"You're not an idiot."

"Why, thank you." A dimple appeared on his cheek.

She wondered if his grandmother still believed he was the golden boy who could do no wrong. Sooner or later it would catch up with him.

"What did you even need that money for?"

His eyes narrowed. "I'm done with that, okay?"

"Like that helps me."

Del had never cared for Eric like he wanted. He was a coworker. He made the customers laugh. She admired him for his smooth selling skills and memory, but that was it.

"I could try to change her mind if you'd reconsider my offer."

She pushed the door hard against his shoulder. "We're done here."

"We don't have to be."

"Don't you get it?" She glared at him. "I didn't have any other way to make a living. And, thanks to you, no one else is hiring me."

"I'm—"

"No you're not." She poked a finger at his chest. "You're not. So you can take your bull and get out of my face before I really lose it."

Eric held up both hands, finally backing up. "Whoa, whoa. Fiery tonight, aren't we?"

This time she did slam the door.

Returning to the sofa, she picked up her pot of spaghetti. The butter had gelled, and the noodles were cold. She ate it anyway.

≈

Cuchara, Colorado

Private investigator David Kirsch loved his job. A stimulating challenge awaited him with each case, and many presented a good excuse to buy a new high-tech gadget and deduct it from his taxes. His cabin was littered with the latest money could buy. From night vision goggles to GPS tracking devices as small as a finger, his inner geek reveled in it all.

He pulled the truck into the driveway of his cabin up in the woods of Cuchara and sat for a moment staring at the structure. This most recent case had him grasping at straws. He'd spent the last month tracking down this elusive Natalie woman. Lo and behold, he'd found her daughter right under his nose in Elk Valley. She had been his last chance, and he was pretty sure she was telling the truth. Which left him back at square one. All he had to directly connect him to Natalie was an email address he'd dug up. But that couldn't tell him her exact location, which is what his client wanted.

Kirsch turned off his dash cam and gave his surroundings a good check. He'd moved into the cabin last year. Remote and quiet, it was just the way he liked it. If he was gonna do half his work on a computer he at least wanted to be comfortable.

He grabbed his camera off the seat. He'd been tracking the girl for a week hoping for clues to her mother's whereabouts, but nothing turned up, which is why he'd risked talking to her in person.

Kirsch bounced his keys up and down in his hand as he walked up to the cabin door. He'd be glad when he closed the book on this case.

Inside, he deposited his gear on the living room recliner and headed into the kitchen.

When he flipped on the light, a man stepped out of the shadows. He could've doubled as a football lineman.

"Wondering when you'd get here."

David stared the intruder down, hoping the man's brain didn't match his brawn.

"Rough day at the office," he said.

The huge man came closer. What hornets' nest had he jumped on this time? He'd riled enough people in his day, but no one had ever dared break into his home. What happened to the security system?

David refused to blink. He would be the lion who protected what was his no matter the cost.

"We can make this real easy," the intruder said. "I ask you questions, you answer, and then I'm on my way."

"Sure you don't want to stay for a drink?"

Sarcasm might buy him time to get to his gun case.

"My boss is getting antsy," the guy said. "And you're holding out. Where's Natalie McGuire?"

"I'm not finished with my investigation."

"I think you are."

David calculated how long it would take to dive toward the man and land a crippling blow. If only he was a few feet closer. He'd clock this guy and teach him a lesson about messing with David Kirsch. This thug was getting nothing from him.

At least that's what he thought before it all went downhill.

6

Elk Valley, Colorado

Del shivered and pulled her blankets tighter, tucking them in under her side. Her heat had been turned off last week. It hadn't been a problem until that cold front moved through bringing in autumn's chill.

She rolled onto her back. First it was that investigator and then Eric's strange appearance at her door. She hadn't seen him since she'd lost her job. Why had he picked today to harass her? And her parents—every time she thought of them she wanted to weep.

A bump came from the living room.

Del opened her eyes. What now? She'd locked the door. There was no reason to be hearing anything at this hour. Since the walls were thin, she sometimes caught the faint undertones of the Lopezes' arguments or the beat of a song playing too loud on the stereo, but they usually went to bed early.

Listening hard, she chalked it up to her imagination, but then she heard it again. Del climbed up on her elbow. That sounded more like a knock, as if someone tapped her door with

25

their foot instead of their hand. Images of Eric coming back flashed in her mind, and a spritz of fear spread through her chest. She wasn't entirely sure what the guy was capable of. Not something she wanted to find out in the middle of the night.

Del threw off her covers, wrapping her arms around herself, and tiptoed into the living room. Hunger still gnawed at her stomach despite her pasta dinner, and she tried to tune it out.

Thump.

There it was again. Definitely coming from her front door.

Del marched over and turned the deadbolt. There were no windows on this side of the apartment and no peephole either. But she wouldn't sleep if she didn't know. Cracking open the door, she peered out into the night. For a moment she saw nothing but darkness. Switching on the porch light, she jumped back when she saw a huge, lanky dog leap to its feet.

"What the—"

Before she could register why a dog would be at her door, something else moved on the ground and Del saw it was a little girl lying on her side. She stirred then slowly sat up. A frayed nylon leash hung around her wrist and connected to the dog's collar. A duffel bag lay under her head.

"What are you doing out here?" Del whispered. She didn't need to wake her landlords.

The girl, who couldn't have been older than nine, squinted in the bright porch light. She quickly scrambled to her feet and reeled the brindle-colored dog closer. Its head nearly reached her chest. A greyhound? They both stared up at Del with sleepy, questioning eyes.

"Are you Del?" the girl asked.

"Who are *you*?"

"Callie. And this is Utah."

"Do you have any idea what time it is?"

The girl nodded. "Late?"

Del glanced down the stairs looking for a car in the drive-way. Where had this girl come from?

"How long have you been out here?"

Wiping her nose with the back of her hand, the girl shrugged.

Del sighed. "Did you run away from home?"

The dog leaned against the child, causing her to almost lose her balance. She rested her hand on its neck. "Laura brought me, but she left."

"Who's Laura?"

"My dad's girlfriend."

"She *left?*"

"Uh-huh."

"Why?"

Glancing at her scuffed Converse sneakers with purple stars drawn on the white toes, the girl's shoulders trembled. She looked up at Del again, and her face scrunched up.

A gust of night air swirled into the apartment, and Del took in the little girl's jeans with holes in both knees. She wore a faded corduroy jacket, but that couldn't be doing much to keep out the cold. Somewhere a door slammed, and Del flipped off the porch light. If her landlords caught wind of a dog any-where on the premises, Del would be out on the street in a heartbeat.

"Can I . . . come in?" the girl asked.

This was not what Del needed. She couldn't get sucked into this kid's sob story. If the cops came looking for her, Del could get into serious trouble.

"Just for a minute," Del said. She locked the deadbolt behind them and turned on the kitchen light. "Get talking, kid. Why are you at my door?"

"I . . ."

Del waved her hand. "What's your name again?"

"Callie," the little girl said.

"How old are you?"

"Eight."

Del crossed her arms and cocked an eyebrow at the young runaway—that had to be what she was—and her skinny dog. The animal sat on his haunches beside the girl, staring straight into Del's eyes as if warning her to tread with care when it came to his charge.

"Let's try this again, okay?" She came over and crouched down in front of the child. "Why did you run away?"

"I didn't run—"

"Kid, it's okay if you did."

"I didn't!"

Del rubbed her tired eyes. Definitely not what she needed. Maybe if she took a more authoritative approach she'd get the truth.

"Okay, you didn't run away, but that doesn't explain why you're lying on my doorstep at one in the morning."

"I didn't want to wake you."

"Well, you did."

"Sorry." Callie sat down in the middle of the floor with the dog resting his head in her lap. She started rummaging in her Adidas duffel bag, which looked like it was three times as old as she.

"So let me get this straight," Del said. "Your dad's girlfriend dropped you off in the middle of the night, and you came up to my apartment for help?"

"She told me you lived here."

"What?"

Callie removed a stuffed lion with buttons for eyes and set it on the floor beside her. The dog sniffed it.

"Wait a minute." Del knelt down in front of the girl. "What are you talking about? This Laura person told you *I* lived here?"

Nodding, Callie handed her a photograph. "You're Del, right?"

She glanced down at the picture. "Yeah, but—"

Del stopped short. It was the same woman the PI had shown her.

Her bio mom.

7

Twenty years ago
U.S. 20, Massachusetts

Natalie stuck to the speed limit so they wouldn't attract attention. Adam had changed into a muscle shirt and shorts and now sat beside her with Javier hovering over his shoulder. They alternated between laughing and whooping and high-fiving each other as she drove.

Javier surprised them with a bottle of champagne complete with plastic flutes. He popped the cork from the back seat, sending it flying into Adam's shaved head.

"Ow!"

"Sorry dude, but we did it!"

"We're not done yet," Natalie said.

"Hard part's over though."

The guys downed their champagne and even she indulged, despite her driving. She needed something to relax her nerves before they made the drop in less than an hour. They were running on fumes and now champagne. No matter. They could crash for a week if they wanted after this.

"I can't believe it," Adam said.

"Piece of cake," Javier responded.

Adam held out his flute for a refill. "A very expensive piece of cake."

All the planning, the lying to family and friends. It had paid off. After tonight they'd each be a hundred thousand dollars richer. Half had been paid when they were hired, the rest would be exchanged tonight when they turned over the loot. Not bad for three college dropouts.

"Did you get what we wanted?" Natalie asked.

"Had to leave the big version of *Self-Portrait*."

She muttered a curse. Rembrandt's 1629 painting would've been the icing on that piece of cake Javier was talking about.

"How much do you think they're worth?"

Adam shook his head. "Don't know. Don't really care, do you?"

"How is he even gonna sell them? No dealer in his right mind would touch them."

Javier snorted. "Who said anything about selling?"

"Why else would—"

"The thrill of owning something priceless?"

"No *reputable* dealer would touch them," Adam added.

As they reached their rendezvous, a truck stop near Shrewsbury, Natalie felt a wave of exhaustion. But when the Mercedes van pulled up beside them and the two men got out, she woke up fast. He'd actually come himself? Was he crazy?

"Is that who I think it is?" Javier mumbled.

"Idiot," Adam responded.

"Rich idiot," Natalie said, trying to sound like her friends and mask the warmth rising up her neck. Since he'd dumped her, she hadn't seen Grant Hudson in person for weeks. All their communication had been strictly business on the phone.

He approached their van, the lights from the truck stop illuminating his face. Natalie had always thought he looked like Brad Pitt in *A River Runs Through It*, and when he had smiled at her from across the cafeteria two years ago, she'd melted despite her better judgment. She melted tonight too.

"Hello, Nat," Grant said as she stepped out of the van and met him beside the cars.

"What are you doing?" she whispered. "If anyone sees—"

"I had to say good-bye."

"We already did. There's nothing more to—"

Grant leaned in and kissed her gently on the lips, effectively cutting off her protest.

"One last time," he said softly, handing her the envelope she knew contained their final payment. Then he turned away and helped unload the van. Within three minutes they were done, and the two vehicles sped away from each other in opposite directions.

While Adam and Javier toasted again, Natalie kept her eyes on the road and pretended she didn't still love Grant Hudson.

∽

Hudson Family Estate
Milton, Massachusetts

"She wasn't good for you."

Grant spun around in his aunt's leather office chair, quickly tucking Natalie's photo into his shirt pocket. Kissing her had brought back so many memories.

At four o'clock in the morning he'd thought himself alone for at least another hour, but as usual, ex-governor April Hudson was full of surprises.

Dressed in a maroon, silk bathrobe, every coiffed gray hair in place, the elder Hudson smiled. "You did the right thing."

"Did I?" Grant couldn't help the edge in his voice.

Blood still raced through his veins from what he'd done earlier that night. He couldn't have Natalie because she wasn't from the right background, but he could pull off the greatest heist in the country. His aunt might control whom he married, but she couldn't control this. He'd risked everything just because he could. Had it been worth it?

"She would only have pulled you down." His aunt came into the study and turned on a lamp, illuminating the built-in oak bookshelves hugging each wall and the oil portrait of herself hanging behind the desk. She'd had it commissioned while still governor. She patted Grant on the shoulder, lasering him with her eyes. "You are made for greatness. That's what I've always said. Sometimes you have to give up the things you love most to reach the greatest heights. Especially if they have long hair and pretty legs." April Hudson chuckled. "Where you're going, there'll be plenty more women. You won't be able to drive them away."

Grant stood up. When his parents died in a plane crash, his aunt and uncle had taken him in and raised him as their own. At six years old his head had spun when he'd first set foot in this mansion and tried to comprehend its size. But April Hudson was a drill sergeant. He couldn't breathe without her approval, and it had stifled him.

"Get some sleep." April Hudson said.

Was he still a child? Grant pushed past his aunt out into the hallway. Later, in the quiet darkness of his own bedroom, Grant curled up in the deep windowsill like he had as a boy. He rested his face against the cool glass, straining for a view of the bay just beyond. Sometimes when the window was open he caught whiffs of the sea, and he would imagine himself a gull gliding above the whitecaps.

The moonlight bathed the ten-acre lawn stretching toward the massive wrought-iron property fence with spiked rail points, an eight-foot-high reminder he could never escape the Hudson name. Grant closed his eyes. April Hudson thought she could control him, but if she had any clue . . .

A sliver of a smile came to Grant's lips. Oh, it *had* been worth it.

8

Present

Elk Valley, Colorado

Laura told me to show you the photo if you didn't believe me."

Del grabbed the picture from the little girl. "How did you get this?"

It was definitely the same woman the PI had shown her. In this photo she was older and her hair was darker, but it was clearly her.

Callie scooted closer on the thin carpet and rested her hand on Del's leg, pointing at the photo. "That's my mommy."

She pried the girl's hand off her thigh.

"And yours too," Callie said.

Del waved the photo in front of Callie. "*This* is your mother?"

Another sleepy nod from Callie. "I don't really remember her."

Del's mind whirred, and she climbed to her feet again. It made no sense. And yet it did. The hard possibility hit her like a tornado.

"Are you serious? This woman is your mother?" She felt like she had to verify one last time in case she'd misunderstood. Del held the photo up to Callie's nose.

"Uh-huh. Which means you're my sister."

This wasn't happening. Not now.

The little girl was fading fast, her eyes drooping. Del prodded the girl's shoulder to keep her awake. "Why didn't you stay with Laura?"

"She didn't want me."

"Why not?"

Callie looked up at her, eyes quickly filling with tears. "I don't know."

Del knelt down beside the girl again. She was screwing this up big time.

"This is just . . . I didn't know I had a sister, okay?"

Callie bobbed her head a few times, and Del sighed. First the bombshell of being adopted, and now this?

Callie pulled the big dog closer, and the animal leaned into her again. In the light Del could better see his mixture of brown, black, and white.

With a feeble smile Callie stroked the dog's back. "He won't bite."

Del gave him a pat on the head. The Lopezes would have a fit if they knew she had a dog in here. "Laura isn't looking for you?"

Callie kept her eyes on Utah. "She's just glad I'm out of her hair."

"What about your dad?"

"He's . . ." Callie pet the dog faster and wouldn't look at Del.

Had she said the wrong thing?

"He died," Callie said.

Del blew out a breath. "I'm sorry, kid."

"I miss him."

She nodded and focused on the whimpering little girl sitting in front of her. She didn't want to upset her more, but she needed to know everything she could. If the girl's father was dead, and no one could find her mother, was this girlfriend Laura her legal guardian?

"When did your mom leave?" Del asked.

"I was little."

"Did Laura try to find her?" She didn't think the girl would understand the rules of custody, but she might've heard the adults talking at some point.

"Dad didn't know where she was," Callie said quietly. "I don't think Laura does either."

Del hesitated then reached out and touched Callie's arm. Like that could possibly comfort a kid who'd lost her father and couldn't find her mother. She oughta know what *that* was like.

She stood up again and paced the small room. "I'll be honest with you, kid. I have no idea why this girlfriend of your dad's thought I was a good person to take care of you."

Callie came over and placed her hand in Del's. "It's okay," Callie said. "We'll be together."

"That's not—"

She stopped herself from expounding on just how dire her situation was. And now she felt the coldness of the girl's fingers. Without heat, she couldn't fix that either.

"Del?"

She held her eyes closed for a second then plastered on a game face. "Okay, first things first. You gotta get some sleep."

"I'm hungry."

Del nearly rolled her eyes. "Of course you are."

"So's Utah."

She went to the fridge and pulled out the bread. "Peanut butter sandwich?"

Eyes lighting up, Callie eagerly climbed up onto one of

two rickety chairs Del had scooted up to the kitchen counter island. Callie didn't seem to care about the dirty pot and junk mail scattered on the surface. Neither did Utah. He stuck to the girl like Velcro, his little ears perked and eyes following Del.

Placing the sandwich in front of Callie who immediately broke it in half and handed one side to Utah, Del tried not to let her panic show. She hadn't known how this food was going to hold out for her, much less between two people and a dog.

Callie stuffed her mouth with a huge piece of sandwich and let out a sound Del thought meant she liked it. She looked like a ground squirrel, cheeks bulging with nuts.

Enjoy it, kid, because there's not much more where that came from.

Jumping off the chair, Callie came over to the sink and without asking for permission filled the only cup on the counter—Del's cup—with water from the tap. She lowered it to Utah who started lapping at it and spilling half of it onto the linoleum floor.

"Kid!"

Callie jumped. More water spilled. "I'm sorry, I—"

"Never mind." She could mop it up later.

Callie let Utah have his fill, then quickly refilled the cup and drank from it herself. Del tried not to cringe.

She stared at the girl and dog. Curse that Laura woman for dumping her with this responsibility. Maybe the PI would be worth calling back. Then again, he'd need to be paid, something she couldn't possibly do. Would the Lopezes be willing to take the kid in temporarily?

Del rubbed the back of her neck. Callie's shoelace was untied, the hem of her jeans frayed. Her hair looked like it hadn't been brushed.

"Where did you come from?" Del asked.

Callie looked up at her, lips still wet with water. She wiped them with the sleeve of her jacket. Her pale forehead crinkled as if trying to understand exactly what the question meant.

"Where do you live?" Del clarified.

"Laura lives in Pueblo. I stayed with her after my dad . . ."

"When did he die?"

Callie dipped her chin. "Two weeks ago."

Before she could respond, Callie ran over and wrapped her arms around Del's waist. Her shoulders started shaking.

At a loss for what to do, Del gave Utah a questioning look. He cocked his head, and she mouthed "thanks" to the dog.

"It's all right," Del said, hoping the girl wouldn't get snot on her shirt.

"He's . . . dead." Callie clung to her like she was a Titanic life raft, and Del stood there with her hands resting on the girl's back. She didn't know anything about taking care of a child. Should she pile her in the car tomorrow morning and drive her back up to Pueblo and Laura? At least Callie knew the woman.

Callie finally let her go. Her face was soaked, and so was Del's sweatshirt. Utah came over and started licking away the girl's tears with his huge, pink tongue.

Del knelt down in front of her again. She didn't want to upset her, but talking might help.

"What happened to your dad?"

"He was going to pick up a horse. The trailer wasn't hooked up right, I guess, and he crashed."

"He was a cowboy?" She needed to focus on the positive here.

"The best."

"Then listen to me." She reached for Callie's hand. She better get this right or she'd end up with a blubbering child again. "Your dad—"

"His name's West."

"West." Del looked right into the girl's teary eyes. "He was doing what he loved, isn't that right?"

Callie let one side of her mouth curl up a little. "Rodeo was his life."

"Okay then." She squeezed the girl's fingers. "He wouldn't have wanted to go any other way. I know it." Actually, she didn't know that at all, but she could pretend. What father worth his salt would leave his little girl alone with a girlfriend who didn't care?

"But I want to see him again."

"And I'm sure he'd like to see you, but he's in Heaven now. You wouldn't want him to leave there, right?"

Callie paused too long about that one, and Del quickly thought up something else. "Your dad would want you to be strong, don't you think?"

"Yeah."

"Then let's try to do that tonight, okay?"

"What about tomorrow?"

"We can deal with that when it comes."

Callie smiled, and Del realized she'd said "we." Perfect. She'd given the kid false hope. But what else could she do at one o'clock in the morning with a little girl who was probably so exhausted she couldn't even think straight? In the morning they could deal with cold, hard life.

"You need to get to bed," Del said. That's what adults said to kids, right?

Callie didn't put up a fight. "Can I go potty?"

"Uh, sure."

She showed her the bathroom—Utah and her duffel bag went in with her—and Del leaned against the wall outside. It wasn't Callie's fault, but she couldn't deal with another problem.

"Del?" Callie's voice came from behind the closed bathroom door.

"What?"

"You're out of toilet paper."

"Under the sink."

She heard the cabinet open. Something fell over, probably

her almost-empty bottle of shampoo. She was pretty sure there was one roll left. She'd taken two from the gas station restroom last week.

A minute later the toilet flushed.

Callie stumbled out, her bangs still wet from an obvious face washing.

"You didn't use my toothbrush, did you?"

The girl shook her head. "I have my own."

"Good."

Callie looked up at her expectantly. Right. She didn't know where she was sleeping. Del glanced at the thread-worn sofa, half tempted to set her up there. But one look into the little girl's emerald eyes—the same color as her own—and Del walked her toward her bedroom. She patted the bed, and Callie climbed up, crumpling onto the pillow.

Without hesitation, Utah jumped up too.

Del grabbed for his collar, but Callie clutched at her arm. "Please, let him stay."

"It's my bed."

"He's clean."

She eyed the lanky dog who'd plopped down beside the girl and already rested his head on Callie's stomach. He looked up at Del with the same pleading eyes as Callie.

Del sighed. "We're gonna need to talk again in the morning."

She took the thinnest blanket for herself and backed up to the door. Callie had already closed her eyes, and that's when Del realized the kid was still wearing her clothes and jacket. Not much she could do about them, but she went back to the bed and gently slipped off Callie's shoes and placed them on the floor beside the bed.

Utah thumped his tail once.

Del crept back into the living room and lay down on the sofa, curling up as tightly as she could.

9

Twenty years ago
Logan International Airport
Boston, Massachusetts

So this is it?" Natalie climbed out of the taxi and joined Javier and Adam at the terminal curb. It had been three months since the heist, and now it was time to go their separate ways.

"I'm gonna miss you guys," Javier said, adjusting the strap of his backpack. He was headed for Scotland on a dream backpacking trip across Europe.

She fought back tears.

"It's okay, Nat." Adam elbowed her. His flight left first, a nonstop to LA where he hoped to start a career as a personal trainer for the stars. If anyone could make it out there, he could.

They'd all agreed this was the best way to go, but that didn't mean she had to like it. The fact was her heart was breaking at the thought of parting with the best friends she'd ever had. But the more they had thought about it, the more they each realized this wasn't the life for them. None of them wanted to live on the run, and what were the chances they could pull off something like a museum heist more than once in their lives?

Natalie swiped at her eyes and dropped her own suitcase to the pavement. A light drizzle dampened the pavement, and she hoped her friends would think she was just removing a little rainwater from her face. They had no idea she hadn't told them everything.

"Hey." Adam patted her on the arm then leaned in close. "If they haven't found us by now they never will, Nat."

"What about Grant?"

Javier cursed. "If he talks, he goes down with us."

They'd had this conversation a dozen times over the past few months. Even though they had no idea what Grant had done with the paintings, they could still name him as the man behind the heist.

Natalie hugged Javier and Adam and then watched them purposely walk out of her life. Even as she walked out of theirs. It was time to move on. A flutter of dread floated over her as she boarded her flight to Colorado and gently rested her hand on the growing belly she'd carefully hidden under her oversized sweater.

❧

Twenty years ago
Harvard University
Boston, Massachusetts

When Grant Hudson stepped up to the podium at his alma mater, he felt a bead of sweat glide down his temple. He stared out across the packed audience cheering for him. Hundreds of clapping hands roared in his ears, and a strength he hadn't expected surged through him like heroine. He raised his arms and the students, teachers, and fans gradually sat down. Someone whistled.

"We love you, Grant!"

He smiled. This was it, what he'd dreamed about since he was eight years old pretending to give speeches to the squirrels in the woods behind the Hudson family home. He would follow in his aunt's political footsteps. They might not always see eye to eye, but he knew there was a reason April Hudson had won her elections by a landslide. It certainly wasn't because she'd fallen in love and let a spouse from the wrong side of the tracks tie her down.

Grant cleared his throat. "You make a guy feel right at home," he said to the crowd. He caught eyes with his aunt in the front row who looked up at him approvingly. Even through the glare of the lights her wink was unmistakable.

10

Present
Elk Valley, Colorado

Del opened her eyes to see Callie's face only inches from hers. She jumped, nearly yelling out loud.

"Sorry," Callie said.

Del groaned, resting her arm over her eyes. "About gave me a heart attack."

"Do you always sleep this late?"

"What time is it?"

"Nine."

"What?" She clambered to sit up. A wave of dizziness hit, reminding her that she hadn't eaten enough for the past week.

"I'm hungry," Callie said.

Utah rested his head on Del's leg. He wagged his tail.

She sighed.

"Can we have another sandwich?" Callie seemed to have recharged since last night and was as bouncy as a yearling filly.

She waved the little girl toward the refrigerator, and Callie skipped over and began to make herself breakfast.

Del sat on the edge of the sofa for a moment. This was a big problem. They would run out of food and what then?

Should she just take this kid and her dog down to the cops and let them deal with her?

Callie plastered peanut butter onto bread slices—she had six of them laid out already—as Del imagined how that conversation would go.

"Is everything you told me last night true?" She rested her head in her hands, and her voice came out muffled.

Callie didn't answer, and Del finally got up and went over to the kitchen island. Callie spread the peanut butter on the third slice, her tongue sticking out in concentration. The jar was almost empty.

"Is it?" Del repeated.

The girl nodded, still focused on the bread. She finished and carefully placed one of the empty bread slices on top. With a grin she handed it to Del.

Del took it. "Your dad's girlfriend didn't say anything else?"

"She didn't want me."

Del bit into the sandwich. It could really use some jelly, but at least it would silence her growling stomach. "Why aren't you in school?"

Callie shrugged.

Del sat down at the island. "We need to be serious here."

"Okay."

"I don't even have a job."

"Okay."

"No, it's not okay."

"I could get one!" Callie jumped up onto the stool and handed the second sandwich to Utah, who ate it in three big gulps.

"You can't—"

"I'm really good with animals."

Del eyed the greyhound sitting patiently beside the girl. "I can see that."

And she could also see this conversation wasn't going at all in the direction she'd planned. This girl had to realize a life with her wasn't an option. Dashing those hopes needed to be done and quickly. Look at the mess she'd made of her own life. Adding a child into the mix was not going to help things.

Someone knocked on the door. Hard.

Del startled, grabbing Callie by the arm. "You have to hide."

"What? Why?" The little girl's eyes got big.

"My landlord. Come on." Del pulled her into the bedroom and pointed at the closet. "Quick, get in there."

Callie still held her peanut butter sandwich. "What about Utah?"

The knocking got louder.

"Him too."

She shoved both of them into the bare closet, sliding the door shut.

"I'm scared!"

"It's all right, just please don't come out until I get you."

A quiet whimper came from behind the door. "It's dark."

"Trust me, kid."

She ran out of the bedroom, shutting the door behind her, and went to answer the persistent banging. When Del flung the front door open, she expected to see Mr. or Mrs. Lopez ready to give her another piece of her mind.

Instead, she faced not only them but a uniformed cop too.

"Del Mangini?" the cop asked.

She cleared her throat. "Yeah?"

"I'm Sheriff Newman."

"Okay."

Her heart pounded as she gaped at the man. His gut hung over his belt, and his fleshy neck bulged over his collar. Clean-shaven with the bulk of a bear, his hard eyes bothered her the most.

Get a grip, get a grip. You haven't done anything wrong.

"I understand you owe the Lopezes three months' rent."

"I—"

"Don't even bother denying it," Benny Lopez said.

Blinking her eyes, Del faced them with as much confidence as she could. "I promise if I had it, I would give it to you."

"Like I keep saying, not our—"

Newman lifted his hand. "I don't have authority to evict you," he said. "But I would suggest you resolve this matter as quickly as possible."

She decided now was a good time to just play along and ignore Tiffany's eye roll. "I understand."

The cop held her gaze, and she felt him sizing her up. He glanced past her into the living room, but she stood her ground. No way was she letting him in.

"Could I come inside for a moment?"

The hairs on the back of her neck bristled. "Why?"

"Just procedure."

"Procedure for what?"

"Are you hiding something, Miss Mangini?"

She rested her hand on the doorframe to appear nonchalant, but it also made a nice visible barrier showing she wasn't allowing anyone inside without her permission, cop or not. She just hoped Callie stayed put. Who did this guy think he was anyway?

Please don't move, kid.

"No, I'm not," she said. "And I'd appreciate it if you'd leave me alone. All of you."

They stared her down. Finally, Newman gave a slight nod and turned and walked back down the treated lumber steps. The Lopezes clambered after him demanding he arrest her, evict her, get rid of her.

Del slammed and locked the door, rushing back into the bedroom.

"We gotta go," she said as Callie and Utah slipped out of the closet.

The little girl looked up at her with complete trust even as Del grabbed her meager belongings and threw them onto the bed. She didn't have time to try anything else. She'd pushed her luck as far as it would go with her landlords, and now with this kid in the mix she couldn't risk police involvement. Not until she figured out what to do.

"Go grab any food you can find in the kitchen," Del ordered. "Put it all in that plastic grocery bag on the counter. Grab the silverware and dishes you find too, and put them in another bag."

Callie scampered off as if sent on a fun scavenger hunt, Utah trotting after her. Which was just as well. Del didn't need the kid to see the frantic tears building up in her eyes.

She'd been down this road a million times in her mind, but she'd always been able to stuff down the worry, convincing herself she just had to make it through another day. She could always do that, right? One more day. And somehow she always managed. Even with hunger and eviction hounding her like a wolf, she got through. But now she couldn't ward off the panic. It was upon her, and if she let it, it would overtake her and wrestle her to the ground.

Del grabbed her canvas suitcase with the torn piping and broken zipper and crammed her clothes inside. She was no beauty queen, even though her mom always said she was pretty. Her wardrobe consisted mostly of sweats, jeans, and tees, but she made sure her one dress—she'd worn it to her high school graduation—was packed so it wouldn't wrinkle. She might need it for a job interview.

Everything fit with room to spare. She went to the unfinished dresser with the burn mark on its side and cleaned out the hairbrush and comb, two belts, and a pocketknife that had been her dad's. She tucked them in the suitcase's side pockets.

Stripping the blanket and sheets from the bed and sofa, she piled them beside her suitcase. She did the same with the bathroom towels and threw the toilet paper roll into a plastic bag of its own.

The last thing she packed she hadn't looked at for three years. Del stood on tiptoes and pulled the sealed plastic bag from the top shelf of her closet. The two pristinely folded American flags would never leave her possession. Someday she'd open the bag, but it wasn't today.

She found Callie in the kitchen, triumphantly holding up the bag containing the last food Del had. How they were going to make do with that, she didn't know.

One more day . . .

"Where's your duffel?"

"By the door."

Del took in the living room. Nothing there she couldn't leave behind. Was she missing anything?

"Where are we going?" Callie's hair was still messed, and her T-shirt with a prancing pony outlined in glitter had a peanut butter stain on the pony's tail.

"I don't know." Del saw Callie's forehead scrunch. "It'll be an adventure, okay?"

"Okay!"

"Just wait here for a second."

Del opened the door a crack and peeked out. No sign of the Lopezes or the cop. She could see her Chevy still parked in the driveway.

Callie waited with Utah's leash wrapped around her hand two times.

"He has to go potty," Callie said.

The dog wagged his tail. She swore he could understand the girl.

"He'll have to wait," Del said.

"He can't."

She ground her teeth together. "Listen, we have to get out of here fast. We can find somewhere for him to go later."

And it better not be in my car.

"But—"

"No!"

Callie flinched, and Del pinched the bridge of her nose. She wasn't trying to scare the girl, but she had to understand. Del reached for her hand then decided against it.

"Callie, I need you to do exactly what I say."

She swallowed hard but gave Del a nod.

"It's really important."

Another nod, but she wouldn't look Del in the eyes. Utah shook, his collar rattling. He bumped into Callie's leg and threw her off balance.

"I'm sorry," Callie said.

"Let's just get out of here, and then we can deal with everything else." Del hefted her suitcase and took the bag of food from Callie along with the girl's duffel. "My car's down there. What I need you to do is run—literally run—to it when I open this door. Utah too."

Callie wiped her nose with the back of her hand.

Please don't start crying, kid.

Del tried to lighten her tone. "I'll race you."

Adventure sparked in Callie's face again. "I'll beat you."

Del almost laughed.

"Okay, kid." She opened the door. "Ready?"

"Uh-huh."

"On the count of three." Del gave her apartment one last sweep with her eyes. When she'd first moved in she was full of hope that her future could erase the jumbled mess of grief her life had become. That she could move on and make a life for herself alone. That maybe she wouldn't always *be* alone. But now the room was an empty shell, holding nothing but broken dreams.

"One."

There was no going back once she crossed this threshold.

"Two."

Callie giggled.

"Three!"

She flung open the door, and Callie zoomed past her, dragging Utah. Del pounded after them. She feared the Lopezes would see them escape. They could sue her for the rent, couldn't they? Could you put someone in jail for running away like this?

Del jammed the car remote over and over so it would be unlocked by the time they got to it. Utah actually made it first, and Callie yanked the door open for him. He leapt onto the front seat, and Callie climbed in after him across the console into the passenger side.

"Get him in the back," Del ordered.

Callie complied. Del threw their luggage back with the dog, tossed the food onto Callie's lap, then ran back up the stairs for the blankets and sheets. She threw them on top of the luggage and dove into the driver's seat. She started the car and backed out of the driveway as fast as she dared.

Only when they pulled out on Main Street did she lift her hand up to Callie for a high-five. The girl slapped it.

"Ow," Del said.

Callie giggled again. Then silence hit the car, and Del could feel her pulse in her fingertips gripping the steering wheel. She tried to loosen them.

"Where are we going?" Callie asked, peering out the window. She still held Utah's leash, and the dog stuck his head between them from the back.

"I don't know," she said.

"How can you not know?"

She braked at the stop sign. This was crazy. Stupid. What if this girl had been kidnapped and she would be charged for it? Callie would've told her that, right?

"But how can we—"

"I said I don't know!" It came out louder and harsher than she intended.

Callie scooted closer to the door.

Del didn't bother trying to come up with a way to pacify her. She just couldn't deal with all of this. Who in their right mind would dump off a kid with a complete stranger? And did that mean her biological mother wanted nothing to do with either of them? Del understood that adoption could be a selfless act to give a child a better life. Yet she still felt rejected. And what about Callie? This was even more of a rejection for her.

Callie rustled the plastic bag as she pushed it onto the floor. She held her arms across her chest and leaned against the door.

"Just give me a minute to think," Del said.

Callie didn't answer.

Money was the problem. Del thought again about selling the car, but with no cash for a hotel, they'd have to sleep in it. Elk Valley didn't have a homeless shelter, but Walsenburg might. They could go there, but that would use up—she glanced at her fuel gauge—too much from her quarter tank.

"We'll be okay, right?" Callie's question came out a whisper.

She glanced over at her and faked a smile. "Sure we will, kid."

11

Outskirts of Elk Valley, Colorado

W here are we?" Callie mumbled, clutching at her seat belt. "Nowhere yet."

"I wanna go home."

Del sighed. She pulled over at the edge of town, turned off the engine, and faced the girl. "I'm sorry for yelling at you."

The fabric of Callie's jeans suddenly seemed fascinating to her. She stared down at them. Utah was lying on the back seat with his head on Del's suitcase, but his eyes bore into her.

Del touched Callie's shoulder, but she pulled away.

"I'm not very good at this," Del said.

"I want my daddy." Tears brimmed in Callie's eyes.

"Sure you do," Del said. "I want mine too."

That seemed to hush Callie for a second.

"Your daddy died?" Callie asked softly.

"Three years ago."

"How?"

With her thumbnail Del traced the groove around the Chevy logo of her steering wheel. She didn't tell the girl she'd lost her mother on the same day. "It doesn't really matter." That wasn't true, but she didn't want to talk about it. She had enough on her mind.

Callie sniffed, and Del felt a small hand on her arm. That's when she knew where she needed to go. She started the engine again.

"I've got a surprise for you," she said.

"Really?"

Then she remembered something else. "Doesn't Utah have to go?"

"Go?" Callie's nose wrinkled. "Oh, yeah!"

"Take him over to that grassy area." Del pointed out a patch beside the road.

Callie quickly obeyed, and a minute later a much happier Utah climbed back inside the car. He stuck his head between them again, and Callie petted his neck.

"Where did you get him?" Del asked.

"Shelter."

Callie plugged in her seat belt and reached for the bag of food. "Can we eat another sandwich?"

"Wait for lunch."

"But I'm hungry."

"We have to save something for dinner."

She wasn't sure if Callie heard her as she started digging into the bag for the peanut butter and bread. Del needed to find a job. Fast. She'd applied everywhere already, but she'd have to try again.

"Tell me about Laura." She'd get Callie talking to get her mind off the food.

Silence.

She glanced over at Callie and saw her give a small shrug.

"Is she nice?"

"She's okay," Callie said.

"What do you mean?"

"Dad liked her."

"But you didn't."

"She wasn't nice to Utah."

Seemed like a sensitive subject. Del turned onto the familiar dirt road. "She didn't hurt you though, right?"

"No."

"Would you have wanted to stay with her if you could?"

Callie stared out the window. "You don't want me, do you?"

"That's not what I meant."

"It's okay. No one does."

Del slowed the car as she maneuvered around the deep, weed-infested ruts. This kid was more perceptive than she thought. And she was right in some ways. Del did not want the responsibility of a child on her hands. Callie deserved better. All Del could offer her was uncertainty.

"Just look at me, kid." She waved at the back seat. "This car is all I've got."

"Okay."

"I don't think you get it. This is it." She tapped the dashboard with her fingers. "I don't even know how we're going to eat tomorrow."

Callie lifted up the plastic food bag. "There's plenty here."

She shook her head. "I'm not the right person to look out for you."

"But you're my sister."

There *was* that. Del gave Callie another good once-over. There was some resemblance. Callie's eyes mirrored her own for sure. Had they gotten them from their mother?

"Don't you want to have a nice place to live?"

Callie was getting good at shrugging. "Laura's place was nice, but it wasn't home."

"And you think this is?"

"I like to travel," Callie said softly.

Del laughed but not because anything was funny. "Well that's good, 'cause that's what we're gonna have to do."

"Why don't you have anything?" Callie looked up at her as if it was the most innocent question in the world. To her it probably was.

Pulling over, Del shoved the gearshift into Park. "Because I'm a loser?"

"No you're not."

She opened her door and got out, gesturing for Callie to do the same. "I lost my job."

"How?"

"Do you always ask this many questions?"

Callie jumped out with Utah in tow. "Dad said I was inquazative."

Turning her head so the kid wouldn't see her smile, Del locked the car. "Inquisitive?"

"That's what he said."

"Describes you to a T."

"So how'd you lose it?"

She came around to Callie's side. "Someone said something about me to my boss that wasn't true."

"Like you didn't do something you were supposed to?"

"Worse."

This girl really deserved better than what she could offer.

"That's not nice," Callie said.

"Totally agree with you."

Del stood for a moment and stared up at the Spanish Peaks in all their glory. Today a few clouds drifted above them creating dark, shadowy patches over the pine forests lining their slopes. Soon snow would dust the crags.

"Do you like horses?" Del asked, guiding Callie and Utah toward the aspen grove. She scanned the area for that vigilante cowboy, but so far the coast was clear. They wouldn't hurt or touch anything. And it wasn't like the place was posted.

"I asked Dad for one last year."

That's right. She'd forgotten her father was a rodeo guy.

"Take it you didn't get one."

Callie's mouth turned down. "Said we couldn't afford it, but he always bought Laura things."

"Horses *are* expensive."

"Do you have one?" Callie's shoulder brushed against Del's arm.

She laughed again. "I just got through telling you I have nothing."

"I thought maybe that was your surprise."

At the barbed wire fence she held down the bottom wire with her foot and held up the top two for Callie and Utah to carefully pass through.

"Are we trespassing?"

She started to lie but couldn't.

"We're just looking," Del said. "I don't own them, but there's a herd of horses around here that I've kind of become friends with."

"Really?"

"They're not here all the time, but—"

"Look!" Callie poked her finger beyond the trees. Through the spindly trunks Del saw the majestic forms of the only friends she actually had. She'd never told anyone else about the horses.

Del led Callie toward them. She wasn't sure what they'd think of Utah. "Will he bark?" Del asked.

"He's been around horses," Callie said.

"Right. Rodeo dog."

"I always had to be careful he didn't get into trouble, 'cause not every horse likes a dog licking them on the nose."

Callie laughed, and Del smiled at the sound of it. Sweet. Another reason the kid was better off without Del. She didn't want her to discover that hunger pangs could feel like a rat gnawing the inside of your stomach.

Del noticed how the sunlight made the girl's dark blonde hair nearly glow. Hair Del hadn't brushed out and that needed it badly. She tried to focus on the horses and not on the fact that she knew nothing about taking care of children. An eight-year-old still needed plenty of guidance. Independent or not, Callie was just a little girl who would yearn for a mother's touch, a mother's love, sooner or later.

But theirs hadn't seen fit to know either of them. Del sighed as they got closer to the herd. Maybe it was better that way.

They broke through the aspens, and the horses turned toward them.

"Beautiful, right?" Del noticed that even Ghost, as skittish as she was, was approaching Callie and Utah. Curiosity might've killed the cat, but it got the horse in trouble first.

Utah didn't make a sound but stared at the huge animals lumbering toward him, wagging his tail eagerly.

Callie met the lead mare Queen first. Del started to instruct her how to be careful around the animals, but then she stopped herself. It sounded like the kid practically grew up on the rodeo circuit. She probably knew a thing or two about horses.

"Do you ride?" Callie asked, rubbing Queen's shoulder with the same ease and affection she had with Utah, who was touching noses with the horse. When his tongue touched her, Queen jumped but ducked her head down again toward the dog. She sniffed Utah's back and nuzzled his fur.

"Not anymore," Del said.

"Why not?"

"Don't have a horse to ride."

"So get one."

She scratched Knight under the chin where welts from a million bug bites were probably itching him like crazy. "Kid, I can't even afford food."

"I prayed for a dog," Callie said, looking up with a big grin on her face. "And I got one. I bet if you prayed for a horse you'd get one."

Del focused on scratching Knight. "I think God listens to little girls like you more than big girls like me."

Callie seemed to think about that for a moment. With one hand holding Utah's leash, the other petting Queen, Callie looked like she belonged on the set of *Dr. Dolittle*. Or deserved an apprenticeship with St. Francis of Assisi.

"He doesn't *always* listen," Callie finally said softly. "Or my dad would still be here."

Del moved over to Lady, giving her a good firm pat on her shoulder. Perfect. She'd said something wrong again. "Or things like that have nothing to do with God at all," Del tried. "But I don't really know much about that stuff."

"Me either," Callie said. "But I went to cowboy church with my dad a few times at the rodeos."

The last time Del had been in church was at her parents' funeral. And before that she could only remember a handful of Christmas Eve and Easter services. But by watching enough TV she'd picked up a few things about God and religion. One of her friends in middle school was a devout Christian who always told her God loved her. Del never really gave it much thought until after Mom and Dad died and she wondered if Heaven were real like her friend had said.

She said hello to each horse, introducing them to Callie, before she decided they better not press their luck. They really were trespassing.

"We better get going," Del said.

Callie was stroking Knight's nose. "We just got here."

"I don't think we're actually allowed to be doing this."

Callie raised her eyebrows at Del, like she was the adult and Del the child.

She smiled. "Don't give me that look."

"Will we get in trouble?"

"Only if we're caught."

They walked back to the fence line, and Del held up the wire for the girl again. The second she was across Callie yelled, "I'll race ya!" and took off toward the car.

She followed the girl and her dog at a slower pace. The visit had given her what she hoped—a reprieve from her troubles. But it didn't take long for them to come crashing back. Callie's dad's girlfriend wasn't a good option. If the woman hadn't cared enough to keep her, she didn't deserve the responsibility. But could there be another relative?

Del watched the little girl's hair fly behind her as she ran, the greyhound keeping pace even though he could've outrun her in a heartbeat. When she'd suggested another guardian in the apartment the kid had lost it. What would she do if Del got serious and started looking for a more suitable arrangement for her?

She couldn't tell her about it; that was for sure.

Callie ran right past the car and kept trotting down the road, laughing as she went, until they were almost out of sight. Utah jumped on her and barked, seemingly enjoying the chance to stretch his legs as much as his owner. Suddenly Callie came to an abrupt stop, Utah pulling his leash to its full length. Both of them were staring at something she couldn't see.

"Del?"

The girl's voice had gone from excited and bubbly to shaky and scared in a moment.

What in the—

Del started to run. Last thing she needed was for either of them to get bit by a rattler or for that dog to flush out an angry badger.

"Del!"

Beside the kid in a few more strides, Del instinctively

placed her hand on the girl's shoulder. She heard the flies first. An insane buzzing, much louder than flies should be. It sounded like a swarm.

Then she saw the red T-shirt on the ground.

Del grabbed Callie by the shoulders, turning her away. Keeping her gaze on the mound of clothing, she pushed the girl toward the Chevy. "Go back to the car."

"But—"

"Now."

"What is it?"

"I don't know." But she had a good guess.

"Why can't I—"

"I said now! There are things kids shouldn't see, all right?"

"What about you?"

"Please go back to the car." Del pronounced each word slowly. She needed her far, far away from this.

Finally obeying, the girl made it back to the Malibu, watching from a distance. It was good enough.

Del smelled an odor she'd never forget. The buzzing increased, and she approached the source—thousands of flies swarming around a mound she knew was a body. She desperately hoped it was a dead deer or a cow, even a horse. But she knew it wasn't.

She covered her nose with her sleeve and cautiously stepped closer. She almost puked what little she had in her stomach. The man's body lay on its side at the base of a tree. She could only see half his face, but where his eyes and mouth should've been was a writhing mass of maggots.

"Stay where you are, Callie!" she called, holding her hand up in case the girl decided to come back.

"What is it?" the girl called.

"Just stay there!"

He wore dark jeans and a red Rockies T-shirt. Just like—

Del's heart pounded in her chest. The private investigator.

Despite the disfiguration of decomposition, she saw the resemblance.

She ran back to Callie. "We have to go."

Had she kept his business card? Would the police come looking for her? How had he died?

"It was a body," she finally said.

Callie looked as horrified as Del felt.

"Get in," Del ordered, ripping the leash from the little girl's hands and pushing Utah inside. She rushed around to the driver's side.

"But it's a crime scene," Callie protested. "We can't just leave."

"We have to."

"Isn't that against the law?"

She had no idea, but they couldn't stay here. Not when the person who discovered a body was usually the prime suspect. They'd rip Callie away from her, and she was suddenly finding that idea unacceptable.

"We'll call it in or something," she said. "Anonymously."

But couldn't they trace cell phones? She'd let her plan lapse, but she still had the phone ready for a 911 emergency. No, they couldn't use that, and she didn't even know if pay phones existed anymore.

"Was it . . ." Callie's nose wrinkled. "Gross?"

"Yeah."

"I thought I smelled something."

Del swallowed down the cold saliva building in her mouth as she thought of the bloated body. "Please. Let's not talk about it for a minute."

She made a three-point turn and gassed out of there as fast as she could without spinning out of control.

12

Eight years ago
Denver, Colorado

Parties made Natalie nervous. The fancy dresses, sparkling champagne, handsome men, dazzling women—it wasn't her world, and it never would be.

Taking a sip from her champagne flute, she pressed close to the wall near a display of well-lit paintings. For twelve years she'd tried to forget her old life, but sometimes all it took was an event like this to carry her back.

Natalie stared at the bubbling liquid, remembering that night long ago when Javier handed her a glass from the back seat of the van. The FBI still hadn't found the artwork, and Natalie hoped they never did. She'd made a new life for herself and now took joy in the simple things. The past was buried; she'd made sure of that. But it still sometimes fought to reach the surface.

She shook her head and took another small sip. She was here for the horses. She wished her friend who ran Mountain-top Horse Sanctuary hadn't gotten sick and enlisted her to be down here in Denver for this fundraiser gala. She'd thought of every excuse in the book why she was the wrong woman for the job and couldn't possibly go in the director's place.

Every excuse except the truth, and that was something she could never tell anyone. Not her coworkers, her baby daughter, or even her husband. Especially not her husband, who thought the nest egg she'd brought to their marriage was inheritance money from her great-uncle.

Enough time had passed that she didn't worry as much about being found, but it still crossed her mind every time a friend snapped a photo or someone tagged her on Facebook. Had she changed enough over the years? Her hair was now shorter and lighter, and she had gained a few pounds.

At least she wouldn't have to make a speech. That honor would go to her colleague, Randy. She spied the older cowboy standing across the room in his black Wranglers, bolo tie, and black felt Stetson, looking as uncomfortable as she felt.

He caught her eye and ambled over to her side of the room.

"I'm too old for this kind of thing," Randy said in his deep, southern drawl. "I should be out throwing hay, not gallivanting around with rich folk."

"Think about all the horses you'll be able to rescue with their money."

He patted her arm with his calloused fingers. "I always have liked the way you think, sweetheart."

She warmed at his kind words and tried to straighten the strap of her dress which kept slipping off her shoulder. Shortly after her daughter's birth she and West had moved to Lyons where he could practice his rodeo skills under a rich friend's covered arena, and she soon found the horse rescue group. She was making a difference in the lives of animals who didn't have a voice, and that made her feel good about herself. She'd changed, and she hoped it would be enough to make up for what she'd done.

"That guy looks like a penguin," Randy said under his breath, nodding in the direction of a cluster of dinner jackets and tuxedos.

They could be famous actors for all either of them knew. "You're lucky they didn't kick you out for wearing jeans," she said.

Randy laughed. He was a good man, but he didn't truly know her any more than anyone else did.

She lifted her champagne glass in a toast. "To the horses."

Their glasses clinked.

"I'm just glad that senator's taking the mic first." Randy took a sip from his glass.

She stared at him. "Senator?"

"Yeah, maybe he'll be long-winded."

"There's someone else speaking?"

"Last minute decision." Randy nodded toward the cluster of men they'd been talking about. "Good exposure for us, though I didn't know he was into horses."

Natalie's throat tightened. How likely was it after all these years?

"Maybe it's just a photo op, since he's in town. They say he's fixin' to run for president some day," Randy said.

"Senator Sanchez?" she asked hopefully.

Randy shook his head. "Hudson."

That's when she saw him. His wavy hair was slicked back, his starched shirt as white as new paper. He was chatting and smiling, probably charming everyone he met. What was the senator from Massachusetts doing here in Colorado? She felt sick to her stomach. Grant Hudson stood only a few feet from her. As handsome as the day they met. As dangerous as the night they parted.

"Do you ride, Senator?"

Grant plastered on a smile at the gentleman's question. "Horses are magnificent creatures," he replied, hoping the response would satisfy. Truth was he had no time for animals. Or this gala. But he was in need of some good press, and his re-election campaign advisor was nagging him to show a more personable side. The Hudson name could only go so far. His family's getaway chalet in the Sangre de Cristo Mountains often brought him to Colorado, and Aunt April had arranged with the media to make sure his constituents in New England knew about his generous donation to the horse rescue. He could hear her voice behind him talking to a group of rich old bags who'd no doubt be writing checks by the end of the evening.

Grant moved farther away from his aunt and glanced across the room at the artwork displayed on the walls. These hicks wouldn't recognize real art if it bit them in the—

Grant froze. He blinked.

The woman across the room. He would know her any-where.

Their eyes met. Could it be?

Hers got bigger. He allowed himself one moment to admire her still beautiful curves before he slammed the doors of his heart and walked across the room toward the woman who could ruin everything he'd worked tirelessly to build.

Her frantic glance toward the exit brought a grin to his face, and this time it was genuine. She wanted to run. Good. He needed to have that effect on her.

In a few long strides Grant was in front of her.

"Natalie," he said, infusing his voice with charisma. *Set her at ease. Make her drop her guard.*

She stared at him like one of the flighty beasts this organization supported. The years hadn't marred her beauty, and a pang of regret scratched at his soul once more.

"Grant," she whispered.

"How many years?" he responded, holding out a hand.

Natalie backed up.

He chuckled, closing the space between them again. "Relax. I'm just introducing myself to the talented woman running this fundraiser."

"What are you doing here?" Her eyes darted to the exit again.

"I've come a long way, Nat. But the campaigning never stops. Everything I do or say is scrutinized." Grant looked deep into her face, lowering his voice to a conspiratorial whisper. "If they knew about you, for example, I'd be cooked."

The woman he'd once planned to marry took another step away from him, then another. They'd made a promise to never speak of the past, to never enter each others' lives again. He'd thought she was gone forever. But seeing Natalie in front of him alive and well and living her own life taunted Grant.

Yes, they'd promised, but as a politician he'd learned promises were made to be broken.

13

Present
Elk Valley, Colorado

They ate cornflakes in a gas station parking lot. Del hated to use up all the milk, but it would spoil anyway if they didn't. She pretended to be full and gave most of hers to Callie.

Utah needed to eat too, but all they had left was the pasta. She dumped half a box into the pot she'd remembered to bring along, topped it off with a bottle of water she'd left in the car last week, and let it soak for an hour before trying it on the dog. He ate it all.

"Full yet?" Del asked as Callie finished off her third bowl.

"I'm thirsty."

"Yeah. We gotta fix that."

Del scrounged in the car and found two more empty water bottles in the trunk. "We need to clean ourselves up too."

Utah wasn't keen on being left alone in the car, but it was cool enough to leave him unattended for a few minutes.

They got the key from the gas station attendant—it was attached to a wooden spoon—and Del closed them in the filthy bathroom around the side of the building.

"Don't touch anything," she said to the girl.

Soiled paper towels and toilet paper overflowed from the
trash can under the sink, which was rust-stained around the
drain and corroded on the handles. A few flies buzzed up in
the corners of the room, which made her think of the dead
body again.

Not now. She needed to focus. She would help Callie clean
up and then worry about making some money. That was enough.

There were still a few clean paper towels left in the dispenser,
and Del took them all, wetting them under the faucet. "Wash
your face and hands," she said, handing a wad to Callie.

She scrubbed her own face as best she could without soap
then carefully refilled the water bottles without letting the mouth-
pieces touch the spigot.

Callie wiped her arms with the towels then tossed the crumpled ball into the trash can like it was a basketball and she the
star player. She was too young to think of the ramifications of
discovering a rotting corpse or sleeping in a car. To her it was
probably all an adventure, and Del was going to take care of
things.

This couldn't go on long.

"Did you get enough to eat?" Del ran her fingers through
her hair, reminding herself to dig out the brush from the bag
of belongings she'd hurriedly slugged into the back seat.

"Yeah."

"Think Utah did too?"

"*He* never thinks so."

Del checked the girl over. They couldn't look homeless.
She blew out a long breath at that thought. She never imagined
she'd associate homelessness with herself, but in the past few
months it had been hovering so close she'd tasted it every night
when she lay down. Now that it was here, it lost some of its
power over her. Maybe it helped that she wasn't alone.

"Come on, kid," she said, urging Callie out the door with
a light push. "Let's go ask inside about some work."

"You're gonna work in a garage?"

"If it pays."

"Can you fix cars?"

"I can change a tire." Del glanced down at Callie and saw a flash of admiration on her face.

"Can you teach me?"

"Maybe sometime."

Utah's head popped up in the Malibu window, and he followed Callie with his gaze like he had a torpedo locked on her. He wasn't the only one watching them. Del saw a mechanic with a shaved head and grease-stained coveralls eyeing them from under the hood of a truck. Another with tattoos covering his arms wiped his fingers on a red rag.

"Why don't you go wait with Utah?" Del suggested.

"Don't you need my help?"

She pointed toward the car. "He needs you more."

Callie grinned. "You're probably right."

Watching the girl cross the parking lot, Del was hit with another wave of desperation. "Lock the door!" she called.

She strode across the parking lot and walked into the glass-fronted garage office. Empty soda cans littered the counter. A woman as equally imposing as the men she'd seen in the garage sat in a chair with wheels. Her gray, short-cropped hair and creased skin made her look older than she probably was. The mini-TV beside her blared a NASCAR race.

"Help ya, hon?"

"Um . . ." Del forced confidence into her steps and approached the counter. "I need a job."

The woman looked at her like she'd just announced she was Miss America.

"I can do pretty much anything," Del added.

"Fix a headlight?"

"Uh . . ."

"Change oil?"

77

"Not exact—"

"Rotate tires?"

"I can change a tire."

The woman hmphed, which caused her to cough. "Unless you can give these pit guys"—she waved at the TV—"a run for their money, I can't help you."

"What about office work?"

"What do you think *I* do?"

Del fingered the chipped Formica counter edge. "Everyone could use an extra set of hands, right?"

"Why don't you talk to Rodney out there."

"Which one is he?"

"Shaved dude."

Del thanked the woman and walked out into the garage where the racket of power wrenches and the aroma of oil and grease met her senses. Someone swore in Spanish from under an amped-up pickup. She didn't see anyone like the woman described. Del crouched down beside the truck.

"Hey."

The mechanic underneath jumped, dropping his oil filter wrench.

"Sorry," she said.

He muttered something else, and Del had a feeling it wasn't complimentary.

"I'm looking for Rodney," she said.

"Why?"

"I need a job."

"We're not hiring."

"Gal in the office said to talk to him."

The mechanic slid out and wiped his fingers on a grease rag. He was probably only a year or two older than she.

"Is he here?" Del asked.

Standing, the mechanic threw his rag onto the hood of the truck. The stitched name on his coveralls read *Josè*.

José lowered his voice. "You don't want to talk to him."

"Why not?"

"Just don't."

Del crossed her arms, feeling indignant. She needed money, and if this garage could pay her something—even if she had to scrub oil off the concrete—she would do it. "I'm in a bind here," Del said. "I need a job, and I need it fast."

"You don't—"

"José!" A voice yelled from across the room.

The young mechanic answered back with a volley of Spanish. Then he lowered himself back onto his dolly, all the while keeping his eyes on Del. As he disappeared under the truck again, he whispered, "Just leave this place, *chica*."

She decided to try the other mechanic, and he pointed her to the back of the garage where Rodney was apparently on a smoke break. She found him sitting on an old truck tire, a cloud of cigarette smoke surrounding him. His short-sleeved blue work shirt had a tear in the pocket, which contained the rest of his cigarettes still wrapped in cellophane. A spiderweb was tattooed on the side of his head.

"Rodney?" Del let the door slam behind her.

He didn't look up and took another drag. "Yeah?"

"Your office manager said to talk to you about a job."

Rodney laughed. It sounded like something was stuck in his throat.

She didn't want to ask him what was so funny.

"I need mechanics," he said, blowing smoke at her. "You're not one."

"I can do a lot of things."

"Yeah?"

"Or maybe you know someone else who's hiring."

"I might."

A spark ignited hope inside Del. "I could really use anything."

Finally turning toward her, Rodney kept his cigarette clenched between his lips. "Anything?"

She thought of Callie sitting in the car waiting for her. "Almost anything."

"You're pretty." Rodney took out his cig and pointed at her with it. "Someone like you could be a good salesman, am I right?"

"What do you mean?"

"First I gotta know what you're about." Rodney sighed and looked off toward the edge of the parking lot where a dumpster sat with weeds growing up its sides.

Maybe Josè was right. An uneasy feeling crept up Del's back. A warning. She'd felt the same way before Eric made his move.

"I have a friend," Rodney said. "He and I move merchandise together."

She was starting to understand where this was going.

"You know what?" Del took a step backward. "Never mind."

Rodney shot to his feet. He threw his cigarette on the ground. "Thought you were desperate."

Del spun toward the door. "Not that desperate."

His muscular, inked arm shot out in front of her, blocking her escape. "Look," Rodney said. "You have no idea what you're refusing."

"I think I do."

"A girl like you could make a killing, and I'd split the profits with you."

"And this so-called merchandise?"

"You'd have first dibs."

Del clenched her jaw. "Not what I meant."

Rodney lit up another cigarette. "See, I don't know you, but I'm willing to take a chance."

"I'm not." Del grabbed the doorknob.

Rodney reluctantly removed his arm.

She couldn't get out of that place fast enough. Del flew past José climbing out from under the truck again. "You were right," she said but didn't wait to see if he heard.

At the car she jumped inside and locked the doors.

"Did you get the—"

"No." Del threw the car into Drive. "I could never work in a place like that anyway."

"So where will we try next?"

She decided to let the question hang in the air. She had no answers for this kid.

"What do we have left?" She pointed at the grocery bag Callie had dropped on the floor. The girl pawed through it as Del zipped out of the parking lot and back onto the road. She wondered if José was selling drugs too.

Callie waved around a can of baked beans. "I found these in your cabinet. And this too."

She produced a can of corn Del had no memory purchasing. Had it been left behind by the previous tenant? She didn't even want to know the dates on those things.

"And we have the water," Callie said.

Barely enough for one meal.

She glanced down at the gas gauge. Closing in on an eighth of a tank. She needed to get out of Elk Valley, where she'd exhausted every possible chance of employment, but that was impossible without more gas. They'd need every drop if it got cold and they ran the heater at night.

Del felt the panic expanding in her chest.

∾

The Perfect Blend Coffee Shop
Elk Valley, Colorado

"You can't help it, can you?"

Abby Dawson looked up, pulling her concentration from the police log she was reading on her iPhone. "What?"

"Once a cop, always a cop."

"Sorry." She set the phone on the outdoor coffee shop table and faced her friend, Christy Williams.

Christy removed the plastic lid from her paper cup. Her light brown hair rustled as a gust of wind drifted by. When Abby first met her she'd been growing out a blonde dye job and struggling to stay sober after years of addiction. Now she was the strongest person Abby knew. It was Christy's lunch break, and Abby berated herself for not being better company.

"It's in you, Ab." Christy held her cup under her lips, breathing in the steam. "You could go back to it, you know."

Abby sunk her teeth into her moist brownie and chewed a few times. After the death of her brother, Christy's fiancé, Abby resigned from her position on the force to take over the family's used bookstore. But Christy was right—her cop instincts were ingrained in her like her fingerprints. She had enjoyed the break from all the crime, but something still stirred in her when she listened to the scanner or caught up with one of her old buddies still working the beat.

"Wouldn't be the same," Abby said.

She knew Christy understood. Everything changed when someone you love died. Christy herself had moved down here to Elk Valley to be closer to her sister's ranch, and Abby spent practically every weekend visiting the small town herself, a four-hour drive from her place in Longmont. With just enough art galleries and ski shops sprinkled amidst the cowtown charm, Elk Valley was growing on her.

"So." Christy pointed at Abby's iPhone. "You gonna let me install that GPS app?"

Abby hesitated, then handed over her phone. "You do realize this goes against everything in me."

"You'll never lose your phone again. Trust me." Christy tapped at the screen.

"A hacker wouldn't need an app."

"Yeah, yeah."

"A phone number in the wrong hands . . ."

Christy rolled her eyes. "Criminals aren't hiding under every rock, you know."

A few minutes later Christy headed back to the bookstore she herself owned in town, and Abby climbed into her Acura parked at the curb. She had an appointment with a realtor to see about renting in the area.

Turning up her police scanner as she pulled onto the street, Abby's attention was immediately diverted by the code from the dispatcher.

10-54.

Possible dead body.

In Elk Valley? The worst criminal activity she'd heard around here was some local kids trying to start a meth lab and blowing up a barn instead.

Abby listened for the location and did a quick U-turn at the light. The realtor could wait.

⌒

Police Station
Elk Valley, Colorado

Sheriff Newman was heading out the station door when the

call came. He turned around and scooped up the desk landline. This better be important.

"Newman," he said.

The voice on the other end was deep and authoritative. He only said a few words, but they were enough for Sheriff Newman to get the point.

14

Eight years ago
Lyons, Colorado

Natalie looked down at the sleeping baby curled up in her crib, and her heart surged with fear. Her little girl. She'd do anything to protect her, but would it be enough? Her past was racing to catch her, and she wasn't sure if she would escape.

In the darkness of the nursery, the only light a slight crack coming from the door, she rested her hand on the little girl's head. "I love you, sweetheart," she whispered then turned and walked out.

What came next would be the hardest thing she'd ever do. Downstairs, her husband West would be sitting in his favorite recliner reading a Patterson thriller before bed. A cup of coffee would be cradled in his fingers, their cat asleep on his lap. He had no idea he was about to be hit with a tidal wave.

But she knew it was time. He needed to know the truth.

Last night at the fundraiser she'd fled to her hotel room, leaving poor Randy alone to fend for himself in an ocean of wealthy socialites. For the past twelve years she'd carefully followed Grant's rise into politics. When he was elected to the U.S. Senate she worried someone would vet him and discover their secret, but he'd set his sights even higher now, and all the pundits said someday he'd be throwing his hat into the race for the presidency. They'd be looking even harder for dirt then.

Why he'd been at that fundraiser she might never know, but the shock of seeing him had done one thing—it convinced her to come clean with West. As hard as this might be, she had to do it before he found out some other way.

She descended the stairs silently and found her husband just where she'd expected him. West didn't look up from his book as she came behind him and draped her hands on his shoulders.

"I'll be up in a minute," he said.

"I need to talk to you."

He looked up. His hair was still wet from his shower, and he smelled of fresh soap. "About what?"

She came around and knelt beside his recliner. Reaching for his hand, she squeezed his warm fingers. Her heart raced like she'd just gotten off the treadmill.

"Do you love me?"

A smile played at his lips. "What?"

"Love me." She couldn't look into his dark eyes. "Do you?"

"Of course."

She always knew it would be difficult, and it was her own fault. If she'd had the guts, she would've been honest with him from the beginning. But there'd always been a niggling feeling that she would lose him if he knew.

"I have to tell you something."

West closed his book. He scooted to the edge of the recliner, massaging her hand. "You've been weird ever since you got back."

"When I was in the city I saw someone I used to know."

"Okay."

She hesitated. If she did this, there would be no going back. Everything she'd carefully covered up would be out in the open, and she would never be able to change it. Maybe it was about time.

"Honey?"

"Grant Hudson."

West chuckled. "Really? What was he doing there?"

"I don't know."

West reached for his book again. "Kinda like to meet the guy myself."

She stared at the tear in the fabric of West's jeans. He'd gotten it caught in a fence last week helping Randy replace some rotten posts. Her ruddy-faced cowboy was as different from Grant as the desert was from the ocean.

"I knew him a long time ago," she said softly.

Her husband's hold on her hand loosened. "Knew him? What do you mean?"

"West, there are some things I haven't told you."

His eyes narrowed. "How well are we talking about?"

She finally met his gaze and was suddenly overcome with how foolish she'd been. How selfish. She'd wanted to start fresh, and West had given her that. He had deserved the truth from day one.

"How well did you know him?" he repeated.

"I was a lot younger," she said. "I . . ."

Her husband took hold of her hand and squeezed. "What does Grant Hudson have to do with you?"

"I don't know where to begin," she said.

"The truth would be nice."

"West, I—"

"Talk, Nat."

She did.

Hudson Private Jet

April Hudson's bony fingers dug into Grant's arm. "I thought you dealt with her."

He pried her hand away. "I did."

"I may be old, but I am not blind." Her face inches from his, April's eyes were as piercing as when he was a child. "I saw her clear as your nose last night. What does she want?"

Grant sighed and focused on the city lights twinkling beneath the jet. He might be Senator Hudson to everyone in America, but he was still April Hudson's "boy." At sixty-seven she kept pace with women half her age and had taken it upon herself to manage his campaigns or play close advisor to those who did. He owed much of his political success to her tireless work.

Which is why he chose his words carefully. "Don't you trust me?"

His aunt laughed, her glasses dipping to the end of her nose. "Not when it comes to women."

Grant patted her arm. "Don't worry."

"Too late," she said. "I told you that girl was bad news. What you ever saw in—"

"She won't be a problem."

If Natalie wouldn't accept his generous offer of compensation for her silence, like she'd made abundantly clear last night, it might be time for something more drastic.

15

Present

Cuchara, Colorado

Abby Dawson slowed her Acura as she approached the cabin up in Cuchara, gravel popping under her tires. David Kirsch. That was the dead guy's name. She really shouldn't know it, but Christy was probably right. She'd never be able to stop being a cop, at least not in her head. She'd made two phone calls and had the guy's name and address within fifteen minutes.

She'd kept her distance at the scene where they were loading the body into the coroner's van. They would not appreciate meddling. She knew that. She'd made sure she wasn't contaminating anything. Her first thought was that the guy offed himself in the woods, but then she overheard one of the medics say he'd been shot in the back of the head.

Abby flipped off her headlights and parked far enough from the cabin so as not to be seen but not so far that she'd have to hoof it in the dark more than a couple hundred feet. She was surprised there were no police around. Could they have scoured the place already?

She climbed out right as her cell phone shrieked, and an oath flew from her lips before she could stop it. The screen lit up with a photo of Christy's face.

Punching the Answer key, Abby whispered, "What?"

"Where *are* you?"

That's when she remembered. She was supposed to be at the ranch for dinner.

She sighed into the phone. "I'm sorry. I got caught up in something and completely forgot."

"You okay?"

"Yeah, but . . ." She closed the car door and started walking toward the cabin. Was there a light on inside?

"Should we save you something?"

That definitely *was* a light.

"I'll call you back," Abby said. She didn't give Christy a chance to respond. She'd have to apologize for that later.

She slipped her cell phone into her back pocket and took a moment to focus on her surroundings. The sun had set a few minutes earlier, and she could barely see the faint purple hue of the western horizon peeking through the pine boughs. A few stars glowed through the branches, and a faint breeze brought the scent of dry pines to her nose. The cabin was surrounded by them, towering toward those stars. She could see why the guy chose this setting. An investigator would face a lot of the same grime as a cop, and a retreat like this would be the perfect place to unwind and decompress.

So why was he lying in the morgue with a bullet in the back of his head?

Abby crossed her arms over her chest and felt the comforting bulk of her shoulder holster. Even though she was retired from police work, she almost always carried. Sometimes in her purse, other times on her person, only once in a blue moon did she leave her gun at home. It had become as much a part of her as her hair.

Her ex-husband Michael called her obsessed, but Abby just called herself prepared. You never knew when crime would creep up on you like a snake on an unsuspecting mouse. She never wanted to be the mouse.

She headed down the driveway, staying close to the trees and off the gravel. Instinct told her something was off, and there was no backup to call. She shouldn't even be here. But she knew the sheriff had given her the runaround when she'd called earlier. She hadn't expected him to give her any information, but he seemed awfully sure it was a suicide already.

Abby kept her eyes glued on the cabin. It was gut instinct, pure and simple. This case was something big. She knew it. A quick internet search had pulled up next to nothing on David Kirsch other than his business web page. Why would someone kill him?

As she got closer to the cabin, a light burned bright in the front window. Had Kirsch left it on? That was possible, except she could've sworn the windows were dark when she first pulled up.

What was a small-time private investigator doing that apparently made someone want to stop him?

Abby's cell rang again, and she quickly silenced it. She'd talk to Christy later.

The light flicked off.

Her heart thumped in her chest. Someone was in there.

She crept closer. Maybe the guy had family going through his things. She remembered when her brother Hunter died, how her father had rashly sorted his clothes the day of the funeral. Emotions ran the gamut at times like that. You did things which didn't make sense. Things you might regret. She should know.

One of the pine trees offered cover as she watched the cabin. A truck was parked near the front door. Kirsch's? She couldn't see the plates in this light or else she'd commit the numbers to memory for a later search. Maybe she could work her way around to have a closer look. She still had friends on the force who owed her favors.

A shadow passed across the window.

Something didn't feel right.

Yeah, and an ex-cop creeping around outside was normal? She smiled to herself, ready to march up to the door and knock.

A twig snapped behind her.

She spun around just in time to see a dark hulk of a man two feet away. There was no time to draw her gun. Abby's fingers got as far as the snap on her holster when the man swung something at her head.

Pain flashed through her skull. Abby's last thought before the blackness swallowed her was that she'd become the mouse she swore she'd never be.

16

Outskirts of Elk Valley, Colorado

"Warm enough?"

Del tucked the blanket around Callie as best she could from the front seat. The little girl lay on the back bench with Utah curled up somewhere under the blanket with her. Del had stuffed their limited gear on the front passenger seat.

"Are *you?*" Callie asked, her voice sleepy.

"I'll be fine."

"It's gonna be okay, right?"

"Don't worry, kid." It was the only comfort she could manage under the circumstances. "I'm going to drive us a little bit farther, but I want you to try to sleep."

Callie nodded, and Utah snuggled under the blanket. She heard him let out a soft sigh.

Del turned around and started the car. They'd spent the rest of the afternoon in town with Del re-knocking on the same doors she'd already darkened over the past few weeks. The only business close to hiring was the deli, and that opening wasn't available until next month. She didn't have that long.

All through the daylight hours she'd managed to keep up a good enough front for Callie, but now that it was dark and Del was alone with her thoughts again the gnawing worry renewed with as much vigor as her empty stomach.

She drove them to the outskirts of town where she remembered seeing a dirt road that led to some hiking trails. Del pulled onto the grass beside the path, turned off the engine, checked to make sure the doors were locked, and leaned back in her seat. She pulled the thinner blanket and sheet over herself and tried to tune out her thoughts. They'd be safe here. She could start the engine and have them moving in seconds if someone showed up.

One day at a time . . . that's the only way she could deal with this.

"Del?"

She kept her eyes closed. "Yeah?"

"Did you ever meet Mom?"

Del stared up at a small rip in the car's ceiling upholstery, barely visible in the darkness. "No."

"Did you want to?"

She rolled over onto her side. She wasn't sure how much to share with an eight-year-old. "I didn't find out I was adopted until yesterday."

Callie got quiet. Del could feel the car moving as Callie shifted on the bench seat.

"You'd want to be told if you were adopted, wouldn't you?" Del said.

"I guess."

She thought back to growing up, how she'd been one of the few kids at school who wasn't from a broken home. Even though Mom and Dad both worked, they coordinated so she was rarely home alone. At least twice a week they ate dinner together, and she couldn't remember ever going to a soccer game where one of them wasn't cheering her on.

"I had great parents, but I still wish they'd told me." Del tightened her covers around her shoulders. "Do you remember anything about her?"

A sniff came from the back seat.

Del twisted around onto her elbow but could barely see Callie's face in the darkness.

"I . . ." Callie's voice cracked. "I wish I could."

Her heart ached for the girl. What would it be like to not remember anything about Mom? She couldn't imagine it.

"You have that picture," Del said.

"Why did she leave?"

With a sigh, Del wrapped her arms around herself. "People do stupid things. She probably regretted it but by then was too ashamed to come back."

Del hoped that was true.

"Didn't she love me? I mean, I would never do something like that to Utah. He needs me, just like . . . just like I needed her."

"Maybe we should get some sleep."

"We could try to find her."

"Needle in a hay stack, kid."

Callie's face was suddenly inches from hers. "The internet?"

"I don't think it's that easy."

"But we could—"

"Bad idea, okay?"

"I just—"

"She doesn't want to be found." Del squeezed her eyes shut again. She really needed some sleep.

"How do you know?"

If a private investigator couldn't find her, what chance did they have?

"I just know," Del said.

〜

"Del?"

Her eyes still closed, Del shifted in the front seat. Had she drifted off? She'd tilted it back as far as possible but knew she was going to be feeling this in the morning.

"Del?" the whisper came a few inches from her ear.

"What?"

"I can't sleep."

"That's because you're talking." *And keeping me up while you're at it.*

"I'm tired, but I can't get to sleep."

Del groaned and opened her eyes. Out here in the country, there were no city lights and the moon had barely risen.

"Only way you're gonna get to sleep is if you close your eyes and quit talking."

"I'm scared."

"It's gonna be all right." How many times had she said that today alone, to herself as well as to Callie? She wondered if the girl had stopped believing her like she'd stopped believing herself.

"It's dark."

"There's the moon."

"I'm still scared."

Del rolled over and made out the little girl curled up on the back seat with Utah still cuddled up against her. Somehow she had to keep her from freaking.

"Is Del your real name?" Callie asked.

"Yes."

"It's not short for something?"

She blew air through her lips. "We need to get some sleep."

Callie went quiet. The blanket rustled, and Utah groaned.

"I'm sorry," Callie whispered. "I know I always talk too much."

"You're fine."

"Laura said I did."

"No, you don't."

The girl sniffed, and Del felt like an ogre for making a little girl cry. After what she'd been through she deserved better. Much better than Del, that's for sure. She'd given her a night sleeping in a car with nothing in her belly but cornflakes and no promise of anything but a can of beans in the morning. That wasn't a life for a kid. She needed stability. A family. People who'd be able to give her everything a kid needed, including love. She wasn't too old to be adopted out, right? Plenty of loving parents must be looking for children just like her to add to their families.

But thinking about adoption only made her think of Mom and Dad, and she knew if she went down that road she'd end up crying like Callie.

"Delaware," she finally said.

Callie didn't answer.

"Del's short for Delaware."

Another sniff from Callie. "Really?"

"Yeah, and you gotta promise to never tell, okay?"

"Why, don't you like it?" The girl said it with a tiny giggle.

Del couldn't help but smile. "I mean it, kid! Tell no one."

Callie sounded like she was trying to cover her mouth but laughing in her hand. In a flash Del reached back and started tickling her, which only made her laugh harder.

"Promise!" Del kept tickling.

"I promise! I promise!" Callie wriggled and squirmed and kept on giggling.

Del was laughing too. When was the last time she'd laughed like this?

"My name's California," Callie said.

"That's pretty."

"Dad liked Callie better though."

She wondered if their mother had been the one to name them. How else could they explain both of them having states for names?

"Good night . . . Delaware," Callie said.

"Kid!"

The muffled laughter of a child made something in Del feel warm. She could not let herself get used to this.

A few minutes later she heard Callie's breathing slow. But Del was wide awake. When she saw headlights turn in the distance and slowly come toward them, she bolted straight up in her seat.

17

Eight years ago
Lyons, Colorado

West didn't speak to Natalie the next morning, and she didn't blame him.

"Comfortable, little one?" Natalie cupped her little girl's rosy cheek and buckled her into her car seat. A pang hit her as the child cooed. Not a day went by that she didn't think of her firstborn daughter. She'd be turning twelve this year. Was she happy? Had her parents told her she was adopted? She'd left it up to them to decide, but now she wished she'd made some stipulations.

Natalie climbed into the Subaru and headed for home, shoving the painful maternal yearnings into the deep crevice she'd forced them into year after year. She'd thought she would never love again. Or bear another child. But then she met West. Now that she finally told him everything, would he forgive her for the mistakes of her past? Was it fair to ask him to?

On the verge of tears, she brought the Subaru to a stop at a four-way intersection. A blue pickup with huge tires came up out of nowhere and hugged her bumper. The driver wore sunglasses and a cowboy hat like half the guys in this ranch town where she and West spent their time when they weren't traveling the rodeo circuit.

"What's your problem?" Natalie said to the rearview mirror as he gunned his engine.

Creeping forward, she hoped he would pass her. But he kept on her bumper like a pitbull on a bone.

Her baby chattered from the back seat, and Natalie cast a quick glance at her. Oblivious, as she should be.

"Almost home, kiddo."

She sped down the two-lane road. The blue pickup kept on her tail.

Natalie rolled down her window and waved the driver to pass, but that only seemed to enrage him further. He darted out into the opposite lane, came up beside her with his engine roaring as if he was going to cut her off, then dropped back.

Slowing down, she hoped he'd get the message she wasn't in the mood for playing chicken. The tap on her bumper threw her toward the steering wheel. Her seat belt locked against her chest and she checked the baby again, heart racing.

Natalie dove for her cell phone in the console and was about to punch in 911 when the phone shrieked in her hand. She didn't recognize the number, but sometimes West used a friend's cell if he forgot to carry his.

"West? I need—"

"Hello, Natalie."

Her blood chilled. It wasn't West, and the man's tone was glacier cold. That's when her stomach dropped and she knew. How many years had she spent running, and now her worst fear was coming true? Seeing Grant at the party had opened up a fissure into her past she could not close.

"Pull over."

"Who is this?"

"Pull *over*."

She punched the gas, glaring into the rearview as her baby started to wail. Who else could've sent this man but Grant? "You can tell your boss his secret's safe. I told no one, and I don't plan to."

"Except hubby."

The words landed like a punch to the face. How could he—

Slamming into her bumper again, the truck kept pushing. She jammed the brakes and smelled rubber.

"Stop it! Please!"

Silence.

"I have a baby in the car!"

Natalie threw the cell phone onto the seat, desperate to hold the wheel steady. The truck swung up beside her and in one quick move sideswiped her, sending the Subaru, Natalie, and her child flying toward a telephone pole.

They hit hard, and the baby stopped screaming.

18

Present

Outskirts of Elk Valley, Colorado

The pounding in Del's chest increased as the headlights approached, dipping and bouncing with each bump in the dirt road. She checked on Callie's still form and prayed Utah wouldn't start barking.

She sunk low in her seat. It wouldn't be all that unusual to come across an abandoned car. Whoever was driving would probably just pass them by. But what if it was the police? Maybe she should start up the engine and drive away.

The car sped up, its lights nearly blinding Del. The covers stirred behind her, and Utah's nose appeared by her elbow. A low growl came from his throat, and she quickly rested her hand on him.

"Shh," she whispered, hoping he would listen to her.

Raucous laughter floated through the air as the car passed by. Del flipped up her seat and started the engine.

"What's going on?" came Callie's sleepy voice.

"Just moving," Del answered.

"Why?"

"Because." She didn't want to scare her, but she didn't

want to deal with a bunch of drunken teenagers any more than she wanted a cop knocking on her window. They'd have to find somewhere else to sleep for the night.

She drove out onto the country road, ever mindful of her sinking gas gauge. Tears pushed into her eyes, and she blinked them away. It would do no good to cry.

"Try to go back to sleep," Del said.

"I wasn't asleep."

"Then start trying again."

"We're in trouble, aren't we?"

"We'll be fine. I'll come up with something."

"I'm scared."

"We're okay."

"Who were those people back there?" Callie's face appeared at Del's elbow, and the little girl stared out the windshield as Del drove them down another dark, endless road.

"I have no idea," Del said.

"Where are we going?"

She almost screamed at the girl's incessant questions. "You need to lie back down, okay?"

Callie obeyed, and Del pulled off onto the grass beside the road, right up against the fence. She needed to get some sleep, even if only for a few hours.

"Del?"

She counted to five. "What?"

"I feel sick."

Join the club. "What kind of sick?"

"I think I'm going to throw up."

Del sat up so fast she banged her hand into the console. "Are you serious?"

Callie didn't answer, and Del frantically jumped out of the car and flung open the back door to find Callie sitting up, a strange look on her face. Without thinking, she scooped her up and deposited her outside the car.

The little girl stood there for a moment, illuminated by moonlight. Then she dropped to her knees and puked in the weeds. Del swallowed hard against her gag reflex. She knelt down beside Callie, resting her hand on her back.

"Just get it out, kid."

"I'm . . ." Callie tried to talk but was overcome by another round of retching.

What was she supposed to do in a moment like this? Del patted Callie, but it felt like a hollow gesture. She'd never been good with kids, but she should've known better than to feed her the junk they'd had for dinner.

Del grabbed a water bottle from the cup holder in the front of the car and closed the back door to keep Utah from running off. Last thing she needed was to chase a loose dog. She handed the bottle to Callie, who sat down and took a few tentative sips.

"Better now?" Del asked.

"A little."

"You can sit for awhile."

"I'm sorry, Del."

"It wasn't your fault." *It was mine.*

Callie took another sip from the water bottle.

"Swoosh it around and spit," Del said. "It'll get rid of some of the taste."

Callie obeyed then scooted closer to Del. A cricket screeched out a song somewhere nearby, and a breeze rustled the dry grasses.

"Is Utah okay?"

She must be feeling better to be thinking about her dog. "He's fine."

"I'm better now," Callie said.

"Good."

"Was it the cornflakes?"

"Maybe the milk."

"But *you're* not sick."

Because she gave most of hers to Callie. "I've got a lead stomach," Del said, leaning up against the Malibu's back tire. It was nearly midnight and they hadn't even begun to sleep. She had a little girl with an empty stomach relying on her for everything, and Del had already let her down by feeding her something that made her sick. What would be next?

Before Del could get up Callie crawled over and cuddled up against her, resting her head on Del's shoulder. Then she started crying.

"Hey, don't do that. We're gonna be all right, I told you."

"I miss my dad."

Del wrapped her arm around Callie's slender frame. "I know."

It was the only thing she did know.

Del's eyes flew open. Where was she?

She tried to move and groaned from the effort. Sitting on the hard ground with her back up against a tire probably wasn't the best place to fall asleep. She took in a deep whiff of the cold night air, and Callie stirred beside her. She'd fallen asleep too.

Raising her eyes to the sky, Del let the tears she'd been holding in all night for Callie's sake fall down her cheeks.

"I don't know what to do," she whispered. "Can You help us?" It felt weird to utter a prayer, but she had nowhere else to turn.

She didn't really expect an answer. But as the wind blew across her face, rustling the dry grass and teasing her nose with the scent of fall, a brief glimpse of hope settled across her and blew away just as quickly.

She had to get Callie into the car. It would be too cold to sleep out here without blankets.

But Del couldn't bring herself to move much less wake Callie. She would sit for a few more minutes and hope the little girl could enjoy some peace. Del closed her eyes and let herself drift too. She dreamed of home.

The next time she started awake it seemed even colder, and her right leg tingled from lack of blood flow.

"Kid."

Callie shifted but didn't wake. Del gathered the girl up in her arms. She struggled to open the back door while holding her but finally managed. Callie wrapped her arms around Del's neck and tucked her head against her chest without opening her eyes.

Del swallowed hard. She could not take care of this girl the way she deserved, but the thought of leaving her with a stranger, or even that woman Laura, was starting to feel wrong too.

Utah jumped up as the door swung open, and Del slid Callie onto the back seat beside him. He quickly settled with her under the blankets Del placed over both of them. Slipping into the driver's seat, Del pulled the door closed as quietly as she could.

Callie had slept through it all.

Letting out a long breath, Del checked the locks twice before wrapping a blanket around herself. Morning would be here in a few hours, and she'd have to figure something out.

19

Cuchara, Colorado

"What are we going to do with her?"

The voices came like ghosts in the smothering darkness. Abby tried to open her eyes, but her lids felt glued shut.

"You're the idiot who knocked her out."

"What was I supposed to do?"

"Think! She sees our faces, and it's over."

"So we dump her."

"Yeah, and look how great that went with the other guy."

Other guy? Gears clicked in Abby's head. Had these men killed Kirsch?

Abby instinctively knew not to move, not until she could make sense of her surroundings. A pounding in her head slowly brought her around, and she remembered standing outside the cabin and seeing the man behind her. He'd hit her with something.

She cracked open her eyes and, thanks to the moon, saw a tire. Gravel. The legs of two men. She lay on her side, probably near the truck she'd seen earlier, crumpled on the rocky driveway. They must've dragged her over here. Would they have searched her?

She could feel her shoulder holster strapped to her chest, but she couldn't tell if the Beretta was still hidden under her leather jacket. If it was, these boys were in for a big surprise.

A boot kicked at her arm. She held in a groan of pain.

"Just leave her, and let's get going."

Slowly, with the care of a surgeon, Abby inched her fingers toward her holster. She realized the truck's door was open, and the minimal light from the interior would keep her in shadows, at least as much as she could be with the moonlight. They might not see—

"You just gonna stand there?"

"But—"

"Grab some rope. I'll get duct tape."

Abby's fingers grazed her holster, touching cold plastic. Yes!

"But where're we going to—"

"Just shut up and—"

In one quick scramble Abby was on her feet, gun brandished. "Hold it!"

Two men dressed in black stared back at her. One had the shoulders of a football player, the other wore a skull cap pulled down tight. Both froze. That was their first wise choice of the day.

"Either of you make a wrong move, and I will put a bullet through you."

Quarterback's lip curled. She saw the whites of his eyes dart toward the truck. He probably had a weapon in there.

"Think I'm kidding?" Abby forced herself to push through the dizziness threatening her balance. He must've hit her hard. She probably had a concussion.

"Get on your knees." Abby widened her stance, desperate to keep from puking. She'd faced worse than these two before.

She had no choice here. If she blacked out again, who knew what they'd do to her? If she could just grab her cell phone to call those boys in blue, she'd be golden.

"I said on your knees, both of you!"

The men slowly lowered themselves to the gravel. She saw Quarterback wince as some of the rocks dug into his flesh.

"What were you doing in the cabin?"

"None of your business," Skull Cap said.

Abby let an expletive fly, surprised the word felt caustic to her conscience. Her vocabulary as a cop had included plenty of salt. But lately she'd tried to weed the words out, especially around Christy, who though she never once said anything about her language had been more of a Christian influence to Abby than anyone she'd ever known. She made the concept of God's forgiveness actually appealing.

"Hands on your heads," Abby ordered.

The men complied. And the truck's interior light blinked out. In the split second before Abby could grab her phone out of her pocket and use it for a flashlight, she saw the shadows of the men jump to their feet.

Abby fired the Beretta at the ground in between Quarterback's feet. The muzzle flashed brilliant in the night, and the sound caused her ears to ring.

"Hold it!"

They didn't.

One of them rushed her with such force that she was on the ground again, struggling and fighting against him.

Abby slammed her elbow against where she thought the face of her attacker was. It connected with something that crunched, and the man growled in pain, pulling away from her.

For one second Abby was free, and she did the only thing she could in her compromised position.

She ran.

Knowing she wouldn't make it to her car, she took advantage of the darkness and tore into the woods.

The trees would hide her.

Behind the trunk of a massive pine, Abby dropped to the ground, pulling in gulps of air, her gun ready.

But the men didn't follow.

She saw their silhouettes standing by the truck. Heard their mumbled conversation. Watched them jump into the truck. Tires spun, and the vehicle shot away in reverse leaving Abby alone and shaking.

20

Outskirts of Elk Valley, Colorado

D el, wake up."
For the second time in twenty-four hours Del jumped awake, Callie's face inches from hers.

"Will you quit that!" She pushed herself up onto her elbow, trying to infuse her voice with a joking tone.

"I have to go," Callie said.

Morning sunlight streamed through the fogged windows, and Del could see her breath.

"Okay, just give me a minute." She fell back into her makeshift front-seat bed and tried to get her bearings. Basic needs—that was what it boiled down to. They had clothes and at least a temporary shelter. What they didn't have was food, or not much of it. She'd have to focus on how to feed this kid.

Utah's long nose shoved under her arm. Del sighed. And the dog.

She dug around in the junk on the seat beside her for the toilet paper and presented it to Callie. "I'll keep watch. Don't go far."

Starting the car, she blasted the defrost, and a minute later she exchanged places with Callie and relieved herself in the grass beside the Chevy, hoping no one chose that moment to drive by.

Callie jumped out again when she was done, and both of them quickly brushed their teeth and tried to wash their faces with the icy water from the gas station.

"How's your stomach?" Del handed Callie the comb she dug out of the glove compartment.

"I'm hungry."

"All we've got are the beans and corn, and I'm not sure that's going to feel good on your tummy."

"They sound good to me."

Del laughed. "You're great, kid."

"So are you."

She tried not to let Callie see her beaming at the words. After everything she'd said yesterday, Callie thought she was great? She rooted around in the plastic bags, hoping they'd brought the can opener.

She found it in a bag stuffed under the seat. After opening both cans, she dumped two thirds of each into a cup and handed it to Callie with a plastic fork. Utah sat drooling beside the little girl, his leash wrapped twice around her arm. He licked his lips, staring up at the cup. Callie glanced at Del.

"I'm getting his next," she said, trying to ignore the pangs in her own gut as she tapped the rest of the food onto a paper plate and set it in front of the dog. He scarfed it down like he hadn't eaten in a week.

"What about you?" Callie paused, fork mid-bite.

Del shrugged. "Not hungry."

"But . . ."

"I'm fine. Just eat."

Callie obeyed, apparently believing her fib. She decided to straighten up the car rather than watch the girl eat the last of their food. By the time Callie was done, Del had everything but their clothes stuffed in the trunk. She downed a bottle of water hoping it would fill her stomach, but it only made her nauseous.

Beg, borrow, or steal. That's what it came down to, like it or not.

Del rounded up Callie and Utah.

Callie snapped on her seat belt. "Where are we going today?"

"Town," Del said.

"You gonna ask around for a job again?"

She closed her eyes, willing herself not to snap as Callie started up her ask-every-question-imaginable game again.

"Your dad was right about you," she finally said, driving them back to the main road.

Callie's eyes opened a little wider.

"You should be a detective."

"Like Nancy Drew?"

"Yeah, you two would get along well."

After a few moments driving in silence, Del decided she needed to know more about this girl's situation. "Tell me about Laura," Del said. "What's so bad about going up to visit her?"

Callie stared down at her hands. "I don't want to."

"Why?"

"Because."

"We might not have any other choice."

"She hated me! Just like my real mom."

"Your mom did not hate you," Del said.

"Was it because I'm ugly?" Callie's voice was barely a whisper.

Del pulled the car onto the shoulder, checked the rearview, then threw the gearshift into Park. She swiveled around in her seat and took both of Callie's hands in her own.

"Callie, listen to me." She squeezed the girl's fingers with each word. "You're beautiful. The prettiest girl I know."

Callie nodded, a tear escaping down her cheek.

"I don't have all the answers, okay? But I know that your mother, *my* mother, did not hate you. She loved you. Why she left, I don't know. Maybe someday we will."

"Where do you think she is?"

"I have no idea. I wish I did."

Del thought of the PI dead in the woods. He'd been looking and came up empty. And dead. Did his death have anything to do with his investigation?

"What would you say to her if you met her?" Callie asked softly.

Nothing she could repeat to a little kid. Del started driving again. "No idea. What about you?"

The little girl thought long and hard as she stared out the window. They passed a spread called Lonely River Ranch, and Del wondered if Callie didn't want to answer.

"I still love her," Callie whispered. "I'd want her to know that."

21

Six months ago
Hudson Mountain Chalet
Westcliffe, Colorado

And that, my boy, is how it's done!" April Hudson raised her wine glass, and Grant met it with the rim of his own. "Cheers!"

"Best speech you ever gave," his aunt said.

Grant carved a slice from his tenderloin steak and glanced out the massive A-frame window of the mountain chalet. He'd specifically requested Marcy serve them dinner here by the window rather than in the dining room or even his study. This view inspired him. Once again he had taken up the political torch for his family. No other Hudson had achieved his status, not even his aunt, and tonight he was on the cusp of his greatest achievement. He would announce the creation of his presidential exploratory committee tomorrow.

The sun was just ducking behind the mountains, and the golden rays glinted off every snow drift sloping down to the lake. It took three full-time employees to keep the Hudson getaway in the Sangre de Cristo Mountains running year round. For the past fifty years, any Hudson family member in need of a reprieve or an escape from life could find refuge here in the peaceful mountains.

Now the cabin was Grant's alone since he'd bought it from his aunt, and he carefully guarded it from visitors. Politics was in his blood, but even a Hudson needed a place to hide once in a while.

Grant savored the bloody steak and eyed his aunt. Despite their differences, she had been right. The allure of power had seeped into his veins, and he'd devoured it with every election victory.

"We'll meet with the others in the morning," Grant said between bites.

"You know I've always had great plans for you," his aunt said. "I've groomed you your whole life for this moment. Congress was a drop in the bucket compared to what you'll face if you set your sights on the Oval Office."

Grant laughed. "If?"

His aunt didn't respond.

"Isn't this what you've always wanted?" Grant asked. "A Hudson in the White House?"

April Hudson leaned forward, resting both elbows on the table. A fork in one hand, a knife in the other, she pointed both at her nephew. "They will rake you over the coals. Anything in your past will be brought to light."

Grant bristled. "I can handle the tabloids."

"You know what I'm talking about."

He knew exactly what she was talking about. She'd wanted him to have Natalie killed twenty years ago, and he couldn't do it.

"You have no chance if they find out."

"And you worry too much."

"I'm dead serious, Grant."

He stared down at the meat on his plate.

"Are you hearing me?" April Hudson's dark eyes lasered

in on Grant as if he was a little boy again, unable to eat when she looked at him that way. She could still bore a hole right through him and make him squirm.

"I realize the risk."

A disgusted sigh came from the elder Hudson as she slammed her silverware onto the table. She jabbed her arthritic finger toward Grant's face. "Take care of her, or I will."

22

Present
Elk Valley, Colorado

Del parked the Malibu in the overgrown lot behind It's Only Natural Foods, her stomach in knots. She'd thought about bringing Callie in with her to buffer the conversation—who wouldn't want to help a cute kid?—but then thought better of it.

"You stay here," Del said, pulling her key from the ignition slot.

"Why? I want to come with you."

"Because." She got out and closed the door before the girl could come up with a good argument. She needed to do this alone, out of earshot of an impressionable child.

The parking lot could've used a new coat of blacktop years ago, and several chunks of asphalt were missing around the back door of the shop, but It's Only Natural Foods customers didn't care. As long as Patricia Thompkins kept stocking the shelves with organic grains, essential oils, and the best gluten-free fudge west of the Divide, she'd stay in business.

Del glanced back at Callie, who'd climbed over into the driver's seat. By the way her lips were moving she was talking to Utah, who'd hopped into the passenger seat. For Callie. That's why she was doing this.

As she opened the door, instrumental music heavy with chimes and pipes met her ears at the same time the incense reached her nose. The store stocked plenty of trinkets and candles alongside the foods, and there was usually a pot of herbal tea at the checkout counter alongside a carafe of fair trade organic coffee.

Del passed through the storeroom where pallets of goods waited to be stocked. It had been her job to take inventory of new shipments, though Eric did a lot of the actual stocking. Maybe he wouldn't be here.

"Patricia?" She passed through the vitamin aisle. The music got a little louder. Patricia usually kept the CD player up by the register on top of the refrigerated case of goodies, many of them either sweetened with agave or honey.

She found the woman measuring homemade granola into single-serving bags she sold for as much as it cost to eat a pancake platter at the diner.

"Can I talk to you?"

Patricia Thompkins swung around, palm on her heart, then laughed. "Oh, my word. You gave me a—" Her smile disappeared when she saw Del. "What are you doing here?"

The woman's long gray hair flowed past her shoulders in waves over a multi-colored tunic, and the bracelets she wore clinked together each time she moved her arm. Years of sun exposure had dug crevasses into her face, but there was always a sparkle Del had envied. For all her kookiness, she enjoyed life and she wanted her customers to as well.

The words Del had planned to say faded on her tongue as she looked into the eyes of her former employer and saw the narrow glare of hurt. Del knew Patricia felt she'd betrayed her.

"I didn't do it, you know." Her words would fall on the deaf ears of a loyal grandmother, but Del had to say them anyway.

"You shouldn't be here," Patricia said, returning to her granola. She picked up a bag and hefted it in her hand. She rarely used a scale and could guess measurements to the ounce.

"I need help."

"Answer's no."

"Please hear me out."

Patricia spun around again. "Why should I? I can't believe a word you say."

If Del pointed the finger at Eric again, it would only make things worse. Patricia treated him like a son, and he'd taken advantage of the woman, expecting the blindness of her love to win out. It had. Blood was thicker than the truth, apparently.

"I lost my apartment," she said softly. She wouldn't bring Callie into this unless she absolutely had to. The fewer people who knew about her the better.

"I'm sorry to hear that."

"And I haven't been able to find another job."

Patricia tied the granola bag with a twisty tie and set it on the growing pile on the counter. The sweet, nutty smell made Del's mouth water.

"I'm kind of in a bind, Patricia. Would you consider—"

"No."

"Could I just borrow a little money?"

The woman's eyes flared. She crossed her arms and faced Del again. "How dare you even come in here after what you did. I trusted you."

She stared at the floor, the sting of Patricia's words made even harsher because they weren't based on facts. This woman thought she was a thief when she'd only been trying to do the right thing.

"I wish you'd believe me," she whispered.

Patricia grabbed her by the arm. "I thought you were a good girl."

What did that mean?

"It'll come back to you." Patricia pointed at her. "These things always do."

She ground her teeth together to keep from snapping out something she'd regret. *Walk away. Don't look back. She doesn't believe you and probably never will.* Del pulled away from her and almost slammed into Eric.

"Whoa!" He held up his hands. "Where's the fire?"

"Shut up." She tried to slip past him.

Eric didn't move. "Maybe we should talk."

She glared at him.

"She asked me for money," Patricia said to her grandson.

"Well, that's rude." Eric's words held a teasing tone.

She shouldered her way around him, shaking her head. This had been a bad idea from the beginning, but she'd been too desperate to see it. She'd hoped Patricia might soften when she saw her. The fact that she didn't probably meant Eric had more control over the business than Del realized. She would not grovel in front of him.

Outside she made a beeline for the car.

"Did you get anything?" Callie asked eagerly, sliding over and pushing Utah into the back.

Del shook her head. "We'll come up with something else."

"Why is that man watching us?"

"What?" Del spun toward where Callie pointed.

"He pulled up right after you went inside."

A dark sedan was parked at the edge of the lot. A man wearing a skull cap was at the wheel. Del got a quick glance at his face before he looked away.

"Maybe he's a customer," she said.

"With binoculars?"

Del quickly started the car. She'd put as much distance between them and It's Only Natural Foods as possible.

23

Cascade Street Bed & Breakfast
Elk Valley, Colorado

Abby checked out of the bed and breakfast with a raging headache. She walked outside, squinting in the sunlight. She'd called 911 the moment she gathered her bearings last night, and the sheriff personally came and took her statement, promising to do everything in his power to find her attackers.

But the local news this morning called David Kirsch's death a suicide. Was someone covering the whole thing up, or had she heard those paramedics wrong? Either way, why had the sheriff let that suicide story get out after what she told him she'd overheard last night? Abby walked over to her car to find Christy Williams leaning against the bumper.

"What are you doing here?" Abby unlocked the vehicle with her remote.

"Checking up on you."

"I'm fine."

Christy came over and immediately noticed the scratch on Abby's cheek. So much for hiding it with makeup. "What happened?"

Abby threw her suitcase in the trunk. She called Christy

from her room last night and profusely apologized for missing dinner. She blamed the headache that still held her in its vice. "Aren't you supposed to be opening your store about now?"

Christy crossed her arms. "Brynn's taking care of things. But Ab, come on. Where were you really?"

"What?"

"You said on the phone you got caught up in something then called me at ten o'clock to say it was a headache?" Christy shook her head. "You think I don't know that look on your face? Something's up."

She unlocked the car doors. "I don't want to drag you into it."

"A little late for that."

"Can we get some coffee first?"

Christy laughed.

Ten minutes later they were sitting at Christy's kitchen table above the bookstore nursing mugs of Peet's Brazil Minas.

"Spill," Christy said.

"You're not gonna like it."

"Yeah, I've heard that before."

Abby held her mug up to her nose and took a deep whiff of the rich brew. She knew what Christy would say, but who else could she tell? Abby reluctantly shared everything with her friend, and just as she expected, Christy was speechless, eyebrows raised in disbelief.

"You could've been killed!"

Abby raised her hand. "But I wasn't."

"Why do you do things like this?"

"I can't help it." She took a sip from her cup and nearly scalded her tongue. "It's what I do."

"You could've called me."

"And let you talk me out of it?"

"Ab, I'm serious." Christy reached out and grabbed her hand. "You can't do this kind of stuff on your own."

"Which is why you're coming with me when I go back to the cabin."

With a groan, Christy shook her head.

"This was obviously more than a suicide, and I want to know the truth." Abby stood up then winced. "After I take some Tylenol."

～

The cabin's ominous aura had faded now that it was daylight. Abby slowly drove down the narrow, gravel driveway, searching the woods. So far the coast was clear.

"Wouldn't the police have checked all this?" Christy asked.

"Why did those creeps come back if they killed him? What were they looking for?"

"Are you sure you heard them right?"

This time Abby pulled the Acura right up to the cabin. It felt safer.

"You're gonna try to get in, aren't you?" Christy said.

She smiled. "Read my mind."

"For the record, that's breaking and entering."

"I won't break anything."

Christy got out of the Acura muttering under her breath.

"Stay in the car if you want."

"And let you get clonked on the head again? I don't think so."

Her hand on her gun, Abby marched right up to the cabin and knocked. "Might as well try the easy way first," she said.

"I'm not bailing you out if the cops come."

"Fair enough."

"And I'm not lying if they do."

Abby elbowed her friend. "Shut up."

Her uneasiness increased with each moment she was on

this property. Christy was right. This was definitely breaking and entering, and Abby didn't have a badge to explain her way out of it.

"Sorry if this goes against your Christian morals," Abby whispered.

"It should go against yours too."

"I'm not a Christian."

Christy shifted her weight, causing a board on the cabin's porch floor to creak. Before her friend could respond, Abby held a finger to her lips. She knew that wasn't what Christy wanted to hear. Christy had come close to convincing her to at least give God a try, but Abby was still on the fence about the whole surrendering her life thing. And she hadn't been able to reconcile all the evil she'd seen in the world with a God who was supposed to care for her.

Abby picked the lock, and they stepped into the cabin. The faint smell of wood smoke drifted through the otherwise stale air. Two pairs of men's hiking boots lay right near the door waiting for David Kirsch to come home.

"What are we looking for?" Christy whispered.

"Not sure."

Which was the truth. Chances were the local authorities had already swept the place and taken anything that would've provided clues, but Abby knew better than anyone things could be missed. She also knew she probably shouldn't be doing this or dragging her best friend into it, but those thugs last night made it personal now.

"In and out in five," Abby said.

"What if he has family?"

"I'll apologize if they show up."

Christy sighed.

"Look, someone nailed me in the head last night and would've done worse if I hadn't gotten lucky." Abby led them through the mud room and into the living room where two leather sofas, half a bookshelf, and a media center that would've made her daughter drool beckoned.

"I have a right to know what happened now," Abby whispered.

"Just hurry," Christy said, glancing around like she expected the cops to come barging in any moment.

Careful not to touch anything, they moved from room to room finding nothing out of the ordinary. Abby wasn't sure what she'd expected. The killer's name written in blood on the wall? Forensic evidence was probably already collected or contaminated by now. Yet this guy had been murdered, she was convinced. What had he been doing to make him a target? A PI's life was usually a lot more boring than the TV shows made it out to be, following an unfaithful husband or wife or researching an insurance claim kind of boring. So who knocked this guy off?

"Two minutes, Abby."

They skimmed the bedroom, which was a lot neater than she would've expected for an apparent bachelor. Even the toothpaste was carefully squeezed with exactly one half of it missing.

"Neat freak," Christy observed.

"Except in here." Abby walked into what looked like the man's office, where all cleanliness and order went out the window.

A huge oak desk cluttered with books, printouts, and three used coffee mugs took up nearly one wall. The barren space in the middle of the desk was probably where the computer and monitor had been. Police no doubt bagged it. She was surprised they hadn't taken the papers too. Maybe the cops were the ones who made the mess.

She took a pen from her pocket and moved some of the papers around.

"Anything?" Christy asked, still whispering.

"Doesn't look like."

A lot of the stuff seemed to be personal reading, like a copy of the *New York Times*, and pages of *Boingboing* blog posts printed on recycled paper.

Christy hunched over the desk. "Eclectic guy."

Abby went over to the filing cabinet and, using a paper towel, opened the first drawer. "I bet there's something around here."

The drawers were completely empty. Great.

"What about this?" Christy held a piece of paper out to Abby.

"I told you not to touch anything!"

"Just look."

She reluctantly took the paper from Christy. It was blank. "I don't see anything."

"Move it around in the light. See the indentations?"

Someone had written on whatever sheet had been above this one so hard it came through.

Before Abby could stop her, Christy picked a pencil out of the mug of pens on the desk.

"Let me see it again," Christy said.

It was too late to worry about fingerprints. Abby gave her the paper, and Christy gently ran the lead of the pencil over the paper. The indentations became faint white lines.

"It's an address." Christy handed it back to Abby.

D. Mangini, 1560 Main Street, Elk Valley, CO.

"Know him?" Abby asked.

"It's not *that* small of a town. But I do know the street," Christy said.

"Then let's get out of here."

24

Present

Lame Horse Bar & Grille
Alamosa, Colorado

"Here you go, ma'am." The perky bartender with Lucille Ball hair slid a mug of beer across the counter to Natalie McGuire. She took it to a table in the corner. There, sitting alone, she opened her laptop. She didn't have many friends and therefore didn't get many emails, but she usually tried to check them once a week.

When she opened the Google Alert for "West McGuire" the headline hit her with the force of a cage fighter's punch: Local Rodeo Star Dies in Freak Accident.

Natalie frantically clicked to the article, each word slamming her in the heart.

West McGuire, 44, of Pueblo, CO, tragically died in a freak trailer accident on his way to pick up a new reining horse prospect. "It's tragic," rodeo coordinator Richard Hunt said. "No one expects for something like this to happen."

Natalie found his obituary with a few more mouse clicks, and she had to squeeze the slippery beer mug to steady her hand. There was no mention of Callie. She dove for her purse and yanked out her cell phone. Where was her daughter? Oh, please God. Let her be okay.

Natalie still had West's old number, and she dialed it without hesitation. Whoever had his phone would know, right? On the third ring a woman picked up.

"Hello?"

"Is this West's phone?"

There was a long pause, as if the woman was checking the incoming number to see if she recognized it.

"Who is this?"

"I'm so sorry to hear what happened, but I need to talk to someone who knew him."

"I'm his . . . *was* his girlfriend."

Natalie closed her eyes. Of course West would've moved on. It's what she'd told him to do. "His daughter, Callie. Where is she?"

"Who did you say you were?" The woman's voice was instantly wary.

"Is she okay?"

"I'm sorry, but I can't—"

"I need to know!"

The bartender sent a glare in her direction, but she didn't care.

"My name is Natalie. I'm West's ex-wife and Callie's mother."

Silence.

"Please tell me if she's okay."

When she heard no sound in her ear, Natalie looked at her phone.

Call ended.

Without thinking, she grabbed her mug and launched it at

the wall. It shattered, sending beer and foam dripping down the wood paneling. She tossed a twenty at the bartender and ran from the building.

25

Elk Valley, Colorado

Del could barely think straight with her stomach so empty. It came in waves. A few minutes would pass and she'd be able to concentrate on driving, then she'd find herself feeling weak and snapping at Callie or plowing through an intersection without stopping.

"Are you okay?" Callie finally asked when Del forgot to hide her hunger and held her stomach with her hand.

She managed a nod, but she knew this couldn't go on.

"I've always wanted a sister," Callie said, looking up at Del like she was a movie star. It made her heart ache as much as her stomach. She knew she was about to disappoint the girl.

Del had parked them in front of the library, hoping maybe a librarian would know of a job opening. No one did, and after prying Callie away from one of the computers, they were back in the car.

It was already two o'clock. Way past lunch time.

"I can wait to eat," Callie said with a firm nod.

Del sighed, starting the car. "No, you can't."

They pulled away from the curb. It was time. There was no other option.

"Where to next?"

"Kid, we don't have a choice. Your dad's girlfriend lives in Pueblo. We'll call her and have her pick you up."

Callie's silence was worse than if she had cried. She stared down at her hands, and her lip twitched.

"Laura will feed you. I can't."

"You have to eat too," Callie whispered.

She'd deal with that later. For now she had to get this little girl, her half sister, settled with someone who could care for her. At least Laura wasn't a stranger. She knew Callie, and Del couldn't imagine anyone refusing to feed a kid.

"She took me to *you!*" Callie's chin lifted, and she glared at Del.

"And you haven't eaten a good meal since."

"I don't care."

"You should."

"I'll run away."

Del pounded on the brake at the stoplight, her tires squealing. Utah flew forward, and Callie caught his fall with her arm. Her face was turning red.

"You can see how desperate things are, right?" Del said.

"She hated me."

"I seriously doubt it."

"I want to stay with you!"

"I don't care!"

But she did. That's what made this so hard. She couldn't be a decent human being and allow a child to live like this, sleeping in a car and not knowing where her next meal would come from.

Wiping at her eyes, Callie turned toward the window.

"You need someone who can actually take care of you,"

Del said. "That isn't me. Maybe once I get a job and some money I can come back for you."

Callie swung around. "Please don't make me leave."

"I don't want to, but I don't have a choice."

"I promise I'll talk less."

Del gave the car gas, and they were moving again. "Why do you even want to be with me?"

Callie didn't answer, no longer looking at her.

"I'm no good for you. Don't you see that?"

"You're my sister," Callie whispered.

"Half sister."

"Stop!" Callie's plea went straight to Del's heart.

"Why? What the—"

"Over there." The little girl pointed out the window. "Look."

All Del saw was a white church on a street corner. "What?"

"The sign."

She leaned over toward Callie's side of the car. A small sign was stuck in the ground, a green balloon on the post to draw attention.

Fellowship Lunch
11:00-2:30 p.m.

"They have food in there." Callie's eyes brightened. "We don't have to go to Laura's."

"We can't just—"

"Del, please."

"That's for people who go to this church."

"We can at least look."

It was the furthest thing from Del's mind to walk into a strange church, but the girl did have a point. They would have food. And it might buy her a few more hours to figure out if her other idea was even possible.

Callie went for the door handle.

"Wait, wait." She quickly scanned the street then pulled up to the curb. She grabbed Callie's arm. "You have to promise me you're not gonna ask a million questions."

"Okay."

"And you do not tell them we have no food."

"I know."

"Or that we slept in the car."

Callie smiled. "I won't."

26

Faith Community Church
Elk Valley, Colorado

They left Utah in the car and walked toward the church entrance. Del tried to smooth out her wrinkled shirt and hoped she didn't look as grimy as she felt. Callie ran ahead of her, almost skipping, and Del tried to infuse her steps with enough energy to keep up.

The second they entered the small lobby Del wished they hadn't. People were going to ask questions, and she was going to have to answer. Or lie.

Straight ahead was the sanctuary with corridors on either side. Callie didn't hesitate and started down the hall on their right.

"Come on," Callie said over her shoulder.

"Slow down."

"I smell food!"

A white-haired man in jeans and a ribbed gray sweater walked toward them, and Callie quickly met up with him.

"We're looking for the fellowship lunch," Callie explained.

The man bent down to her, listening carefully. "Well, my dear, you've come to the right place." He pointed to one of the rooms beyond. "Right in there."

"Thank you," Callie said.

Del gave the old man a polite smile. "Hold up, kid."

"He said it's right in there."

She allowed Callie to lead her by the hand, and together they made their entrance. Several long tables had been set up, and against one wall was an assortment of crock pots and casserole dishes. Almost everyone in the room looked old enough to be their grandparent, and most of them seemed engrossed in their own conversations. That could work to their advantage.

Callie honed in on a plate of cookies, and before Del could stop her she stuffed half a chocolate chip cookie into her mouth. She could hardly scold the girl. And maybe Callie had the right idea anyway. Pretend like they belonged and ask no questions.

Del reached for a plastic plate sitting in a stack and quickly handed one to Callie too. "Just fill up your plate, and then let's go."

Callie eagerly scooped macaroni and cheese alongside a wedge of lasagna dripping with mozzarella. She piled three rolls on top and squeezed as many apple slices in the cracks as she could. Del had no trouble filling her plate either, and they both took extra rolls for Utah.

No one seemed to notice them until they headed for the door.

"Excuse me."

A middle-aged woman with short, obviously dyed black hair approached them, a frown on her face. She wore an apron and held a large serving spoon coated with goopy cheese.

Del glanced down at her food then tried to meet the woman's stern gaze.

"Are you church members?"

She cleared her throat. "Um . . ."

"Because this lunch is for our seniors group."

"We saw your sign outside," Callie said. Her plate was tipping dangerously toward the floor.

The woman used the spoon to point at them. "Yes, well that's so they know where to go."

"It didn't say it was just for seniors."

If Del wasn't mistaken, she was almost sure Callie was smiling extra big on purpose.

"But do you go to church here?"

Callie thought for all of a split second. "No."

"Then you need to put it back," the woman said.

Del's mouth watered at the yeasty smell of the rolls.

"Put it back?" Callie glanced up at Del.

"You can't just come in here." The woman pursed her lips.

"But I thought—"

"It's only for the seniors," the woman said.

This is exactly what she feared. Del sidled next to Callie. "Listen, I'm sorry for the mistake, but we've already got the food on our plates. Can't we just—"

"I'll take them." She reached for Callie's plate, and the little girl started to give it to her.

Del stepped between them. They could not lose this meal.

"It's just two plates of food," she said.

"Didn't you hear me?"

"Brenda, is there a problem?"

A bald man with a tattoo sleeve on each arm stood up from the nearest table. He seemed to be the only one in the room besides Brenda who wasn't a senior.

Brenda pointed her spoon at their plates again. "These two just came in here and took this food. I told them it's for the seniors lunch and that they need to give it back."

The man came over. He met eyes with Del. "Not a big deal, Brenda, but thank you for your concern."

"But—"

"There's plenty left," the man said.

Brenda backed down, but she managed to give Del a piercing glare before she walked away and began covering the food on the tables.

"Feel free to sit down and enjoy your meal," the man said, introducing himself as Pastor Walt.

"Do you mind if we don't stay?" Del was self-conscious enough with Brenda giving her the evil eye and half the seniors now zeroing in on the two young people who'd stolen their food. She knew if they sat down they'd be bombarded, and she wasn't sure she could rein Callie in enough to keep her from saying too much. As soon as someone discovered she was taking care of her half sister out of the trunk of her car she knew the jig would be up.

Pastor Walt smiled, and Del wasn't sure if she liked it. The way he stared made her feel like he knew what she was up to.

"Are you sure about the food?" she said before he could respond.

Walt patted his belly. "Enjoy it, kids. I think I've gained ten pounds since they started inviting me." He pointed at the lasagna on her plate. "Evie has won awards for that."

Del nudged Callie with her arm, edging her toward the door.

"Thank you!" Callie said.

Pastor Walt gave her a salute. "If you girls need anything, you're always welcome."

Inwardly, Del winced. She'd been right. He did suspect something.

"What about forks?" Callie whispered as they rushed back down the corridor toward the lobby.

"In the trunk."

The little girl grinned the whole way to the car and had already eaten half a roll before Del could unlock it.

Utah almost knocked Callie's plate out of her hands when she tried to get inside, and Del had to set hers on the roof and shove him into the back seat so Callie could buckle up.

"Can't we eat first?" Callie asked as Del jumped in and started the car.

"I'm pulling up the street."

She didn't want that pastor or any of those elderly men and women seeing them devouring the food at the curb.

"He was nice," Callie said.

"That food really was only for those people."

"I don't care. I'm so hungry I could . . ." Callie glanced at Del.

"What?"

"I could never eat a horse."

Del laughed.

27

Elk Valley, Colorado

Things always looked different with a full stomach. Del used her fingers to scrape every last drop of the lasagna off the plastic plate, and then she let Utah lick it clean. They'd given the dog all the rolls and a few bites of everything else too.

"Can't believe I'm doing this," she said with a chuckle.

"He likes you."

She shrugged. "My parents weren't really animal people, so I never had a pet."

Settling back into her seat, Del closed her eyes. She could take a nap so easily right now.

"What happened to them?" Callie asked.

"I really don't want to talk about it."

It was better to focus on how to feed this kid tomorrow. One meal could tide them over until morning maybe, but it would be the same hunger after that. This food was just a Band-Aid on a much bigger problem.

"We could come back for tomorrow's lunch too," Callie said, as if reading her thoughts.

"I doubt they have it every day. And if they see us again

they'll ask questions. No one's gonna let you stay with me if they find out we're homeless."

She wished she had something to pawn or sell.

"Where's that picture of your mom?" Del asked, tilting her seat back.

Callie dug around in her pocket and handed it to her.

"I wish I remembered her," Callie said. "But she's like a dream."

"Did you ever ask your dad why she left?"

"He said it was to protect me."

Del pulled herself up onto her elbow. "He did?"

"But I never knew from what."

Del stared down at the photo. If she could track Natalie down, maybe they could get some answers.

Callie started to say something then stopped herself.

"What?"

"Never mind," Callie said.

Del leaned toward the girl over the console. "Tell me."

"I don't want to."

"Is it about her?" She tapped at the picture.

Callie nodded.

"Kid, it's important I know everything."

"But you'll take me back to Laura."

"Does she know something?"

"She *might*," Callie said, fiddling with the threads in the tear of her jeans.

"If I'm supposed to help you, I need to know everything."

"You don't tell me everything."

She glared at the girl.

"You don't." Callie pulled her other leg up onto the seat Indian-style.

"There are some things a kid shouldn't know, okay?"

"Like what?"

Del levered up her backrest and faced Callie head on.

"Fine. You know what they're going to do the second they find out I don't have a job or a place to live?"

Callie's eyes were so vulnerable, so innocent, but Del had to get across to her the seriousness of what they faced and make her understand.

"They're going to take you away from me," Del said softly.

"But you're my sister."

"They won't care."

"I'll tell them I want to stay with you."

"It doesn't matter."

Those were the cold, hard facts. She was twenty years old with no hope of getting out of this hole she'd fallen into. It wasn't fair to drag a little girl down with her.

"Do you"—Callie's words caught in her throat—"want me to go back to Laura?"

Good question. Del glanced at herself in the rearview mirror. The whites of her eyes looked dull, and a pinkish hue surrounded her pupils, a sign of her nearly sleepless night. She'd spent the past twenty-four hours worrying about someone else, and in a weird way it had helped get her mind off her own troubles. But sooner or later she would have to face the music and figure out what she was going to do with her life now.

She was surprised to feel her lip quivering. Del tried to get control of herself, desperate to keep from losing it in front of this kid. That would freak her out even more. But what were they going to do? How could she take care of herself much less a kid and a dog? The hopelessness of it all overwhelmed her. She threw open the door and walked around to the back of the car, leaning against the bumper where Callie couldn't see her.

Del hated crying. It made her feel weak and powerless. She squeezed her eyes shut. Then she heard the other car door open, like she knew it would, and in a moment Callie was standing in front of her. Del tried to make a joke about getting dust in her eyes, but it fell like a stone. Callie wrapped her gangly arms around Del's waist and gave her a hug she hadn't known she needed.

"I don't want you to go anywhere," Del whispered.

≈

They walked into the library again and Del asked to use a phone. The librarian scowled but pointed to an extension. Callie had Laura's number and Del punched it in, hoping the librarian wouldn't notice it wasn't a local call. Time for some answers.

On the third ring a woman picked up.

"Laura?"

"Who is this?"

Del paused. She hadn't planned this conversation out beyond hello

"This is Del Mangini," she said.

Silence.

"I believe you already know who I am," she added.

More silence. Del wondered if Laura had hung up, but then she heard the woman sigh into the receiver.

"I did what he asked," Laura said.

Del wished she hadn't let Callie listen in. The little girl was craning beside her to hear through the receiver. Would Laura say something the girl shouldn't hear?

And how had Callie's father even known who she was much less *where* she was? What if her mother had somehow been keeping track of her all these years? Del wasn't sure if that idea thrilled or chilled her.

"A little heads-up would've been nice," Del said, hoping Callie didn't take that the wrong way.

"I couldn't keep her."

"How did West even know where I lived?"

"All I know is he told me that if anything ever happened to him—he rode the rodeo circuit, ya know—I was to take her to you."

Del didn't appreciate the woman's tone. "Did he say anything else?"

Another pause. Laura seemed to be weighing her words. "Look, didn't the kid tell you?"

She eyed Callie, who suddenly seemed to find the pen on the table fascinating. "That my mother is her mother? Yeah, she mentioned that."

"Then what's your problem?"

"Where *is* her mother?"

Laura paused a little too long.

"Do you know where she is?" Del asked.

"How would I know."

Closing her eyes, Del held back what she really wanted to say. "What *do* you know, Laura?"

"She's yours now."

The line clicked.

Del slammed down the receiver then quickly apologized to the disapproving librarian. Grabbing Callie by the arm, she headed back to the car.

"What'd she say?" the little girl asked.

"Nothing."

"But—"

"Absolutely nothing," Del said.

28

Colorado State Fairgrounds
Pueblo, Colorado

Natalie drew in a deep breath of horseflesh, manure, and wood shavings. She strode down the barn aisle at the fairgrounds as if she belonged, but she hadn't belonged in West's world for over eight years. She'd given up the right to tread these floors when she walked out on him and Callie.

A horse nickered as she passed its stall, sticking his eager head out over the wooden half-door. In her old life she would've stopped and given him the attention he wanted. Maybe even a peppermint. But not today.

She'd left to keep her family safe when she knew her past was closing in on her. When she'd been driven off the road and hit that telephone pole she'd only broken her arm, but little Callie had spent a week in intensive care. It had been touch and go, her life hanging in the balance, and Natalie had sworn that if her daughter survived she would do everything in her power to protect her. It would never happen again. The only way Natalie could be sure was to leave. Grant had wanted to hurt *her*, and she could never let her family end up as collateral damage again. As soon as the doctors assured her Callie was okay, she'd made good on her promise. Her heart had never been the same.

Natalie passed through the barn and made her way to the back parking lot where dozens of trailers were parked, ready and waiting for their cowboy or cowgirl owners to return with bruises and buckles.

She passed trailer after trailer, RVs, and campers, but none of them matched the description the rodeo official gave her for the rig of West's girlfriend. Slant load three horse trailer, he said, with living quarters, silver trim, and a hot pink running horse stenciled on the side.

Then Natalie spotted it.

Parked on the edge of the lot and still attached to a red pickup. She marched right up to the door and started pounding. It didn't take long for a woman to yell back, and the whole trailer rocked slightly as someone inside came to answer.

When the door opened, Natalie came face to face with the woman who had replaced her. Her dark hair with red highlights, rhinestone-studded Cruel Girl jeans, and a tight tank top contrasted Natalie's plain, washed-out Levis and blue plaid shirt.

"Laura?"

"My time hasn't been changed, has it?"

Natalie gave her a smile and hoped it didn't look as hostile as she felt. "I need to talk to you."

"Why?" Laura cocked her head slightly, seeming to process she wasn't a rodeo official.

Natalie didn't wait for an invitation and stepped up into the trailer. Laura instinctively got out of her way, then swore.

"What do you think you're—"

"We're gonna talk," Natalie said.

"Get out of my—"

"About my daughter."

Laura glared at her, arms crossed. "Like you have a right."

Natalie held up her hand. "I'm sure you think I'm the worst mother in the world but—"

"You broke his heart."

If Laura had twisted a knife in her stomach, it would've hurt less. Natalie's momentum stalled. She wanted to hate this woman.

"Where's Callie?" Natalie asked.

"You've got a lot of nerve to even ask."

Natalie stepped farther into the compact living quarters of the trailer, her shoulder up against the refrigerator. At least Laura hadn't tried to throw her out. Yet.

"I can't possibly expect you to understand," Natalie said. "But there's more to my story, to West's story, than you can imagine."

Laura stared at her, cocking an eyebrow. "I loved him, you know."

"Where is my daughter?"

Laura's response was to call her a crude name, and Natalie nearly lost it. But getting into a cat fight with this woman wouldn't get her any closer to her daughter. She ran her fingers through her hair trying to remember the last time she'd washed it. She'd let herself go in the past few years, and she knew it. But when you had nothing to live for, what was the point? She spent more time at the bar than her house. Over the years she'd held minimum wage jobs to keep herself from going insane, but she never set down roots by design.

"Look, let's try this again." Natalie leaned up against the kitchen sink. "I'm not trying to—"

"You should leave."

"Just tell me where she is. Is she okay?"

Laura's eyes darted to the trailer door, probably wondering if she had time to call arena security. Her Rodeo Queen belt buckled sparkled as sunlight spilled in from the window.

"I left to protect him," Natalie said softly. "You have to understand. I would never have left otherwise."

That got a snicker out of Laura.

Natalie's gaze dropped to the floor. She wasn't sure how much she should say or how much West had revealed. The less Laura knew the better, but that wasn't getting Natalie any closer to Callie.

If West had shared any of her past with Laura she could see why this cowgirl felt the way she did. What kind of woman abandoned her husband and child? No one would believe it was because of her love for them that she'd left. Even West apparently. At the time she truly believed Grant Hudson had it in him to hurt her family in an attempt to silence her, but had she been wrong? Had she lost her family for nothing?

Tears pushed into Natalie's eyes when she pictured West's crooked grin and imagined kissing the stubble on his cheek. It had barely sunk in he was gone.

"I just want to know about my daughter." Natalie reached into her coat pocket and pulled out a stack of bills. "And I'm willing to pay for it."

Laura started to say something but then stopped. She uncrossed her arms and smiled at the money.

29

The Book Corral
Elk Valley, Colorado

Didn't you already try here?"
Callie stared up at the store's window. *The Book Corral &
Art Gallery* was painted in decorative gold script on the glass,
two bookends sandwiching the words together. The window
display was littered with Dr. Seuss books, and a stuffed Cat in
the Hat almost seemed to be watching them from his perch in
a miniature chair.

"They were closed," Del said.

"Do you like books?"

She sighed. Callie was back to her twenty–million-ques-
tions routine, but at least it kept Del's mind occupied.

"I guess," she said.

"Could I get a book?"

"Do you have money?"

Callie sighed. "I can at least look, right?"

"Sure, kid."

Del opened the door, and a bell jangled as they entered.
She didn't imagine a bookstore would pay much, but maybe it
would be enough to tide them over.

She'd never been inside a used bookstore, and she was surprised at the redolence of what had to be old pages and leather. Barnes and Noble didn't smell like this.

The silence surprised her too. It seemed they were the only customers, and no clerk was in sight. Del walked over to the L-shaped counter where a few books were set on display stands. She noticed a stack of business cards and picked one up. They had the name and address of the store with *Christy Williams* listed as the owner.

"I like animal stories," Callie said.

"Why doesn't that surprise me?"

"Oh, look!" Rushing over to a shelf on the other side of the room, Callie snatched a book and held it up for Del to see.

Misty of Chincoteague by Marguerite Henry. The book had a cute illustration on the cover of a white pony with a brown circle over its eye.

"Can I get this, Del, please?"

"You know we can't."

The little girl's shoulders drooped.

"If I had money for a book we wouldn't be here."

Callie nodded. "I forgot."

How could she forget something Del couldn't erase from her mind?

"May I help you?"

They turned around as a woman, a purse on her arm and keys in her hand, walked into the room.

"Sorry. I've had quite the afternoon. I'm opening up a little late today."

Del still felt awkward soliciting for work, but she didn't have a choice. "Are you the owner?"

"That's me."

"We need a job," Callie said, holding the horse book to her chest.

Christy smiled, and the skin around her mouth crinkled. She was practically old enough to be their mother.

Del rolled her eyes at Callie. "I would've worded it differently."

"But we do," Callie said.

"Know anything about books?" Moving behind the counter, the woman sat down in a rolling chair. She picked up a leather-bound volume that looked like it belonged on the set of *Downton Abbey* and slipped a pencil behind her ear.

"A little," Del said softly, hoping it would be enough. How hard could it be to run a bookstore?

"Unfortunately, I can't afford anyone else right now." She waved at the shelves. "Wish I could. It would be nice to be that busy."

"What about the gallery?"

"My sister manages that, but she's in the same boat."

Del figured as much but for some reason had let herself hope. "Thanks anyway."

The woman eyed her, and Del could practically see the wheels in her brain turning. Did they look homeless? She'd combed her hair and made Callie clean up too.

Christy took the pencil from behind her ear. "What's your name and number? I can call you if something changes, but I don't think it will anytime soon."

"That's okay. I understand." Del turned to leave and take Callie with her, but apparently the little girl had wandered off among the shelves and was nowhere to be seen.

"She looks like you," Christy said. "Are you related?"

"We're sisters."

It felt weird to say it, but Del was surprised at how easily it rolled off her tongue. She'd wished for a sibling growing up, but Mom and Dad were perfectly content with just her. She wondered what they would think of Callie.

"Are you girls okay?"

Del shook herself out of her thoughts and managed a fake laugh. "We're fine."

"Hey, didn't you used to work at the health food store?"

"A while back."

"Their fudge is to die for."

Del relaxed a little. "You don't have to tell me."

Christy hesitated like she was about to say something else but then seemed to stop herself. Del needed to find Callie and get out of there.

The little girl appeared from behind a shelf, ogling the room. "How many books do you have here?"

"Twenty thousand or so," Christy said.

Callie's mouth opened. "Wow."

"With more unsorted boxes still in my back room."

"You must make a lot of money."

That made Christy laugh. "I wish."

"If each book was just one dollar . . ." Callie looked off into space

"Kid, we have to get going."

"But I haven't seen all the shelves."

Callie's voice took on a whining tone, and Del had to remind herself the girl was probably exhausted. "Five more minutes," she said.

An enormous grin spread on Callie's face, and she skipped off to the back of the store.

"You really have twenty thousand?" Del asked.

Christy came around the counter again. "Keeps me busy."

She wasn't sure why, but seeing this woman making a living for herself reminded Del she hadn't thought about her own dreams in a very long time. Did she even have them anymore? When she was little she wanted everything to do with horses, but when their family moved she didn't have much opportunity to be around them. School activities kept her busy through most of her teen years. And then her world ended just before her eighteenth birthday when the ceiling caved in on two firefighters who'd rushed into a burning apartment complex to rescue a trapped old man.

Del pretended to examine one of the books displayed by the checkout. The newspaper had called her parents heroes, but that only made things worse. Every day someone would say something stupid like "they died for a reason" or "you must be so proud of them." She'd been far too angry to be proud. Why hadn't they thought about her before they'd thrown themselves into that danger? Couldn't one of them have stayed back so she didn't have to lose them both?

She stayed with a neighbor for a few weeks until she graduated. With no life insurance and a mortgage for an inheritance, she barely had enough to bury them much less pay for college. She took the little that was left from selling the house and moved out here to Colorado, a state she'd admired for its scenery since grade school.

She'd hoped starting over in Elk Valley would help her forget. She'd be creating new memories with nothing to remind her of her parents. She knew they'd want her to go on and have a happy life, but she hadn't realized how much she counted on them always being there.

Del wandered to the back of the store to find Callie. Selling the car was the only way she knew to get any cash, but then they'd really be homeless. Was there anyone in this town she could trust? Anyone she could ask for help? She fleetingly entertained the idea of going back to that church and the pastor, but telling anyone risked Callie being taken away. She'd been okay with Laura only because she already knew the girl, but after talking to her on the phone Del wouldn't be suggesting that idea again.

"Callie?" she whispered, turning a corner. She found her sitting on a small stool with a book in her lap. She didn't seem to hear Del.

"We have to go." Del rested her hand on Callie's shoulder.

The girl jumped, grabbing the book to keep it from falling.

"Sorry," Del said.

"Do we have to?"

"Utah's waiting."

"I guess he is."

They said good-bye to Christy and headed to the car, Callie holding her jacket closed.

"Before we leave I have to get something," Callie said, bee-lining for the trunk.

"Get what?"

"Something from my duffel."

"Hurry, okay?" Del unlocked the doors. Utah had fogged up the driver's window and left wet nose prints on the glass. She sighed and shooed him onto the back seat.

"You're lucky she loves you," Del said.

Callie got in a minute later, empty-handed.

Del eyed the girl and started the engine. "Thought you needed something."

"Oh, I . . . ended up not."

"But you just—"

"I thought I did, but I guess I didn't."

She flicked on her turn signal, still staring at Callie. "Why do you sound so weird?"

"Can we just go?"

She shook her head. "Fine."

"We don't have anything to eat, do we?"

"No."

"How are we going to get something?"

"I don't know," Del said, pulling out onto the street. She was out of legitimate options. There was nothing of value to pawn, and she had to keep the car.

Del glanced over at Callie who'd grown sullen staring out the window. It was for her. She'd have to feed this little girl and deal with the consequences later.

Laura could barely concentrate through her barrel race. Luckily her gelding knew the pattern better than she did, and they got a second place finish despite her distraction.

Back in her trailer she paced up and down the small corridor between the sofa and table. She'd told Natalie the truth— she really had loved West McGuire. But all his big talk had been just that. Talk. She'd naively assumed he had the means to buy the things he promised her. His bank account said otherwise, and now that West was gone she wasn't gonna wallow in grief. Or raise his kid.

Laura yanked open the kitchen drawer and pulled out Natalie's hundred-dollar bills, which were now all hers. At first the woman had offered her five hundred, but Laura easily talked her up to an even thousand. She didn't feel guilty about it either. A single grand barely scratched the surface of what Natalie could have owed West in child support. And it wasn't like it would do any harm for Callie's biological mother to know where Laura had taken her in Elk Valley.

She'd gotten the better end of that deal. Dropping onto the sofa, Laura stuffed a cushion behind her head and thought about the weird call she'd received the day after West's accident. The man on the other end was trying to find Natalie McGuire. Of course she had no clue where the woman was since not even West knew that, but the man had asked Laura to contact him if Natalie ever came around. He said it was important and that he'd pay her for the trouble.

She grabbed her phone and opened the contacts list. What were the chances she could triple that thousand in a day?

Maybe it was seeing how easily Natalie parted with her money for such a small amount of information. This guy might be willing to pay double what Natalie had. And Laura might be able to get that new truck she'd been drooling over. She could at least give the guy Natalie McGuire's phone number, which she'd saved in her contacts from when the woman called her. What would be the harm in that?

30

Main Street
Elk Valley, Colorado

Natalie cut her SUV's engine and stared up at the address Laura had given her. Could it really be true, was she about to see both her daughters again?

Popping open her glove compartment, Natalie carefully slipped out the two photographs she had cherished for all these years. It had pained her too much to place them out in the open, so she'd kept them in a drawer most of the time. But every day on their birthdays she allowed herself to see her babies.

Natalie stared at the picture of her oldest, Delaware. It was taken a few hours after her birth, right before the nurse had whisked her away into another woman's arms. Natalie touched the tiny, pink hand with her finger. Her only request had been to name her, and the adoptive parents were kind enough to allow it.

Callie's picture was taken at her first birthday party, a puppy-themed adventure she would never remember, but it made West and her feel like good parents. Natalie smiled at the hat with the doggie ears hanging over her child's bright face. She could still hear her sweet giggle and the sheer joy she expressed whenever West or Natalie took her to the petting zoo or the barn. She touched an animal, and it made her happy.

"Oh, sweetheart," Natalie turned her face away to keep her tears from dropping onto the photos.

She got out, and with her heart pounding in her ears, Natalie walked up the brick path to the front door. Some of the paint was peeling around the window frames, but for the most part the home looked tidy save for an ashtray full of cigarette butts near the porch swing.

Natalie knocked. She laid awake many nights trying to imagine what Delaware looked like. She'd be twenty now. A young woman.

A Hispanic gal flung the door open. "Yeah?"

Natalie tried to see past her. Was Callie in the next room? How would she explain to the girl why she'd left?

"Can I help you?" the woman cocked her head, giving Natalie a once-over she could practically feel.

"I'm here to see Delaware Mangini."

With a snort the woman pushed through the doorway, and Natalie quickly got out of her way.

"Delaware, huh. I always wondered what Del stood for."

"Is she here?"

"Not if I can help it."

"I thought she lived here."

"Skipped town owing us rent."

Her heart dropped. "When? Any idea where she went?"

"If I did I wouldn't be standing here talking to you." The woman went over to the swing and sat down, pulling a pack of cigarettes from her back pocket. "Deadbeat, if you ask me. You know her well?"

If only.

"No," Natalie said.

"Quiet. Kept to herself. Perfect tenant at first." The

woman lit up and sucked in a drag. "But we're not running a charity, you know."

"No idea where she could be now?"

"Not a clue." The woman arched an eyebrow. "Who knew the girl was so popular."

"What do you mean?"

"You're the third person looking for her today."

31

Development Outside Elk Valley, Colorado

I'm hungry."

"I know, kid."

It was nearly dark as Del drove them to the outskirts of town. Here the houses were spread farther apart, but they weren't completely isolated. All afternoon Del had tried to keep Callie busy concentrating on anything but food. They played twenty questions, tic-tac-toe, and the animal guessing game Del made up that Callie loved. It was all an attempt to kill the daylight hours until she could carry out her plan.

"Here's what we're going to do," Del said, pulling down a narrow street and scanning the homes. Most had lights on. She parked alongside the road, hoping anyone who passed would think they were stopping to check a map or something. "We're going to sleep here, and later I have to leave you alone for a few minutes."

Callie sat up straighter. "Why?"

"I'm gonna talk to a friend about some food." She couldn't look the girl in the eye as she said it.

"Can't I come too?"

"Not this time."

"But—"

"I need you to guard the car."

"Utah can do that."

"No. You're staying here."

Callie crossed her arms.

"Don't be mad," Del said.

"We need to stay together."

"I won't be long, so just—"

"Who is this person?"

Del sighed. "What's important is you're going to have breakfast tomorrow. And you want that, right?"

At that moment Callie's stomach gurgled.

"See?" Del tried to tickle her, but Callie pulled out of reach. She threw her door open and jumped out of the car.

The door slammed so hard Del flinched, but she dove out after the girl. They could not be running around out here calling attention to themselves. "Callie, come back here!"

She found Callie leaning against the trunk with her arms crossed again.

"What are you doing? Get back in the car."

"You're not my mother!" Callie swung around. Even in the twilight Del could see the fire flaring in her eyes. "I have a say in things too!"

She lifted her hands in surrender. "Callie, I—"

"I'm not a baby!"

"Did I say you were?"

"You treat me like I am." Callie sniffed.

"I'm trying to protect you." Del wanted to touch her or reassure her in some way, but she wasn't sure if Callie would allow it. In her eyes, Del was just being mean. But she couldn't tell her the truth. If someone had to get in trouble, it was going to be Del. And if all went as she hoped, they'd have full bellies tomorrow and enough to keep them going for at least a week. Then Del could concentrate on getting a job.

"I can protect myself," Callie said.

Del glanced up and down the road to make sure they were alone. She needed to do some serious damage control here.

"You're just a kid," Del said softly. "You shouldn't have to."

"I'm almost nine."

"We need each other. Neither of us can do it alone."

Callie squared her little shoulders, looking up at Del. "Then why can't I come with you?"

"Would you just trust me?" Del risked it and touched the side of Callie's head, surprised at the silky feel of her hair.

"I . . . want to."

"I'll tell you what." Del unlocked the trunk. "Get your toothbrush and anything else you need for bed, and we'll talk more in the car."

She didn't like how exposed they were out here, especially when the trunk light went on. Callie unzipped her duffel, got her toothbrush, then dug around a little more and pulled out two books. She held them both tightly to her chest.

Del gave her a slight nudge toward the front of the car.

Callie stomped over and climbed back inside where Utah waited to slather her arm with licks.

"You sure I can't come?" Callie said.

Del rolled her eyes, knowing the girl wouldn't see her. "I really need you to drop it, okay?"

"Why are you always so cranky?"

"Oh, I don't know, maybe it's because . . ." she started to say something snarky about Callie's incessant questions but caught herself. This kid just lost her dad and was dumped by his girlfriend. She had a right to be angry, yet instead she'd gone along with all of Del's wanderings through town searching for anyone willing to pay her a few bucks, and she hadn't once complained about the lack of food or sleeping in the car.

"I'm just tired," Del finally said.

"Me too." Callie yawned.

After sitting for what seemed like hours, Callie opened the book on her lap. A familiar pony stared back at Del. Callie quickly tried to cover it with her hands.

"You're going to return those."

"I'm sorry, it's just—"

"Just what?" Del stuck her face in Callie's. "You stole those books from that bookstore, and you expect me to be okay with it?"

Hypocrite. What right did she have to scold this girl when she knew full well what she herself planned to do in a few hours?

"I never get nice things," Callie said softly. "I just wanted…"

She understood perfectly well why the girl had done it, but it didn't matter. She couldn't let her go around stealing things. "What would your dad say?"

Callie's head dipped. "He'd be disappointed. Like you are."

Del rested her elbow on the ledge of her door and stared out at the deserted street. She could see the blue glow of a TV through the curtains of one of the homes. What would it be like to be in there, warm and comfortable, knowing tomorrow would be just another boring day?

"We'll go back first thing in the morning, and you can explain it to that Christy woman."

Hypocrite. Hypocrite. Hypocrite.

Callie rearranged the books in her lap. "The Bible was free."

She turned toward Callie who held out the smaller book.

"Really, it was. The price says zero inside," Callie said.

Del took the book and tried to page through it, but she couldn't see the words clearly enough. "Get the flashlight in the glove compartment," she said.

Callie dug around until she found it and clicked it on.

"Keep it low," Del said.

Callie pointed the light at the Bible. Sure enough, a neat price of $0 was penciled on the first blank page.

"My dad used to read this," Callie said.

It was bound in faux leather with *Holy Bible* written in gold on the spine.

"Sometimes he'd read it to me at night in our hotel room." Callie bounced the light around. "Can you read it to me now?"

"What?"

The glow from the flashlight caught Callie's earnest face. "Please?"

"You stole a Bible, and now you want me to read it to you?"

"It can be my punishment."

Del tried not to laugh. She couldn't be mad at this kid for long. She grabbed the flashlight and shone it on the book. Not like she had anything better to do, and if it would get Callie to nod off, Del would've read her the phone book.

"Where should I start?"

"I don't think it matters. It's lots of little books put together."

She flipped to the table of contents. "Lots of weird names too."

Del decided to open up in the middle and ended up in a book called Proverbs. She cupped her hand around the flashlight to keep the beam as small as possible and started reading. "A person who is full refuses honey, but even bitter food tastes sweet to the hungry."

"Oh, I love honey," Callie said. "Especially on crackers.

My dad used to get a whole box of Saltines, and we'd plaster them with peanut butter and honey and make little sandwiches."

So much for getting their minds off food. "I thought you wanted me to read."

"Sorry."

She continued. "A person who strays from home is like a bird that strays from its nest."

Callie giggled. "That's us. Little birdies."

"Maybe I should pick a different spot," Del said.

"Try toward the end."

Del flipped over a wedge of pages and squinted down at the small print. "Dear brothers and sisters," she read, "when troubles come your way, consider it an opportunity for great joy."

"It really says that?"

"Yeah kid, it does. Do you want me to stop?"

"Keep going."

Del sighed. "For you know that when your faith is tested, your endurance has a chance to grow. So let it grow, for when your endurance is fully developed, you will be perfect and complete, needing nothing. If you need wisdom, ask our generous God, and he will give it to you. He will not rebuke you for asking. But when you ask him, be sure that your faith is in God alone."

"That's what we need to do," Callie said.

Del slapped the book down on her lap, giving up the idea of reading more than a few sentences without Callie interrupting. "Do what?"

"Ask God for help."

"I thought you said He doesn't always listen."

"I did?"

"Yesterday. Back with the horses."

"Could it hurt to ask?"

Del kept her finger in the book and flipped off the flash-light. Her parents hadn't been religious so she hadn't been either, but she also wasn't like some of her friends at school who ridiculed Christianity. If she were being completely honest, Del didn't know whether to believe or not. Some of the stuff Christians talked about, like people rising from the dead, was freaky.

In the darkness, Del could barely see Callie clasp her hands together and lift her eyes toward the car ceiling.

"Father God, we need some help." Callie's voice was soft and reverent. "I . . . I miss my daddy. Can you . . . can you tell him I love him?"

Del's throat tightened at the words. This little girl was certain her dad was in Heaven, and her innocent prayer made Del wish she did believe.

"Thank you for giving me a sister," Callie continued. "She's taking care of me, but we can't do this alone. Please help us. And . . . I'd really like to see my mom again. Please tell her I still love her. Amen." Callie unclasped her hands. "Did that sound okay?"

Del patted her on the leg. "Just right."

"Think He heard me?"

"What do you think?"

Callie gave a little nod.

"Then don't worry." Del pointed toward the bench seat. "Climb back there and try to go to sleep."

"Will your friend really give us food?"

Del was glad it was dark now, because Callie wouldn't be able to see her face. "That's what I'm hoping."

"Can you get some chocolate?"

"I really don't think—"

"If you can."

She leaned back in her seat and closed her eyes. "Okay, kid. I'll try. Can I borrow your duffel bag?"

∽

Del closed and locked the car door as quietly as she could, hoping Callie would stay asleep. She hated to leave her alone, but she didn't have a choice. Something had to be done, and Del was doing it. She'd exhausted every other resource.

She carefully emptied the contents of the duffel bag into the trunk and slung it over her shoulder. Her heart was pounding in her ears as she checked up and down the lane where they were parked.

Callie had prayed for God to help them, but in the meantime Del couldn't sit back and watch the girl go hungry. There was nothing else to do.

She started walking down the street as if she belonged, her breath billowing around her in a moisture cloud. What would her parents think of her now? She pictured them staring down at her from the Heaven Callie believed in. Were they telling her to find another way? Or were they urging her down the street to care for the little sister she didn't even know she had because of them?

Del kicked at a stone and sent it skidding across the pavement. The moon was out again, illuminating her path. She'd thought through this plan all day, but now that it came down to seeing it through, she was as nervous as a mustang near a rattlesnake.

More lights were disappearing in the windows of the houses, and Del searched for the right one. If her parents *were* watching, they were about to see their daughter become a thief.

32

Cascade Street Bed & Breakfast
Elk Valley, Colorado

Abby couldn't sleep. Every time she closed her eyes she pictured those thugs attacking her and replayed what she could have done differently.

Rolling onto her side, she closed her eyes for the hundredth time. It had been almost a decade since her ex-husband had slept beside her, but for some reason, tonight Abby wished for Michael's comforting arms.

She threw off her covers. Best to leave that thought alone and try not to picture him holding his second wife. Abby pulled on some clothes and padded from her room and out to her car in the bed and breakfast's tiny parking lot. She'd had every intention of heading back home to Longmont this afternoon, but after what happened at the cabin, that was out of the question.

With a sigh she climbed into the Acura and sunk into the driver's seat. Why couldn't she just leave this whole thing alone and let the locals deal with it in their own way?

Because I'm a cop.

Abby tapped a rhythm on the steering wheel. Christy was

right. Twenty years, and it was ingrained in her. For the first time since she'd quit, Abby admitted she missed it. The thrill, the rush, the unpredictability, even the paperwork. Well, maybe not the paperwork.

She ran through the events of the day as she started the car and pulled onto the street. Christy had to get back to town and open her bookstore, but Abby had spent the rest of the day staking out the address they'd found written on the paper. According to the landlord, Del Mangini was a twenty-year-old kid who hadn't paid her rent in three months. She'd run out on them a few days ago, and they hadn't seen her since.

Abby drove back across Elk Valley and pulled up two houses from the girl's apartment again. All the windows were dark except for what looked like the bathroom. A dim glow shone in that window. A night light perhaps?

Abby couldn't let it go. Every fiber in her sizzled with questions. How could she allow something like this to slip through her fingers without trying to find the truth? That's what police work had always been for her—the pursuit of truth. Something greater than herself. She might not be able to make sense of her own life, but if she could bring closure to someone else's, at least she could sleep at night.

Abby smirked in the darkness. Sleep would be nice.

Twenty minutes later, she wondered if Christy was right. She should let it go and get on with her life.

Then Abby noticed a white SUV slowly cruise down the street. It turned around at the end of the block only to loop back and park in the shadows across the street.

Its lights blinked off, but no one got out.

33

Development Outside Elk Valley, Colorado

Del crept around the back of the house, ready to bolt at the slightest sound from inside. No cars in the driveway, no lights in the house. No one home, she hoped. She'd already eliminated four other houses. Even though their lights were out, somehow they seemed occupied.

She pulled out the towel she'd brought along and wrapped it around her hand. She hoped the back door was glass.

This had to work.

Dirt crunched under her boots. She froze, listening again for sounds of a dog, an alarm, anything that meant she had been discovered.

Silence.

A dog did bark, but it was far in the distance. Probably at a raccoon or possum that had wandered into its yard. Del tried to read her watch in the moonlight. Past midnight. She blinked back her exhaustion. Callie needed food.

Time to move.

She crept closer to the back door even as warnings screamed like sirens inside her head. *Don't do this. There has to be another way. You're about to ruin your life! They'll take Callie away from you. What are you going to tell her?*

Forcing the thoughts away, she scanned the back yard. A birdfeeder swung lightly on a hook hanging from the gutter. A picnic table with a potted cactus was a few feet from an outdoor grill.

Bingo.

The top half of the back door was paned glass.

Del squeezed her hand into a fist. This was it. Something she could never undo. There was no going back from here.

She gritted her teeth and peered inside the house. A microwave clock glowed blue, and a dim fluorescent light above the sink gave enough light for her to see the brushed aluminum refrigerator beckoning. The meal at the church had long ago worn off.

God, please. I don't want to do this. But she had to. The only other option was child services or the police, and she wasn't going there.

Del punched the glass through the towel as hard as she could.

It shattered.

She listened for an alarm. When she heard none, she reached inside and unlocked the deadbolt. If there was an alarm, it would probably be on a delay. She had to be in and out before there was time for the cops to respond.

She opened the door and rushed inside. Making a beeline for the refrigerator, she flung the door open and stared at more food than her apartment kitchen had ever held at one time.

Milk, eggs, Pepsi cans, orange juice, salad dressing, mustard, butter.

The options paralyzed her—what would be nourishing yet wouldn't spoil quickly?

She dropped the duffel bag on the floor and began stuffing everything inside. Half a loaf of whole wheat bread, pack of

American cheese, three cups of blueberry yogurt. She threw open the bottom drawer—two green apples, an orange.

In the back she spotted a sleeve of English muffins right beside a pack of ground beef. Her mouth watered thinking of a juicy hamburger, but they had no way to cook the meat. Instead she grabbed a bag of baby carrots and the muffins, her heart pounding in her ears.

Del scooped up the duffel and swung around. Was there a pantry?

There. Over by the window. Two floor-to-ceiling slatted doors built into the wall had to contain something. She pulled one open, wincing as it squeaked. She didn't dare turn on a light and could barely see the labels, but she'd hit pay dirt. Canned goods lined the shelves. Del grabbed them two at a time, laying them in with the rest of the food and desperately hoping they wouldn't clink together.

Can of mixed nuts, a box of Wheat Thins, and—

"Hey!"

She spun at the man's voice, dropping a jar of spaghetti sauce.

It exploded on the floor like a bomb.

Del was gasping in breath. No, no, no. She could not be caught!

"Stop it right there!"

Without thinking or zipping it closed, she grabbed the duffel by the straps and shot across the kitchen floor to the gaping back door. Callie needed her. She had to make it out of here!

She flew through the doorway and out into the yard, past the picnic table, almost knocking her head on the bird feeder.

"I'm sorry!" she yelled over her shoulder.

That's when the gunshot blasted through the night.

Del tripped, dropping the food. Frantically she scooped the duffel up again and was halfway across the yard when the second shot came.

The next thirty seconds felt like a stop-motion film. She made it through a neighbor's yard and into the street, desperately running as fast as her legs could carry her. The duffel felt like it was loaded with bricks, but she was bursting with adrenaline that infused her with strength.

She passed three more houses at a dead run before the pain hit.

Del gasped and nearly fell to her knees at the intense stab in her side. She'd been running so hard, so fast, it was no wonder her out-of-shape muscles complained. Even as the thought that this was no ordinary side-stitch tried to press into her mind, Del kept running. That crazy man could be right on her heels.

So could the cops.

She spotted the Chevy hulking in the darkness, and it was a beacon to her sinking ship. She'd left the trunk unlocked and partially open on purpose.

When she reached the car, all she had to do was throw the duffel inside, slam it closed, and dive for the driver's door.

Del's hand shook trying to get out her keys. She banged on the window. Utah started barking.

"Unlock the door!"

Callie's head popped up.

"Hurry!"

Finally the locks clicked, and Del pulled herself inside, freeing her keys from her pocket.

"What's going on?" Callie's sleepy voice came from behind her.

The ignition. She had to get the key in the ignition. A glance over her shoulder down the street showed the coast was clear, but it couldn't stay that way for long.

"Did you get the food?"

Del held her throbbing side with her left hand and spun the wheel with her right. She almost jammed on the gas pedal, but at the last moment realized that would only draw more attention in the sleeping neighborhood. It took all her will to keep from gunning it.

Sweat dripped into her eyes and she could barely see, but she would keep driving. Hunching in her seat, Del reached for the burn just below her rib cage. She could feel sticky warmth under her fingers.

34

Main Street
Elk Valley, Colorado

Abby couldn't stand it any longer. She'd waited over an hour, but no one emerged from the SUV. Switching off her interior lights, she unsheathed her Beretta, got out, and crossed the street at a jog. Keeping her gun ready but pointed at the ground, she approached the SUV. She didn't want to scare anyone, but she needed to know who else was interested in this Del girl. And why.

Abby approached the driver's window from behind like she was still on patrol at a traffic stop. She tapped on the glass.

A dark figure moved inside. Abby's heart thumped faster as the window slowly rolled down halfway and a woman around her age stared up at her. She was relieved it wasn't either of the men who'd attacked her at the cabin. But this woman seemed nervous.

"Why are you sitting out here?" Abby asked.

The driver reached for the gearshift like she was going to bolt.

"No, wait." Abby raised her free hand. "Wait."

She glanced up and down the street. It was late, and she probably looked like a stalker.

"I'm trying to find the girl who lives over there." Abby pointed at the house.

"Del Mangini?"

Bingo.

"Have you seen her?"

The woman hesitated. "Why do you want to find her?"

Abby tucked her gun into the back of her pants so the woman couldn't see it. "She might be in trouble."

"What kind of trouble?"

"Look, I don't know who you are, but—"

"She's my daughter."

Okay. She hadn't seen that one coming.

Abby's eyes darted toward the house. A light had turned on in a downstairs window. She wouldn't put it past that landlord to call the police, and Abby wasn't ready to talk with the sheriff again.

"Is there somewhere we can talk?" Abby said.

The doors to the SUV clicked as she unlocked them. "Get in."

35

Neighborhood Outside Elk Valley, Colorado

Every breath sent a jolt through Del's body.

"Are you okay?" Callie asked.

She shook her head, checking her rearview and clutching her side.

Callie's little hand rested on Del's shoulder, and it was the most comforting thing Del had felt in a long time.

"I messed up. Really bad."

She eased the car up to the stop sign and turned right toward Elk Valley. They needed to get somewhere with more people. One car out on a deserted road would be like sending up a flare. How long could she and Callie run? But more importantly, Del knew she had to see how badly she'd been hurt.

She parked at the curb on the main street of town.

"Get the flashlight." She pointed toward the glove compartment.

Callie climbed over the console and obeyed.

"Can you shine it on my side?" Del twisted in her seat closer to the girl.

The light hit, and she sucked in her breath at the blood.

Her sweatshirt was torn, and a red patch the size of her hand was spreading through the fabric.

"Del . . ." Callie's voice hitched.

She pulled up the sweatshirt. A deep gash had torn through her side.

Callie started crying. "Don't die. Please don't die."

"I'm not dying."

"But—"

She let go of her shirt with a wince. "I'll be okay."

"You have to go to the hospital!"

"No!" Del didn't mean for the protest to come out so loud. "I can't, okay? We can't."

It looked like the bullet had just grazed her, but it hurt worse than breaking her arm as a kid when she'd fallen out of a tree trying to rescue a kitten. What help was she going to be to Callie in this condition?

Del tried to calm herself enough to think. "I need you to get me a towel from the trunk."

She had to stop this bleeding.

Callie dove out of the car and was back in less than a minute holding out one of Del's bathroom hand towels. She'd used the other matching one when she broke the glass. Had she left that behind?

Headlights pierced through the car, and Del pulled Callie down. "Duck!"

When the car passed, Del started the engine again. "We have to get off the street."

She drove them down an alley until they were behind the businesses of Main Street. A few other cars were parked here, dark and still. She pulled up beside one of them, hoping to blend in. How long before they were discovered? She could go to jail for this, couldn't she?

Del folded the towel and pressed it against her side. Pressure would take care of the bleeding eventually. At least that's what she hoped. But what about cleaning it? They didn't have bandages, and how could they buy any without money? If this thing got infected . . .

Callie started crying. Her pitiful sobs ripped through Del just like the bullet had.

"Kid, don't."

"Everything was going good."

"Going well," Del corrected, trying to sound as if this was no big deal, everything was normal.

Callie got quiet for a moment. Then she rested her hand on Del's arm. "What did you do?"

She deserved the truth. Del hesitated for a second then told Callie everything.

"I didn't know how to feed you," she said softly. "It was wrong. The same way you taking those books was wrong." She sucked in her breath, trying to ignore the flame in her side. "I'm sorry I got mad at you for that."

"I know I shouldn't have taken them," Callie said.

"Good."

Del tilted the back of her seat and ended up getting slathered with licks from Utah. She felt badly that the dog hadn't eaten any more than they had, but they'd shared everything they could with him.

"Callie, go get something to eat from the trunk."

"Really?"

"I'll deal with the consequences later."

While the girl was outside, Del checked her wound again and almost threw up at the sight. It looked like raw meat. They could ask about Callie if she went to the hospital, and she wasn't putting Callie through the maze of social services.

Del pushed harder on the towel. Maybe it wouldn't kill her, but this gash was going to slow her down, and that was something she couldn't afford.

Callie made cheese sandwiches, and she and Utah shared

one of the yogurts. Del could barely eat half a sandwich. Her brain told her she needed the nourishment, but her stomach rebelled.

"What are we gonna do?" Callie asked. She'd climbed back onto the bench seat at Del's insistence and tucked herself and the dog under the blanket. They would sleep here for the night.

"Same thing we have been," Del whispered, squeezing her eyes shut.

"Are we running away?"

She swallowed hard. She'd run to Colorado to escape the grief of her parents' death, but she had to stop now that Callie had knocked on her door. This was no way to teach a kid about life.

"We should get some rest," Del said.

"What about your side?"

"I'll live."

"Does it hurt bad?"

She couldn't even try to fake it. "Yeah."

It took hours, but she finally did doze off. Del woke up to the car door opening beside her. She shot into a sitting position, squinting against the morning sun, instantly regretting the sudden movement. It still felt like someone had touched a branding iron to her side, and she grimaced. Where was she? Hadn't she just closed her eyes? Why couldn't she get her bearings?

"It's all right, Del." Callie's voice soothed, and Del tried to blink away her confusion. The girl stood over her, and Del realized Callie was the one who'd opened her door. Utah stood by her, sniffing the air. He probably smelled Del's blood.

"What are you doing?" Del's voice was groggy. "Get back in the car."

"You need help."

She shifted and pulled up the seat lever. "I'm fine."

"No you're not."

That's when Del realized Callie wasn't alone.

36

Elk Valley, Colorado

"What did you *do?*" Del grabbed Callie by the sleeve. "We were fine. We don't need—"

"You're hurt," Callie said.

A familiar woman stood behind the girl.

"I told you I'm—"

"Please let her help us."

Del gritted her teeth and held back another protest. For all her bravado in front of Callie, she knew they were in deep trouble. She'd done everything she could to keep them safe and had failed miserably.

Callie stepped away, and the woman came closer. She knelt down beside the car, and Del recognized her as the owner of the bookstore they'd visited yesterday. What was her name? Christy. Concern etched her face.

Del swallowed a faint wave of nausea and managed a slight nod. With weak fingers she pulled the bloody towel away from her side.

"Can I take a look?" Christy asked.

She nodded, and the woman lifted Del's sweatshirt for a

better view of the ugly gash. Most of the bleeding had stopped, but not before it had soaked the top of her jeans and even dribbled onto the upholstery, leaving dark stains that would probably never come out. A clear liquid oozed from the wound now, dripping through the crusty blood.

Christy gently pulled down Del's sweatshirt and met her eyes. "You really should go to the ER."

"I . . ." Del glanced over at Callie. "I can't."

"It looks like a bullet grazed you," Christy said.

She guessed what this woman was thinking. It's what she'd be wondering herself. What kind of trouble were they in?

Christy reached for Del's hand. "Are you sure you can't?"

Del nodded again.

"Then let me help you."

She hesitated. If anyone found out she'd broken into a house, even if it was for food, Callie would end up in some strange foster home. Utah would be taken away from her, and Del would sleep in a cell tonight. She couldn't allow that. But she also wasn't much good to the kid doubled over in pain and risking infection each hour that passed without properly cleaning her wound.

She met Christy's kind eyes again. Should she risk everything and trust her? How long could they make it on their own, living out of a car with no money?

Del took hold of Christy's hand and carefully climbed out of the car. She handed the keys to Callie, instructing her to lock it and bring Utah with them.

Del could walk, but Christy held on to her arm anyway. She was glad she did, because she felt unsteady and lightheaded. Everything was catching up to her. Del tried to muster her remaining strength to stay strong for Callie.

The little girl clutched her other arm, and Del gave her a nudge on the shoulder to let her know they were in this together.

"My apartment's on the second floor," Christy said, guiding them over to a door only a few feet from where they'd parked. "We can go up through the store."

In her state last night, Del hadn't realized how close to the bookstore they were. If she had, she might've picked a different place to lay low. She didn't know anything about this Christy woman. What if she'd already called the cops on them and was just playing along until they arrived?

Christy led them inside, past a computer workstation and boxes stacked on wooden pallets. Several rolls of bubble wrap, bags of packing popcorn, and Priority Mail envelopes were stacked on a table. A young woman, her back to them, rolled a tape gun over a box to seal it.

"Brynn, can you go man the front of the store for a little while?" Christy asked.

The twenty-something's eyes widened when she saw Del.

"I'll explain later," Christy said. "Right now, these girls could use some help."

"Got it," Brynn said. "Call me if you need me."

Del wondered how much Callie had spilled to these women before waking her.

Climbing the stairs was more painful than she expected. She was breathing hard by the time they reached the top, clutching her side and hoping she wasn't scaring Callie.

"Once you close the door in here, you can let your dog run around," Christy said to Callie. "There's some cereal in the cupboard and milk in the fridge."

"But what about my sister?"

"We're gonna get her fixed up," Christy said.

Del nodded toward Callie. "Just do what she says, kid."

Christy gestured toward the bathroom off the kitchen. With a grimace, Del slowly walked in that direction. How could she hurt so badly? It was just a graze, right?

Del sat down on the closed toilet, trying to catch her breath.

"I'll be right back," Christy said.

A feeling of panic overcame Del as she clutched her side. What was to keep Christy from reporting them? Had she realized Callie had stolen from her? And Christy already suspected a bullet had done this damage. Del could make up a story about getting mugged and shot by some punk, but she'd be setting another bad example for her little sister if she did.

Sister. She thought again of how she used to pester her parents for a sibling. They'd always laugh and tell her maybe someday. When she got older, she stopped asking and grew to enjoy being the only object of her parents' affection. She wondered if they'd known about Callie and withheld that from her too. Had they been in contact with her bio mother, or was it a closed adoption?

When Christy returned she carried several towels and a shallow Rubbermaid container. She set them on the bathroom counter and pulled a box of gauze packets and a roll of medical tape from the cabinet beneath the sink.

Christy turned on the faucet and wet one of the towels. "I have two younger sisters, so I've had some practice with bandages."

Del suddenly wished she could tell Christy everything. There was something about her that made Del want her advice.

"I suppose you're not gonna tell me how it happened."

But Del couldn't bring herself to give her the truth. Not now. Not yet.

She also couldn't bring herself to make up a lie.

"One thing I've come to learn." Christy tipped a bottle of iodine onto the wet towel. "Secrets never help anybody."

"But sometimes we don't have a choice," Del said softly.

"I used to think that too."

Del gingerly pulled off her sweatshirt. The wound looked worse in the light. It still oozed lymph mixed with blood, and she didn't want to think about the scar this would leave if she didn't get proper medical care.

Christy gave her a sympathetic wince.

"Can you close the door?" Del asked. "I don't want Callie to see."

Christy did and handed her a towel to drape across her lap. While Del held the makeshift basin under the wound, Christy scrubbed it with the iodine rag as quickly as she could, apologizing every time Del muffled a cry.

Finally Christy finished, and Del hoped Callie hadn't heard anything.

"Thank you," Del finally said.

Spreading some sort of ointment into the gash, Christy placed wads of gauze on top. "You were looking for a job. Did you find one?"

"No."

Christy met her eyes, and Del knew this woman had her number. After wrapping her side, Christy handed her two Tylenol tablets, which Del swallowed with a little tap water. She started to carefully re-dress in her dirty sweatshirt, but Christy stopped her.

"Let me get you something clean."

"That's okay, I—"

But Christy was already out the door. She came back with a gray hoodie and helped Del change into it.

They found Callie sitting at the kitchen table with Utah sprawled by her feet sound asleep. An empty cereal bowl was on the table, a half-empty glass of orange juice beside it.

Callie jumped up when she saw Del. She rushed over and squeezed a hug out of Del on her good side.

"I'm fine," Del said, surprised at the husky sound of her voice.

Christy smiled. "Your sister's a tough cookie."

And a stupid one, Del felt like adding. She'd broken into

someone's home, for crying out loud. Somebody was going to find out eventually.

They stood in Christy's kitchen in awkward silence. Del guessed the woman was waiting for her to open up and explain their situation.

Callie looked up at Del, and she knew the little girl was wondering what she could and couldn't say.

"We really appreciate your help," Del said. "If I had money . . ."

Christy quickly waved off the comment. "You could really use a doctor."

"I'll be careful," Del said.

Callie held up the keys. "Can I go get something out of the car?"

She started to ask her what she needed then realized what the little girl had in mind. With a nod she gave her consent, and Callie left Del alone with Christy again.

"Look, I wish I could . . ." Del sat down in the chair Callie had just vacated. "I just can't involve anyone else right now."

"But I might be able to help," Christy said.

"You already have. You have no idea how much. I didn't know what I was going to do."

Christy came over to the table. "Believe me, I know what it's like to be in trouble. You can't do everything on your own."

Del started to formulate her story into something she could share, but before she could get it out Callie returned. Like Del suspected, she carried the stolen books.

Callie hesitantly walked over to Christy. Her bottom lip trembled, but she pushed her shoulders back and thrust the books into Christy's hands. "I took these. From your store."

Christy stared down at her then carefully examined the books, opening the cover of *Misty of Chincoteague*. Callie was blinking quickly and not looking at Del, probably trying to keep those tears at bay. The scene was almost ironic. Her little sister, not even nine years old, was owning up to her mistake and ready to take the consequences.

"Yesterday, right?" Christy said softly.

"Yes, ma'am."

Christy crouched down to Callie's level. "I saw you take them."

The little girl finally met Del's eyes. This was news to her too.

Christy placed the books on the table. "I was hoping you would come clean. I'm proud that you did. That's not easy."

"Are you mad?" Callie stared at her sneakers again.

"Why don't you tell me why you took them?"

"Because . . ." Callie dug the toe of her Converse into the carpet. "I didn't have money to buy them."

It was Del's turn to stare at the floor.

"That's a very honest answer." Christy reached for Callie's hand, and the girl let her. "I have a feeling you know what you did was wrong."

"I do!" Callie's face shot up. "I'm sorry."

"And you're not gonna do it again."

"No, ma'am."

"Okay then, that's good enough for me." Christy returned to the table and picked up the Bible. She handed it to Callie. "But this one was free, and I want you to have it."

"We read it last night, but some of it doesn't make much sense."

"I'm sure Christy has plenty of things to do today," Del said, picking up Utah's leash from the table and hooking it to his collar. He didn't even look up, probably as exhausted as she was from last night.

Callie didn't seem to get the hint.

"We really need to get going," Del said.

"Are you sure?" Christy turned toward Del. "You can rest here for a little while."

"I appreciate everything you've done already." Del meant that and hoped Christy would understand. "But we have things to do ourselves."

"We do?" Callie gave her a questioning look.

They had enough food to last them a day or two now, enough time for Del to figure something out.

Christy grabbed a tablet and pen off the kitchen counter and scribbled on it. She tore the sheet off and handed it to Del. "Please call me if you need anything."

She pocketed the paper and gave the woman a nod.

Christy touched her arm. "I mean that, okay?"

A few minutes later, they were back in the Chevy and Del tucked the plastic bag of bandages, ointment packs, and Tylenol Christy had insisted she take in the glove compartment out of Utah's reach.

Crossing her arms, Callie's jaw was set and she stared straight out the windshield. The Bible lay in her lap.

"What?" Del asked, starting the engine.

"She would've helped us."

"Yeah, and what happens when she finds out the truth?"

"Would that be so bad?"

Says the girl who completely one-upped her by confessing her crime. Del sighed and tried to back out of the parking place without moving her torso. The Tylenol was working, but her side still ached.

"I just want a chance to do this on our own."

"I don't want to lose you," Callie whispered.

Del had nothing to say in response.

37

The Perfect Blend Coffee Shop
Elk Valley, Colorado

How could God make the Earth in seven days?"
Del looked up at Callie from the newspaper she was scouring for job openings. They were sitting at a table in the cozy Perfect Blend coffee shop, and Callie had been pouring over the Bible Christy gave her for the past ten minutes, following along with her finger and repeating the words loudly enough to distract Del.

"I have no idea," Del said.

"Did He really do all that?"

"I guess, if you believe that book."

"You don't?"

Del let out a sigh. "I'm not sure what I believe, kid."

Callie's lips pressed together for a moment. "I wonder what Mom believes."

Good question. Del hadn't really thought about her bio mother's faith or lack thereof. She'd barely thought of her own except Callie kept bringing it up. It didn't really bother her for the girl to want to talk about God, but it did frustrate Del to have absolutely no answers. What kind of kid asked about the creation of the world?

"Why all this talk about God?" Del finally said.

Callie's forehead crinkled, and she stared down at the thin pages of the Bible. "My dad. If he's in Heaven, I want to go there too."

"I'm sure you will."

"But the preacher said only Christians can go."

"What preacher?"

"He came to the rodeo once. I don't remember his name."

Del folded up the newspaper. She didn't know why she expected to find some new opening in the same classifieds she'd read all week. A whiff of pastry teased her, and she wished she had the money to buy them each a scone or a cup of hot coffee. She touched her throbbing side and tried not to think about having to change the bandage.

"Some people say just being good will get you there, kid, I wouldn't worry about it."

Callie glanced out the window, probably trying to see Utah, who was waiting in the car. "It seems important."

"So's finding a job." Del tapped the newspaper. "And I'm out of ideas."

"Can't we ask Christy for—"

"No."

"Why not?"

"Because I say so."

"But—"

"Can't you just trust me?"

Callie stared at her with the face of innocence, and Del wanted to kick herself. What would've happened to Callie if she had been arrested for that break-in? She *had* trusted her every step of the way, and Del wasn't doing anything to deserve it.

"Why don't you want her to help us?"

"Kid . . ."

"She seemed nice."

Del leaned across the table with a wince. "I appreciate what she did, but I've told you why already."

Callie rested her arms on the table, her chin on top. "So what's the plan?"

"I'm gonna get us out of this."

"How?"

"Sell the car."

"But won't that—"

"We don't have a choice."

Callie seemed to ponder Del's words. Then she popped up in her seat. "Yesterday we passed a place that sells cars. Maybe we can go there."

"That's the ticket."

She almost climbed out of her chair when she saw a man with a cowboy hat walk into the shop. She instantly recognized him and grabbed the newspaper, flapping it open across her face.

"Don't move," she whispered to Callie, peeking over the newspaper.

"Why, what's wrong?"

"I know that guy."

The little girl spun around.

"Callie!" she hissed.

"Which one?"

"Turn around."

"If you know him, why don't you want him to see you?"

He glanced in their direction. She couldn't tell his expression through the handlebar moustache. And he didn't exactly look threatening here in the coffee shop like he had on horseback with a rifle in his hand. Del ducked behind the paper again. Why did she have to end up in a small town like Elk Valley? It wasn't exactly Mayberry, but enough people knew each other that word could spread like chickenpox. Even Christy had recognized her from It's Only Natural Foods.

"Um . . . Del?" Callie whispered.

"Let's lay low until he leaves." She kept the newspaper high then realized it was upside down.

"Del?"

"What?" She started to turn the paper around then heard a male voice clear his throat.

She slowly lowered the newspaper. The cowboy was standing over their table.

She stared up at him. He looked ten feet tall. The skin around his eyes wrinkled, and she realized he was smiling.

"Didn't expect to see you again."

His voice was deeper than her father's had been, and for some reason she suddenly felt as young as Callie, her hand caught in the cookie jar. Why couldn't she find her voice? Del swallowed and tried to think of what to say to explain trespassing on his land.

The cowboy reached out his hand. "I don't bite."

"I didn't hurt your horses," she finally said, reluctantly shaking his hand.

His calloused fingers enveloped hers. "But you were trespassing."

Okay, this was not what she needed.

"I think we better get going," Del said, clambering to her feet and gesturing for Callie to do the same.

"What's your name?"

"Not important," she said over her shoulder, taking the newspaper with her. She should've stayed in the car and checked the classifieds there. The less people they came in contact with the better at this point.

"I'm Jim," the cowboy said, but Del was already heading toward the door. She didn't wait to hear anything more from the man.

Callie started to protest at their hasty retreat, but Del grabbed the fabric of her sweatshirt and pulled her out the door.

On the sidewalk, Callie twisted out of her grip. "He was just being nice."

"I can't deal with nice right now."

She couldn't deal with anyone right now. She climbed in the car, trying to hold her side as she bent down, but the pain was still barely tolerable. She started the car and pulled away from the curb.

She had them pointed in the direction of the dealership when she realized with a wave of dread her mistake in leaving her apartment as quickly as she did. She slowed down.

"What?" Callie asked.

"I forgot something at my apartment."

In the bottom drawer of her dresser were the few important papers she'd hung onto. Her high school diploma, birth certificate, and the title for the Malibu. If she wanted to get a fair price, she'd need it.

But would her apartment key still work?

"Hang on." Del did a U-turn at the next side street. When she got to the Lopezes, she smiled when she saw their empty driveway. They were in luck.

"Wait here," she said, shutting off the engine. Her key had to still work.

"I'm coming with you." Callie opened her door.

"Kid, I said—"

But Callie was already out, and Del didn't have time to argue with her. She'd probably lose anyway. The last time she'd made Callie stay behind, Del had managed to get shot.

She gripped the railing to steady herself and hobbled up the stairs as fast as she could. Callie was right behind her. At the door, Del gave one look around then tried her key. It slipped into the lock. She turned the knob, and the door swung open. She gave Callie a quick high-five, and then they were inside.

Regret washed over her as she entered what had been her home for the past year. Its familiarity had been comforting. If only she could have its refuge while she tried to figure out what to do with Callie, her adoption, and a way to make some money.

Del gave her old bed a longing look before reaching for the dresser.

"Why can't we stay here?" Callie plopped on the bed while Del opened each drawer. She would've sworn her papers were here, tucked in a worn manila folder with her father's handwriting on the tab.

"I owe three months' rent."

She pulled out another drawer. Empty except for a stray black sock with a hole in the toe.

"I'll check the kitchen again," Callie said and was off before Del could stop her.

Where in the world was that folder?

She dropped to her knees and checked the bottom drawer. Empty. Del rested her forehead against the dresser. Just like her life. She'd been running from everything now for weeks, barely getting by, barely surviving. But Callie needed her now.

Del raised her face to the ceiling. Even though Callie hadn't been expected, her presence had given Del something she'd never known she needed. There was a reason to make plans now. She needed to do something with her life because a little girl was counting on her.

Standing to her feet, Del squared her shoulders.

Then she heard Callie scream.

38

Del bolted into the living room. What she saw stopped her cold. The man with the skull cap who'd been watching them at the health food store held his hand across Callie's mouth and was dragging her toward the door of the apartment. Callie thrashed against him, and then she must've bitten his fingers because he let her go with a curse.

Callie ran toward Del, but the man dove after her.

Del didn't think. She flew at the attacker, ready to kick and punch and do whatever it took to protect Callie. She didn't even have time to process why anyone would be trying to take her.

"Run!" Del screamed at Callie.

Callie ducked around the man and flew toward the door, but he was faster. He snatched at her sweatshirt and reeled her in, pulling her against his side and locking her there with his forearm. This time when Callie struggled against him, his grip didn't budge.

"Let her go!"

Backing toward the door, a faint grin spread across the

man's face. His skull cap had been pushed up on one side. Taller than she by at least six inches, heavier by a hundred. She didn't really have a chance, but she wasn't letting him take her sister.

Del rushed toward him again, but before she made it across the floor he whipped a knife from his coat pocket and flashed it at her.

"Don't," he said.

"Watch me," she said.

"I'm not here to hurt either of you, but I will if I have to."

Callie stopped struggling, her eyes wide.

"I said let her go." Del's hands clenched into fists.

The man took another step backward, dragging Callie with him. She knew if she let him get outside her chance of rescuing Callie slimmed, but he'd have to navigate the stairs, and Callie might have the sense to trip him.

"What do you want with her?" Del edged closer.

The man's eyes darted down to Callie, but his knife didn't waver.

It was a stupid question she didn't really want him to answer, but if she could get him talking maybe the Lopezes would come home and call the police.

"Not your business," the man said.

"You better believe it is."

He was in the doorway now, and Del's heart pounded as she saw the fear in Callie's eyes, begging her to do something. But what could either of them do with a knife in the picture? Del wouldn't be any good to Callie dead, and she certainly wasn't risking the little girl's life.

If she started screaming the neighbors would hear, but most of them worked during the day, and she wasn't sure if this man was crazy enough to stab her anyway.

God, please help us!

Del gave the living room a frantic glance for anything to

use as a weapon, but there was nothing. She would have to rush him. If she was hurt again, so be it. She'd get the knife away somehow and hopefully live long enough to get to a hospital.

The man must've sensed her intentions, because he pressed the tip against Callie's cheek. "Do not move."

Del held up her hands. "Please . . . don't hurt her."

"Then don't come any closer."

Callie's lip trembled, and Del could only watch helplessly as the man backed out of the doorway.

"Drop it. Now."

A female voice came from outside, and it took a second for Del to realize a woman was standing on the stairs behind the man. Del saw she held a silver gun to the back of the man's head.

A cord bulged in the attacker's jaw.

Callie whimpered.

"I said drop the knife." The woman's voice was as hard as the man's eyes.

He tried to turn his head to see who was behind him, but she must've jammed her gun harder against his skull. He grimaced.

"Now!"

Slowly he lowered the blade. The moment it was safely away from Callie's face, the woman slammed the butt of her gun into his head. He crumpled to the floor just inside the apartment and didn't move.

The woman rushed in and pried the knife from his hand. While still aiming her own weapon at his chest, she kicked his arm.

No response.

Del stared at her in disbelief. She kept her pistol aimed at the unconscious, would-be kidnapper lying on the floor, and for a second Del thought she was going to kill him. But then she knelt down and quickly pulled the belt from his pants. She moved to his feet and removed the laces from his boots.

When she handed her gun to Del and ordered her to keep it trained on the man, Del froze. She stared at the woman's face. The sharp nose, frizzy hair that was now auburn . . . it was her. The woman in the photographs. Natalie.

"You don't know who I am, but—"

"I know exactly who you are."

Natalie looked away, her fingers making quick work of tying up the man who'd nearly abducted her sister.

"You've got a lot of explaining to do." Del purposely veiled her words, since Callie didn't seem to recognize her yet.

"I know," Natalie grunted as she worked.

Callie clung to Del, her face buried in the borrowed hoodie. Del winced as the sting came back in her side but dropped to her knees and held Callie close.

"It's okay, kid." She squeezed her and wished she could keep her safe forever.

"We have to go," Natalie said.

"Who said anything about we?" Del stood up, still holding Callie close.

"Please. My car's outside."

Del stared at the woman who'd given birth to them both, and she knew one thing for sure—everything was about to change.

39

The Book Corral
Elk Valley, Colorado

"Del Mangini was here and you didn't call me?"
Abby was pacing in the back room of Christy's book-store, alternating between waving her hand in the air and running it through her hair. Christy stood with her arms crossed by her computer work station.

"I had no idea who she was until I called the health food store where she used to work to see if I could help her get her job back." Christy's voice was tinged with irritation.

Abby tried to calm down. She didn't want to take her frustration out on her friend. But she'd had two hours of sleep after her encounter with Natalie McGuire and was feeling it. She knew Natalie hadn't told her everything, but at least she now knew this Del girl had family.

"You're sure it was a bullet wound?" Abby asked.

"Looked like a graze."

"And you have no idea where they went."

"She was skittish, Ab. I didn't grill her."

"You should have." Abby held up her hand immediately, wishing to take back the words. "Sorry. I'm sure you did what you thought was best."

Abby's caustic ways often turned people off, and she knew it. Christy was a whole lot better in the human relations department, but Abby was frustrated with this whole investigation that no one asked her to conduct. She knew she should probably let it drop, but if Kirsch really had committed suicide like the media said, why did someone attack her at his cabin?

"You should call Natalie," Christy said.

The phone was already in her hand. The woman had given Abby her cell number last night, and Abby pulled it up and punched the screen. Natalie needed to know her daughter had been here.

∽

Main Street
Elk Valley, Colorado

Del and Callie followed Natalie down the apartment steps at a run. Callie rushed for the Chevy, and Del did the same. They could call the police anonymously if they had to later, but they had to get out of here now.

Natalie swung around, gesturing wildly toward a compact SUV parked behind them. "Get in mine."

"I'm not leaving my car," Del said.

"You have to. They know you're driving it."

Natalie's eyes were wild, and Del realized she was still holding Natalie's gun. In broad daylight. With a man tied up in Del's apartment. If the police or the Lopezes drove up now, she'd be toast.

"What is going on?" Del pointed toward the steps. "Who *is* that guy? And what are you even doing here?"

She was yelling, and she couldn't help it. Her voice pitched higher, realizing what could've happened to Callie. Natalie glanced around like she was expecting to be ambushed.

Callie pulled on Del's arm. "She looks like my photo."

"I know," Del said.

A light sparked in Callie's face. "Mom?"

Callie was staring at Natalie like she was an alien.

Natalie barely got out Callie's name before the little girl threw herself into Natalie's embrace.

"Mom!"

Natalie kissed Callie on the forehead and squeezed her so tight Del wondered if the girl could breathe. "Callie, honey, we have to go."

"I knew you'd come back," Callie said. "I knew!"

Natalie met Del's eyes, tears spilling down her cheeks. She stood, still holding Callie but staring at Del. "Please trust me," she mouthed.

Callie let her mother go. "What about Utah?"

"He's coming with us," Del said.

"Utah?"

"Her dog."

She gave the Malibu one last glance before making her decision. She could always come back for it later, but right now she had no choice. They were in danger here, and her bio mom held all the cards.

They quickly transferred everything into Natalie's vehicle. She relinquished the gun to Natalie, and with Callie and Utah sitting in the back seat and Del in front, Natalie backed the car out of the driveway so fast Del had to grab the door handle. She groaned as the seat belt raked her side.

"Who was that guy?" Del asked again as they pulled out onto the road.

"Shouldn't we call the police?" Callie added.

The sudden burst of a cell phone ring pierced the SUV's interior. Natalie grabbed a smartphone tucked up in her visor. She glanced at the screen and mumbled something Del couldn't hear.

Natalie silenced the phone then slipped on a pair of sunglasses, hiding her makeup-smudged eyes. She'd aged a lot since the photo the PI had shown Del. Her auburn hair was uniform and dark like it came from a bottle. How old was she? Del didn't even know her last name much less her age.

"I'm not sure who he is," Natalie said softly.

Del stared at her. "How did you even know where I lived?"

"Dad's dead," Callie blurted.

The little girl's statement sounded matter-of-fact, and Del worried the girl was more traumatized than she was letting on.

"I know, sweetheart," Natalie said. "I'm so sorry."

Del reached around her seat and caught Callie's hand. She wanted to reassure her, but so many thoughts were swirling around in her head she could barely make sense of any of them.

"So you mean to tell me the moment we choose to come back to my apartment you just happen to show up?"

"Did he say anything?" Natalie turned onto a side street.

"No."

"Yeah, he did." Callie scooted up to the edge of the bench seat. "Remember? He said he wasn't there to hurt us."

Natalie glanced in the rearview mirror. "That might've been true."

"He was trying to take Callie!" Del gripped her side and tried to take a deep, calming breath. It felt moist, like the wound was bleeding again. No surprise. She'd probably torn it open when she rushed the guy.

Del glanced over at the woman who was her mother. "You do realize my parents never told me about you. I had to find out from a private investigator four days ago."

Natalie's face was impassive, hard even, but Del saw a tear trickle down her cheek under the sunglasses. Natalie quickly wiped it away.

"They were good parents," Del said, letting the words sink in. "But they died three years ago."

She waited for a reaction from Natalie, but the sunglasses hid her expression. With Callie in the back seat, Del couldn't ask her what she really wanted to know—why she'd given Del up for adoption and not Callie. But the real reason for the anger and confusion boiling inside her wasn't because she'd given Del up. That took guts, and Del would forever be thankful for the time she had with Mom and Dad. But it was one thing to give a child up for adoption at birth and quite another to abandon a baby. How could she do that?

Del let go of Callie's hand and allowed the silence to spread through the car.

"Are you going to say anything?" Del finally asked.

Natalie was slowly shaking her head. "I'm sorry."

"That's it?"

Callie stuck her head in between them. "Mom, where are we going?"

"Somewhere safe," Natalie said.

"What's your last name?"

Natalie stared straight ahead. "McGuire."

"Mine too," Callie chimed.

"Where *are* we going?"

"Somewhere safe."

"You already said that."

Natalie sighed. "It depends on if we're being followed."

"Followed?" Del swung around, checking behind them. An old pickup trailed the SUV several car lengths back, but trucks in Elk Valley were commonplace.

"I don't know who attacked you," Natalie said. "But I have an idea who sent him."

"Who?"

"I can't say right now."

Callie rested back in her seat again, Utah's head in her lap. Del didn't want to scare the girl anymore, and that's the only reason she didn't press for more answers.

"Are you okay, kid?"

"Yeah."

It hurt to do it, but Del reached back and took the little girl's hand again. Callie squeezed her fingers. She heard a whimper.

"Hey." Del undid her seat belt so she could turn around and see Callie better. She didn't care if Callie's mother was here or not. Right now it was just the two of them, like it had been. Like it might be again if Del got the faintest hint Natalie McGuire was up to no good.

"He . . . he . . . almost . . ."

"But he didn't, Callie. He didn't."

She scrunched up her face. "He . . . almost killed you!"

Del wished she could give her a hug. "We're both safe now."

"You can't get hurt again."

Natalie glanced at Del, but she wasn't telling that story.

"I won't, okay?"

"Promise?"

"You bet," Del said.

They spent the next few miles in silence, and Del tried to make sense of everything that had happened. Why would someone want to take Callie?

Natalie turned the vehicle onto the freeway heading north. She kept her eyes on the road. "I tried so hard to protect both of you, and now look what happened."

"Protect us from what?" Del lowered her voice. Callie's eyes were closed, and she was leaning against the door like she was nodding off. "I need some answers, Natalie."

"I think some people are after me. When they couldn't find me, they found you instead and assumed we were in contact. What better way to flush me out than to threaten my children?"

Del held her hand against her bandaged side. She wondered

if going with this woman had been a big mistake. Who exactly was Natalie McGuire, and did she even want to know?

A sense of dread slowly filled her veins. The good guys didn't go around kidnapping little girls.

"What did you do?"

"It's what I didn't do," Natalie said. "I should've ended something years ago."

Now she was talking in circles, and Del wasn't even sure what questions to ask. "Was it drugs?"

That actually made Natalie laugh. The type of laugh you heard when someone asked a question so far off the mark it didn't even come near the target.

"I made a stupid choice when I was younger." Natalie gave her a look that was more genuine than before. "But it had nothing to do with drugs. I promise."

"And you're not going to tell me what it really was."

"I will."

Del glanced back at Callie. Her eyes were still closed. "Why did you leave her?"

"I had to."

"That's bull and you know it. No mother has—"

"You don't know what happened."

She clenched her hand around the door handle. "She needed you, and you just took off? At least you gave me up to parents who loved me, but Callie didn't—"

"She had her father."

"She needed her mother."

Natalie's expression didn't change, like she'd expected this. "If I could go back, I'd do it again."

"What? How can you even—"

"They tried to hurt me," Natalie said. "While she was in the car. She spent a week in the hospital."

"They. That's all you keep saying."

"It's complicated."

Del gestured out the window at the open freeway. "You're right. I don't know what happened, and I don't know you. Which is why I don't trust a thing you've said."

"I hope you will."

She was getting herself worked up, and that would cloud her judgment if she wasn't careful. Del shut up and wondered what she'd gotten them into.

40

I-25 North
Near Pueblo, Colorado

"Where have you been all this time?" Del asked when she couldn't stand the silence anymore.

Natalie McGuire took a drag from her cigarette and stuffed the filter in the ashtray. "Alamosa. For the past year at least."

Del took a moment to digest that her birth mother had been living an hour away.

Natalie changed lanes. "Your parents . . ."

"Was it a closed adoption?"

"Yes."

"So you never saw me after the hospital?"

"I got to name you, but that was it."

Del remembered how Callie and she had joked about their names the other night. It seemed a lifetime ago.

"My two best friends lived in Delaware and California," Natalie said.

"Who was my father?"

Natalie checked her side mirror.

"Is he alive?"

"He is."

She stared out the window at the barren, brown fields. It looked like a fire had scorched one of them not long before. Charred ground had replaced whatever grass or shrubs had originally claimed the soil. Del's throat felt smaller. Her father was Ron Mangini. The thought of another man giving her life had never entered Del's mind, and she felt guilty that she was actually curious to discover who her bio dad was.

She glanced over at Natalie, unable to keep from comparing her to Kelly Mangini. Mom had a way of instantly making anyone, even a stranger, feel like family. The warmth never left her eyes. When she hugged you, you felt *hugged*. Kelly Mangini cared deeply about people. She'd rather die for a stranger than watch anyone suffer.

Del blinked hard. Which is exactly what happened.

"I wanted to keep you," Natalie said softly.

The SUV slowed with the rest of the traffic as they approached Pueblo, and Del stared at the woman she could've grown up with. "Why didn't you?"

"I made a mess of things, Del. I didn't want to bring you into that."

At least she'd had her. Del would forever be thankful to Natalie McGuire for not aborting her. She could never hate her for that reason alone.

"I'm glad they loved you," Natalie said.

"I've had a good life."

Del glanced back at Callie again, but even when Natalie braked suddenly as a car merged right in front of them, the little girl slept on. Oblivious and trusting, like a kid should be. Del wasn't sure how much to tell Natalie. Despite the urge to box herself off emotionally, Natalie's DNA was a magnet to her own, whether she liked it or not.

"I grew up in Pennsylvania." The words dropped out of

Del's mouth an hour later. "But I moved out here when they died since I'd always dreamed of living near the mountains."

"Colorado must be in our blood then. I've always loved them too."

"How long have you lived here?"

"Since a little before I had you."

There was so much Del needed to know. A part of her didn't want to feel connected to Natalie; the other felt strangely satisfied she and her mother had something in common.

"I fell in love with Callie's father and horses around the same time," Natalie added. "I even worked for a horse rescue organization a number of years ago."

So they shared that as well. Could a love for horses really run in a family?

"When your parents died . . . you didn't have any other relatives?"

"None I wanted to live with."

Her mother came from a huge, dysfunctional Italian lineage, most of them in New York City. Del hadn't thought she could survive long in a big city like that. She needed to breathe fresh air and wrap her arms around a tree if she wanted. And Dad was an only child whose parents died before she was born.

"You and Callie get along well," Natalie said.

"She showed up on my doorstep with a picture of you."

"I just found out about her father." There seemed to be real grief in Natalie's voice.

"She misses him."

"Did she tell you how he died?"

"Truck accident."

"Del?" Callie's sleepy voice sounded worried. "Where are we?"

Pikes Peak hovered to their left, practically glowing.

"Near the Springs, I think."

"I thought you girls might be hungry," Natalie said,

taking an exit and aiming the vehicle toward a McDonald's Drive-Thru sign.

And just like that, Del's opportunity for more answers disappeared.

Natalie told them to order whatever they wanted, and between Del, Callie, and Utah they scarfed down six burgers, two large fries, a Caesar salad, two vanilla shakes, and a super-sized Coke. Natalie ordered a grilled chicken sandwich and only ate half. She kept watching out the windows, scanning each car that entered the parking lot as they ate.

"You really think we're being followed?" Del wiped her mouth with one of the thin white napkins.

"I hope not."

Still aware of Callie's young ears, Del couldn't ask the hard questions like who in the world did she think was after them and what had Natalie done to tick someone off enough to make them want to hurt her. The woman sounded psychotic, but after what happened in the apartment, Del was starting to believe it was possible.

"How long have you known where I lived?"

Natalie stuffed her half-eaten dinner into the greasy McDonald's bag, her face softening. "Since yesterday."

Del didn't ask if it was okay and took the half sandwich out and handed it to Utah. He snapped it up and barely chewed. She would never admit it, but a part of her wanted to hear that her bio mother had been watching her for years, following her achievements and longing for the relationship she'd given up. Not that Del had many achievements to follow.

Maybe Natalie sensed her disappointment, because as she pulled out onto I-25 she started talking again. "I've wanted to find you for years, Del. But I knew if I did, it would kill me to watch you grow up from afar. And I promised your parents I would never make contact without their permission."

"So they did meet you?"

"Once. At the hospital."

Del tried to take it all in. In a way, she understood Mom and Dad keeping this secret. It was something surely every adoptive parent struggled with, but it still felt like a betrayal to realize they'd withheld this vital puzzle piece of her identity. She would've thought they'd at least have mentioned it in their will or left her some document with the truth. But then again, they hadn't planned on dying.

Callie had fallen silent in the back seat. She sat listening to them while stroking Utah's back. The dog had settled down for a nap after his meal. Del was feeling the food's tranquilizing effects too, but she had to stay awake and look out for Callie. Her side was throbbing again, but she didn't have any more Tylenol and wasn't asking Natalie for anything.

"Thanks for feeding us," Del finally managed.

Natalie slipped on her sunglasses again, even though the sun had nearly disappeared behind the mountains. "Why don't you rest while I drive?"

"Where are we going?"

Glancing in the rearview, Natalie changed lanes. "Does it matter?"

"Yeah, I think it does."

"You have to trust me." It almost sounded like she was begging.

Del pulled herself up straighter in her seat. Callie or not, they needed some answers. "You can't possibly expect us to blindly go along with you like this."

"I have to go to the bathroom," Callie interrupted.

Del rolled her eyes. "Why didn't you say so when we were at the drive-thru?"

"I didn't have to then."

"Kid, we can't—"

The SUV shot forward, throwing them back into their

seats. They zoomed around a tractor-trailer in the right lane, and Del watched the speedometer push eighty.

"What are you doing?"

Natalie stared ahead, gripping the wheel with both hands.

A red convertible with a white top was in front of them, but Natalie didn't slow down. She came up on its bumper then swung the SUV into the opposite lane, slamming Del up against the door. Utah lost his balance and tumbled to the floor.

"Slow down, will you?"

"Do you see that white van?"

Del tried to keep her cool so Callie wouldn't sense her fear. "Where?"

"Behind us."

She craned to check while holding onto her seat belt. "No, there's . . ."

Wait. Zipping out from behind the tractor trailer they'd passed was a white . . . something. Yeah, it was a van.

"What about it?" Del asked, already suspecting Natalie's response.

"It's been back there since we left McDonald's."

"Are you sure?"

All Del got in response was a sunglass stare, and then Natalie focused on the road again.

They were going ninety now.

"What are you gonna do?"

"Lose them."

Callie was hanging onto Utah, who'd hunkered down beside her. "How?"

"Hang on."

Natalie weaved around a slowing Walmart truck.

"They're really following us?"

"Do you want to stop and find out?"

Del wasn't sure, actually. It was hard to believe Natalie

wasn't delusional. But she certainly hadn't made up the man in her apartment.

She glared at the side of Natalie's face. "I need to know what's going on, or we're leaving you first chance we get."

She wasn't sure if admitting that was a good idea or not, considering Natalie had a gun in her possession and they'd only just met. It made her wish she'd kept it instead of passing it off.

"Let's get out of this in one piece first, okay?" Natalie steadied the wheel and slowed down to seventy-five.

Callie was practically on her knees staring out the back window. "It's still there."

"We need more traffic," Natalie said.

"Take this exit." Del pointed at the green Monument exit sign.

Her bio mother hesitated.

"Then we'll know for sure," Del added.

They passed the sign, and at the last second Natalie merged into the right lane, speeding down the exit ramp. The tires squealed, and Callie whimpered and clung tighter to Utah.

Stopping behind a pickup at the light, Del searched for the white van. Had they ditched it?

"Looks like we—"

The light turned green, and just as Natalie accelerated Del saw the van swerve down the ramp and head toward them.

41

Monument, Colorado

If you pulled over, what would they do?" Del twisted around. How did they know for sure that white van didn't belong to the FBI or the police?

"Hang on."

Natalie jammed the gas, weaving in and out of the traffic. She nearly clipped the mirror of a black Jeep, and its horn blared behind them. Spinning the wheel, she aimed them down a side street. Del smelled burning rubber. Then just as quickly, Natalie took another sharp turn into what looked like a tire and auto repair shop and pulled up beside a camper in the parking lot.

Natalie killed the engine. The shop appeared to be closed. No lights shone in the windows.

Still clutching the door handle, Del reached back for Callie's hand, and the little girl's fingers dug into her palm.

"Are they cops?" Del managed. Several orange traffic cones were lined up near the first garage bay. Del stared at them rather than her mother.

"No," Natalie said.

"I think we deserve to know who's chasing us," Del said, glancing back at Callie who gave a nod in agreement.

Natalie reached back and pulled a notebook from behind the passenger seat. She handed it to Del. "Some of your answers."

Its cover was worn, its pages soft and fraying. Del opened it to a newspaper clipping glued to the first page. She silently read the article dated twenty years ago:

Thieves Make Off With Over 500 Mill in Stolen Artwork

Boston - August 4: Last night thieves hit the Elizabeth Dutton Stockton Museum and made off with over a dozen priceless works of art. "It's a devastating loss," says museum curator, Michael Shapiro. "We can't explain why someone would do this. We ask that if anyone has knowledge of the crime, contact authorities and bring these pieces back to their rightful home."

The heist appeared to be well planned, according to officials. Security officer John Sutton was on duty and told police he answered the door for two young men he believed to be police officers who demanded he show them identification. Sutton tried to comply, but the officers quickly overpowered him, tying and gagging him. Unable to reach the museum's only panic button behind the security desk, Sutton wasn't found until early the next morning when he was to be relieved of duty.

Originally held for questioning, Sutton was later released and the FBI was called in to handle the investigation. A reward has been offered for any information leading to the safe return of the masterpieces, valued at over 500 million.

"What does this have to do with you?" Del asked.

Natalie stared out the window for a moment as if she didn't hear. Then she turned back to Del. "I was the lookout."

"Are you kidding me?" Del gawked at Natalie.

Natalie slowly shook her head. "I was silent for twenty years," she said softly. "First to protect my own hide, then to protect yours."

"But—"

"There were three of us," she said. "Remember my friends who lived in California and Delaware?"

Del gave a small nod.

"Their names were Javier and Adam. They both died a year ago within two weeks of each other. You'll see their obits are in that notebook as well. The reports all say their deaths were accidents, a drive-by shooting and a hit and run. They were at the wrong place at the wrong time. But I've always wondered if the person who hired us to commit the crime wanted us out of the picture so we wouldn't confess. We always figured we just had to wait for the twenty year statute of limitations. Then we could come out of hiding. But now I'm not sure."

A click came from the back seat, and Callie got as close to Del as she could without climbing up into the front.

"Are they in Heaven with Daddy?" Callie asked.

Natalie gave the girl a sad smile. "I hope so, sweetie."

Del didn't appreciate her use of the endearment. Not after what she'd just admitted.

It was all starting to make sense.

The PI—had he been hired to find Natalie by the person who was after them now?

What if Kirsch had discovered the museum theft, and that's why he ended up dead too? A chill crept up Del's back. That made at least three possibly related deaths.

"I thought if I just walked away from everything and made a fresh, clean start on my own I could forget about the biggest mistake I'd ever made."

Her mother was a criminal.

Del could barely take it in. Did it matter that she regretted her crime? She'd still taken part and kept it hidden all these years.

They waited in the parking lot for five tense minutes before Natalie was satisfied they'd shaken the van off their tail, if it even had been in the first place. She finally rested both elbows on the steering wheel, and Del noticed for the first time she had the same hands as her biological mother. Wide palms, short and stubby fingers.

"I got by for a few years." Natalie's tone dropped. "Javier, Adam, and I made a pact to never commit another crime and to somehow try and make up for what we'd done by living good lives."

Del rested her hand on her throbbing side. "Pretty convenient to make a pact *after* you get away with stealing millions. And I suppose you didn't mind keeping the money you were probably paid either."

"By the time I was ready to confess, it was too late. I had a husband and family." Natalie lowered her head. "If what I'd done came out, everyone who had anything to do with me would face a media firestorm. Not to mention I'd probably go to jail."

"Did Daddy know you stole paintings?" Callie asked.

Natalie started to reach for Callie's hand but then withdrew. "I didn't tell him when I should've, but yes, he knew most of it."

"Most of it?" How dare this woman drag them into her problems. Even if she had saved them at the apartment, it would never have happened if it weren't for her.

"He didn't know I was going to leave."

Callie's lip puckered. "I missed you. Did I do something to make you mad?"

Natalie gently touched Callie's cheek. "Never. I left to protect you from the same people who are chasing us now."

She turned to Del. "I figured they would leave my family alone if I disappeared."

"You were wrong." Del said.

"I'll be the first to admit that."

"You know what?" Del raised her hands as if in surrender. "I don't care. I want out, and I'm taking Callie with me."

"But—"

"The van's gone, and I think it's time Callie and I were too."

"And Utah," Callie whispered.

Del scanned the empty parking lot. There had to be somewhere safe to spend the night in this town. "In fact, here's as good a place to start as any."

"No, wait." Natalie grabbed her arm.

Del jerked out of her grasp, but the effort caused a bolt of pain to fly down her body. She winced and bent forward.

"I'm sorry, I—"

"What did you do with the paintings?" Del asked then held up her hand again. "Never mind. The less we know the better."

"Please don't." Natalie took off her sunglasses and frantically glanced from Del to Callie then back to Del. "I can't protect you if you leave. I just need to get you both somewhere safe, where they'll never find you."

"And then what?"

"I don't know, but you have no idea how dangerous—"

"I think I do." Del climbed from the SUV and walked a few steps closer to the camper beside them. Maybe they could get inside it. Then Del realized that if they left Natalie, they'd be even worse off than before. They had no car now. Even if she hadn't hurt herself, she wasn't sure if she could carry all their gear. Were they stuck with this woman?

The back door cracked, and Callie and Utah climbed out too. Callie came over and wrapped her arms around Del's waist.

"I'm scared," Callie whispered.

Del didn't dare utter *I am too*, but she was. She'd almost lost Callie back there, and this little girl was the only family she had left. Natalie McGuire didn't count.

"What do you think?" Del asked in a whisper of her own.

"She saved me."

"Yeah, but what about the other stuff?" Was Callie old enough to even understand the seriousness of the crimes Natalie had confessed to them?

"She seems sorry."

Del sighed, frustrated with Callie's response and warmed by it at the same time. She'd been the recipient of this girl's forgiveness more than once in their short time together, and the fact that Callie extended it to her mother said a lot.

"I guess we're stuck," Del said. "She holds all the cards."

"Holds all the . . ." Callie scrunched up her face.

"She knows more than we do right now," Del held Callie close, and the feeling of the girl's warm little body against hers hardened her resolve and calmed her rash plans.

"Maybe we should trust her," Callie said, looking up at Del.

"Why's that, kid?"

"She needs us."

That was one way to look at it.

Callie shrugged, letting Del go. "We prayed for help, remember?"

"I was kinda thinking about winning the lottery."

"Del . . ."

The girl's exasperated tone made her smile. "Kidding."

"I asked God to bring back my mom, and He did."

She didn't remember hearing that prayer, but she imagined if she were Callie she might've prayed the same thing. If she had this kid's faith, that is. When she was Callie's age, she didn't have any concept of God beyond the fact that the Bible had some crazy stories in it. People living in a boat for forty days? A sea parting? It was another fairy tale.

If Del had known about Natalie as a child, would she have wished to know her? Mom and Dad gave her everything she needed, a real childhood, but what they hadn't given her was the truth, and their deception, however well-meant, still stung.

"Maybe you should pray some more," Del said, nudging Callie with her hip.

"You too."

"Think I'll leave that in your capable hands."

"I could help you."

Del tried to see Natalie through the windows, but everything was a shadow. She was surprised the woman hadn't jumped out to stop them.

"Del?"

She pulled her eyes away, focusing on Callie again. "Think we should go with her?"

Callie nodded. "She fed us."

"Very true."

Callie beamed up at her again, and inwardly Del thanked God for keeping this girl safe. Somehow they had to make it through whatever came next.

42

Monument, Colorado

"We'll go with you," Del said once they were back in the car. "With three conditions."

Natalie listened intently.

"One, you answer my questions when I ask them." She ticked off a finger. "Two, you seriously consider going to the police, and three . . ." Del stared right into Natalie's face. "We go back to Elk Valley."

Natalie blinked. "You can't be serious."

"I am."

"But they know you live there!"

"Listen." Del clipped her seat belt on again, gesturing for Callie to do the same. "You may be fine with running from these people your whole life, but that's not the way I want to spend mine."

"Del."

"Or we can leave. Your choice."

"Do you realize you might not *have* a life if they find us again?"

"Number two covers that."

"If I go to the police, they could still hurt you to get to me. The cops can't be around every minute of every day."

"We'll be careful."

"How was that going for you when I found you?"

Del didn't want to lose her resolve, but she knew Natalie had a point. And maybe, if it was just her, it wouldn't matter. Her life wasn't much to speak of. But Callie was too vulnerable. She needed to depend on one of them at least, and Natalie lost that privilege when she walked out.

"It's a good town," Del said.

"You won't be able to hide there."

"I don't intend to." She caught Natalie's eye again. "You can end this today with one phone call."

With a sigh, Natalie started the engine. "It's not that simple."

"Why not?" Callie asked.

Natalie's jaw firmed. "If I go to the police, I don't know if they won't take their revenge out on you two."

"We could change our names," Callie suggested.

It wasn't a bad idea, but Del wasn't sure witness protection would be available for them.

When Callie started to say something else, Del shushed her with a look back. Natalie needed to make the next move here. Del had laid out her ultimatum, and she wanted to see what their bio mom did next.

"I'll make you a deal," Natalie said, pulling the SUV out of the parking lot. She was back to her hawk-like scanning.

The white van was nowhere to be seen.

"We find a motel and stop here for the night."

"That's a deal?"

"If it were up to me, we'd already be in Wyoming."

Maybe it was a compromise. One glance at Callie, and Del knew it made sense. She was so exhausted herself she couldn't think clearly for much longer.

"Fine," Del said.

"Can we get another hamburger?" Callie asked.

Del thought about the food she'd stolen, still sitting in the duffel bag. The box of Wheat Thins was calling to her. "We have food, kid."

"Utah's hungry again too."

They stopped at a light, and Del felt like Ghost, the skittish mare from the herd she visited. Natalie's fear had rubbed off on her. Was she being foolish wanting to go back? Elk Valley wasn't anything special, and it certainly hadn't done much for her in the way of employment. But she felt a strange pull to the little town, and insisting they go back felt like a way to take some control back from Natalie. It made her nervous to put so much trust in someone she didn't know.

The notebook Natalie had given her slipped between the seat and console, and Del pulled it out, stuffing it under her leg. She'd read it later. For now, she needed to keep watch.

≈

Woodmore Hill Hotel
Monument, Colorado

Natalie picked a hotel that was nicer than anything Del had ever stayed in with Mom and Dad, who usually preferred camping out in rustic cabins or tents.

As they entered the glimmering lobby with marble floor, Del's exhaustion hit in full force. She wondered how much blood she's lost. Callie had Utah pulled close on his leash, and her eyes darted about like she was afraid someone was going to yell at her for bringing in a dog. His toenails clicked on the marble, and his nose wouldn't stop moving as he sniffed the air, floor, and anything that crossed their path.

The three of them walked up to the counter where Natalie pulled out her wallet.

"Welcome," the chirpy gal behind the counter said. Her tag said her name was Jennifer H. "How may I help you?"

"Do you take dogs?" Callie stood on her tiptoes at the counter.

The clerk nodded. "Yes, though there is a deposit required."

"We'd like a room on an upper floor please," Natalie said.

"Okay, let me see what I can do, ma'am."

Del hoped she didn't look as ratty as she felt. She hadn't changed clothes for two days, and Callie hadn't either. Del noticed the little girl's tangled hair. She should've done a better job watching out for this kid. She was the one who'd been entrusted with her care, not Natalie or Laura or anyone else. She still wondered why Callie's father—West was his name if she remembered right—chose to give her that responsibility when he didn't even know her. But standing behind Natalie at the front desk, Del felt all her inadequacy come to the surface. She hadn't been able to feed the girl, much less give her a roof over her head. No wonder she caught Callie looking longingly at Natalie more than once. To Callie, her mother was like a mythological creature you read about in books but don't quite believe is real. Except in Callie's case, she *had* believed.

Del tried to buck up some strength so she could get Callie settled.

"May I have your name?" Jennifer the hotel clerk said while staring at a computer screen. Her fingers tapped at a keyboard, her long pink nails clacking against each key.

"Susan Stewart," Natalie said without hesitation, handing over a gold American Express card.

Del pretended she didn't notice, but she and Callie exchanged glances. Natalie lied convincingly, and the clerk didn't seem to find anything that would send up a red flag. She just swiped the card and handed it back without fanfare. Taking two room keys from a drawer beside her, she slipped them into a paper sleeve, wrote the room number on it, and handed them to Natalie.

"Your room includes a complimentary breakfast," Jennifer spouted quickly, like she'd given this spiel a million times. "If you have any questions, please don't hesitate to ask. Will you need help with your bags?"

"No, thank you."

Del followed close behind Natalie, shifting the duffel bag to her other shoulder. She and Callie had stuffed enough clothes and food in it to last them until tomorrow.

There was a platter of cookies on a table in the lobby, and Callie swiped a handful before Natalie could notice, sending a sneaky grin Del's way.

They took the elevator up to the seventh floor and found their room. Inside, it smelled clean and fresh with some sort of pine air freshener, and Del was embarrassed at how long it had been since she'd actually been clean herself.

Callie ran into the room and threw herself onto one of the double beds. Utah dove up too and pounced on her, licking her face. She giggled. Del would never get tired of hearing that.

"You can use the shower first if you want." Natalie waved toward the bathroom, setting her rolling suitcase on the luggage rack. Now that the door was locked behind them and no strange men with knives had shown their faces, Natalie's weariness became as obvious as Del's. She wondered again how old her biological mother was but didn't want to ask.

Natalie tried to sound cheerful as she spoke, but it didn't quite reach her eyes. Was she disappointed they weren't heading to Wyoming?

"Aren't we safe here?" Del dropped the duffel on the floor.

"As safe as we can be," Natalie said.

"We ditched the van. How else could they find us?"

Natalie tilted her head, as if she knew of a million ways but didn't have the energy to share them with Del.

Digging around for a clean change of clothes, Del decided to just enjoy the fact that she'd be sleeping in a bed tonight. Then she remembered the bandages she'd stuffed in the Chevy's glove compartment, forgotten in their haste. Great. She wasn't sure if her wound would get worse under a showerhead. She'd have to make due with a sponge bath.

She closed herself in the gleaming bathroom and turned on the fan. That way if she groaned in pain, no one would hear. She lifted her shirt and saw the fresh blood that had seeped through the bandage, along with a yellowish tinge she guessed was lymph mixed with whatever ointment Christy had used. She tried not to imagine infection setting in and got to work cleaning the rest of herself up.

Ten minutes later, she emerged to find Callie sitting cross-legged on the floor outside. She jumped up when she saw Del.

"Mom went to get you some bandages."

Del combed her wet hair with her fingers. She'd tried to wash it hanging over the tub. "You told her?"

Callie gave her a sheepish look. "I knew you wouldn't."

Del wasn't sure why she didn't want Natalie to know. Maybe it was because it confirmed what a lousy job she'd done taking care of Callie. But she couldn't exactly be mad at Callie for telling either. Christy had told her to change the bandage at least once a day, and that wasn't possible without clean dressing.

Someone knocked on the hotel room door, which sent Utah into a barking frenzy. He flung himself at it, and Callie caught him by the collar while Del undid the chain, checking to make sure it was Natalie first.

"Callie told me what happened," Natalie explained when she came in, pulling a box of gauze pads, medical tape, and a tube of Neosporin from a plastic bag. "I hope this is enough."

"Thanks," Del said, shooting Callie another look and reaching for the supplies.

Natalie hesitated, and Del wasn't sure how to read her. She almost seemed afraid to speak.

"Do you need help?" Natalie finally asked.

Del wanted to respond with a big "no," but she remembered how she could barely breathe when Christy had cleaned the wound before. Hopefully it wouldn't be that painful now, but she wasn't in a position to refuse the offer. It was either Natalie or Callie, and Del wanted to shield the girl from seeing her wound.

She gave Natalie a small nod and backed into the bathroom again.

"Be out in a minute," she called to Callie.

When the door was closed, Del stood facing her bio mother. "Can we just get it cleaned and not talk about it?"

She realized how hypocritical she sounded, holding back on her mother while demanding the truth, but she didn't like needing help from this woman.

"How bad is it?" Natalie pulled open the box of gauze pads.

"Grazed."

"I noticed you seemed in pain but didn't want to ask why."

"I was stupid," Del said.

"Callie thinks you hung the moon."

"Hard to believe I've only known her for a couple days."

"Lift up your shirt."

Del obeyed, sitting down on the closed toilet like she had in Christy's bathroom. It was weird how she'd felt a whole lot more relaxed with Christy than she did with Natalie even though Christy was just as much a stranger.

Carefully Natalie removed the old bandage, apologizing as Del winced but getting the job done quickly. At least the wound didn't look worse, but it still hurt to take a deep breath and Del wasn't sure how she would get to sleep with it throbbing. Natalie gave her two ibuprofen tablets. Hopefully they would help.

They emerged a few minutes later to find Callie and Utah sharing the box of Wheat Thins.

"Hey!" Del tried to lighten the mood and dove for the box as quickly as her injury allowed. "Mine!" she yelled in a joking tone.

But Callie was quick. She giggled and ducked away, teasingly holding the crackers just out of Del's reach. Del conceded, dropping into a plush chair at the small circular table by the heater/AC vent.

"You win, kid."

Callie stole the other chair with Utah by her side wagging his tail. That left Natalie standing in the middle of the room staring at them with a look Del *could* read. Longing. As if in that moment she got a true glimpse of what she'd missed. Del wasn't so callous that she enjoyed seeing her suffer through the feelings that were no doubt warring inside her, but she also wasn't planning on consoling the woman. How did they know she was telling the truth about why she left her husband and Callie all those years ago? West was no longer there to corroborate, and Callie obviously couldn't either.

It really came down to trust, and Del wasn't ready to do that just yet, though she couldn't deny Natalie's seeming concern for their welfare. She'd put her life on the line to protect them today. Would she have done that if she wasn't to be trusted?

"So." Natalie sat on the bottom of one of the beds, pulling her leg up under herself. That was all she said, and the one word spoke volumes.

The sun had set, and inky blackness poured through the balcony sliding door. Natalie got up and closed the curtains. In a way, Del was glad someone else was looking out for them.

After she and Callie polished off the entire Wheat Thins box, Del gave a little clap and told Callie to go get ready for bed. Surprisingly, the girl didn't complain. Utah went with her, of course, and she saw the dog's tail disappear through the bathroom doorway.

Natalie sat down in Callie's place with a weary sigh.

"What?" Del finally asked.

Natalie shook her head. "I'm sorry. It's just that I've dreamed of meeting you for so many years."

She wished she could say the same, but it was still barely sinking in that her parents weren't really her parents. Love was thicker than blood, she knew that in her heart. But they were gone, and Natalie was here.

"How old were you when you had me?"

"Twenty-two."

"And my father?"

Natalie sighed again. "He never knew about you, Del."

She decided not to push for a name. She wasn't sure if she was ready for it anyway. "I wish we could've gotten off on a better foot," Del said, meaning it. She might not trust Natalie, but she was curious to understand the woman better. What did they share besides DNA?

Another thought hit Del.

"Do I have grandparents?"

"I haven't seen them in a very long time," Natalie said.

"Aunts? Uncles?"

"I was an only child."

"You're using a fake name."

Natalie didn't seem fazed by her change of subject or bluntness. "I don't have a choice."

Del leaned back in her chair. "I had a choice when I broke into that house. I made the wrong one, but it was still a choice."

"You did what you had to."

"It was still wrong."

Natalie tapped on the table with her fingers. "You may think you know all the answers, Del. I sure did when I was your age. But life has a way of teaching you not everything is black and white."

She was hardly in a position to debate right and wrong, but something small inside her rebelled at Natalie's attitude. She'd done a lot of growing up in the past few years and wasn't afraid to admit she had a lot more to do, but the way Natalie talked didn't sit right. It made her wonder if the young woman who'd looted that museum hadn't changed as much as she wanted Del to believe.

"Why did you do it?" Del asked.

Natalie seemed to know exactly what she meant. Del thought she saw her hand tremble a little before she leaned back and crossed her arms defensively.

"I was stupid."

"Was it the money?"

"That helped." Natalie twirled a silver thumb ring she wore on her right hand. "But it was also about the thrill. And the money, yes, I don't deny that. I was a wild child, and I'm not proud of it. I started stealing things when I was a kid, and it got worse and worse as the years passed. Stealing that art was like a dream come true for me at the time."

Her curiosity got the better of her. "How much were you paid?"

"A hundred grand."

Del's mouth dropped open.

"Each," Natalie said.

No wonder this woman had risked everything, even prison, when she'd committed that crime.

"It wasn't as hard as you'd think either," Natalie added wistfully. "But Del . . ." She leaned forward, resting her arms on the table and meeting Del's eyes again. "If I could go back, I'd never have done it. I lost everything that night. I just didn't know it until it was too late."

"You need to tell the authorities." Del suddenly had the

urge to reach out and touch Natalie's hand, but she didn't. "No matter the consequences."

The statement seemed to break a spell over Natalie, and she regained her composure. "If only it were that easy."

"Why isn't it?"

"Because of who hired us."

43

Before Del could respond, Callie emerged from the bathroom. "Utah needs to go," she said.

Del gave Natalie a look she hoped said "We'll talk about this later" before getting up and taking Utah's leash. They should've walked him before they checked in.

"Where are you going?" Natalie asked.

"Outside." Del said with a shrug.

"You can't—"

"What do you expect him to do? Use the toilet?"

Callie started laughing at that picture, and Del couldn't help grinning at her. If she was being honest, she wished it was just the two of them again. The two of them with some money, anyway. She didn't want to admit it but, mother or not, she wished she'd never met Natalie McGuire.

"It's better I go." Del headed for the door, Utah eagerly in tow. "*They'll* recognize you faster."

Natalie reluctantly nodded in agreement.

Downstairs in the lobby again, Del hated feeling paranoid like Natalie, scanning in every direction before she ventured outside. Was that a white van parked on the edge of the lot? No. It was more like tan. Did that man just give her a once-over, or was he just looking at Utah who was lifting his leg on a bush before she could get him over to the dog walking area?

She'd forgotten it was dark out.

By the time Utah had marked every blade of dead grass and just about pulled her arm out of its socket leaping after a leaf he probably thought was a squirrel, Del was shivering but thinking a little more clearly. She couldn't let Natalie deter her from her ultimate goal—getting Callie and herself back to Elk Valley safe and sound. They'd figure everything else out when they got there. Natalie seemed to have deep enough pockets, and Del wasn't above asking her to help get them back on their feet. It would be like paying a past-due debt.

"Thanks, buddy," she muttered to the dog. "That's just what I needed."

Back on the seventh floor, she found their room and knocked. Callie's muffled laughter drifted through the door. Del knocked again. More laughter, this time Natalie's too. Del felt a twinge of jealousy wash over her, and she tried to suppress it. Natalie was Callie's mother, the only mother she'd ever had. Callie deserved to know her.

At her third knock, Natalie opened the door. "Sorry, we didn't hear you."

"No problem." Del unfastened Utah's leash once the door was closed behind them. He immediately launched himself onto one of the beds, where Callie lay tucked in and resting her head on a huge, white pillow.

"Mom tells a great story!" Callie exclaimed, looking like she'd just been given a pony. "Can you tell it again to Del?"

"Not tonight," Natalie said, an almost guilty expression returning to her face when she glanced at Del.

Utah flipped the covers up with his nose, and Callie lifted them for the dog. He burrowed under and plopped himself in Callie's arms.

Del dug around in the duffel bag for her sweatpants. She

hadn't given much thought to their sleeping arrangements until now, but it was a no-brainer she was sleeping with Callie and Utah.

Natalie took a step toward Callie then stopped herself. "Good night, Callie," she said.

"Night, Mom. I love you."

Natalie pressed her fingers to her lips and blinked a few times. "I love you too."

It was exactly what Callie had said she wanted her mother to know, so it didn't really come as a surprise to hear the little girl say the words to Natalie. But Del still didn't think Natalie deserved her naive devotion. How could Callie accept her so easily?

She slipped out of her blood-stained jeans and into her worn sweatpants and climbed under the covers on the other side of the mattress. Her body screamed for rest even as her brain went into overdrive. Maybe she shouldn't be so hard on Natalie. She had come clean about a bunch of things already, and that couldn't have been easy. She could just as easily have lied. Like she had to the hotel clerk.

Del closed her eyes then opened them again when she felt Callie scoot over. The little girl's warm body was cuddled up against her, her arm draped over Del's stomach. She sighed and gave Callie's arm a small stroke.

"We'll get through this," she whispered.

Callie sighed too, and for a moment all was right with the world.

$\backsim$

When Del started awake, it was Utah who lay against her, heat radiating off his lithe form. Somehow he'd slithered in between them. Callie was sound asleep on the other side, and Del could see her chest rise and fall.

Pushing up on her elbow, she gave the clock a quick glance—1:21—then let her eyes drift over to Natalie's bed. As she focused, she realized the lump in the covers was just the balled-up bedspread.

A rush of panic hit her as she pictured Natalie leaving them high and dry in a Monument hotel room without a car or money. Wouldn't that be the best thing for Natalie? If she was in danger and had been running for the last twenty years, it would be second nature. No matter that she'd be leaving her daughters behind. Again.

Del carefully peeled off her covers and got up, instantly wide awake and trying not to imagine the worst. Had Natalie gone out for a bucket of ice? Then the curtains moved, and Del felt a cool breeze drift through the room. When she caught a whiff of cigarette smoke, she realized Natalie was sitting out on the balcony, the sliding glass door open a crack.

Okay, fine. Now was as good a time as any to continue their conversation. Del pulled the rumpled spread from Natalie's bed and wrapped it around herself. She tiptoed across the room and painstakingly slid the glass door open enough to slip through.

Natalie didn't look up when she joined her on the tiny balcony, their only light the stars and a streetlight at the edge of the parking lot. Del imagined the mountain view was breathtaking during the day.

The tip of Natalie's cigarette glowed, then faded, and a cloud of smoke swirled around her face. Del scooted out the chair across from Natalie and sat down. There was a hotel water glass in front of her mother, a half-empty wine bottle beside it. This explained a few things.

"Couldn't sleep?" Del knew it was a stupid question, but she had to start somewhere.

"Must've been something we ate." Natalie lifted the wine to her lips.

If she'd drank half a bottle, she was probably buzzing.

"I thought you were worried about being found," Del said.

"I am."

She pointed at the bottle.

Natalie nodded slowly. "Help yourself."

"Not what I meant," Del said, though a tiny part of her wanted to oblige and get drunk too. It would feel good not to worry. But instead she pulled the blanket tightly around her shoulders and tucked her bare feet up under herself. She couldn't do that to Callie, and anger flamed inside her that Natalie hadn't thought enough of either of them to stay sober.

"Do you do this often?"

"I do a lot of things I regret later."

"Listen, I get that you made a mistake, okay? What I don't understand is why, if you really are sorry, you haven't done something about it. You could go to police and they would protect you."

"My friends are dead, remember?"

"What if they did die accidentally?"

"They didn't."

"You know that for a fact?"

Natalie laughed, but it wasn't like the laugh Del had heard through the door when Natalie was tucking Callie in for bed. This one came from the bottle, she was sure.

"I know too much, that's what I know." Natalie set down her glass, and it chinked against the metal patio table.

Time to get down to it. "Who hired you to steal the paintings?"

Natalie dropped her cigarette butt in the silver tray beside the bottle, grinding the filter down hard into the ash, like she probably wanted to grind away more than the cigarette. "Let me ask you this." She filled her glass back to the top with dark liquid. "And think long and hard before you answer."

"Fine."

"Do you really want to know who hired us?"

She started to respond, but Natalie cut her off. "Because once you know, you can't ever *not* know."

Del stared at Natalie's shadowy face. Please don't ever let me end up like her, she thought then wondered if it was fair to judge her mother like that. She really didn't know Natalie McGuire, and the woman was obviously eaten up by her past. Del was quickly realizing how different her life would've been if she'd grown up under this woman's care instead of Mom and Dad's. It made her less angry that Natalie had left Callie. The little girl might've been better off with just her father after all.

Del exhaled and tried to shake her judgmental thoughts. "I want to know," she said.

"Did you read the notebook?"

"Some."

There were more clippings about the heist, but at least half the articles seemed to chronicle the political career of Grant Hudson, a man she was hearing about on the news these days. Del hadn't known much about him until his face was plastered across the internet and TV as the media zeroed in on the upcoming presidential primaries.

Natalie said nothing, and Del felt uneasy. Why had Natalie been following the political career of a man as famous as a Kennedy?

"Who hired you?" Del asked.

"Grant Hudson."

44

I knew you wouldn't want to know," Natalie said.

Del remained in the uncomfortable patio chair that was digging into her back, stunned. How could her bio mom have ties to someone so powerful and famous? "Are you kidding me?"

"I'm afraid the poster boy for the American way"—Natalie's words were starting to slur—"isn't what he seems."

"But why in the world would he do something like that?"

"He was living under the shadow of his family." Natalie stared off at something in the darkness. "He felt stifled, and he wanted to do something crazy just to prove he could. He knew I'd always wanted to do something like that too. We were the perfect match."

That made sense in a weird, twisted way. People with insane amounts of money had done strange things. And the Hudsons were rich. Almost like royalty, if America had royalty.

"Then he decided to run for office," Natalie said. "And his criminal past had to be erased. We knew we had to fly under the radar from the beginning, but when Grant's star began to rise, I feared every day they'd try to get rid of me."

"You could've come clean before he got famous," Del said.

"And I would've ended up in prison right along with him."

Del might disagree with Natalie about many things, but she got that. It's why she hadn't figured out what to do about the break-in she just committed herself. If she confessed, she'd be arrested. And if she was arrested, then Callie would be taken away.

She eyed her mother. Maybe they had more than one thing in common.

"And . . ." Natalie lifted the cup to her lips. She held it there for a moment before taking a long sip. "I was in love with him."

"What?"

"We met in college. When he graduated, I dropped out to be with him."

Del rubbed her forehead above the bridge of her nose. This was getting weirder each minute.

"Then his family found out about us." Natalie's words were coming out particularly slowly. "I was from the wrong family, the wrong schools, the wrong economic bracket. Being with someone like me didn't fit with the Hudson family image."

"Did he love you?"

"I thought so," Natalie said. "But his family . . ."

Del squeezed her arms tightly around herself, but the cold was seeping in through the bedspread.

"They threatened to cut him off if he didn't dump me." Another sip of wine. "What was he supposed to do?"

She decided not to answer the question Natalie obviously didn't really want answered. If this Grant guy had any backbone he would've stood up to his family and laid down the law about someone he loved, no matter what they thought about it.

Natalie began to light another cigarette, but her lighter kept misfiring. She finally tossed it on the table, where it clattered and slid toward Del.

"It was also his way of taking care of me," Natalie said. "Two birds with one stone."

"How is—"

"Like I said, I was already heading down a dark path," Natalie continued. "He knew that. In a crooked sort of way, hiring me and my friends was his way of saying he was sorry for ending our relationship. He knew I needed that money."

Del wasn't buying it, but she had to hear this story.

"We planned it for weeks." Natalie no longer looked at Del as she spoke. "And we pulled it off. No one had a clue it was us or that Grant was involved."

"Why would he want paintings like that? He couldn't sell them."

Natalie shrugged. "We didn't care."

"And now you think he wants to kill you?"

Another shrug. "Not him necessarily. More like his family or advisors. I could ruin him, and they know it."

The elusive *they* she kept talking about. Del felt a shiver work its way up her body. The Hudsons wouldn't be the first rich family to have a dark side. Just ask Marilyn Monroe.

But it was still hard to picture something like this happening in real life. Natalie was clearly afraid, and someone really had tried to kidnap Callie. Could this all be connected to what Natalie had done years ago?

"You need to go to the police," Del said. "If the statute of limitations is over, you have nothing to lose, right?"

"Except you two."

Hate to break it to you, dear mother, but you lost us years ago. Natalie turning herself in would put an end to the danger if enough press was involved. Any more attempts on her life or theirs would look suspicious.

"Why would anyone believe me?" Natalie said. "The American people love him. They'll crucify me, and he'll get away with it either way."

"But at least you could stop running," Del said.

Natalie leaned forward, finally looking her full in the face. "Your life would never be the same either."

"I got news for you. It changed the moment I found out my mother wasn't really my mother." Del pulled her legs out from under herself to keep them from falling asleep. She'd noticed Natalie hadn't really asked much about her parents, and that bugged her. Was she intending to swoop in and take their place?

"That's not what I mean," Natalie whispered.

"If you really care about us, you'll do what's right."

"And you know for sure what that is."

"I seem to know a lot more about that than you do. At least I know when I've done something stupid."

Natalie shook her head. She lifted the bottle and tried to hand it to Del. "You really should join me."

"I'm twenty. Or did you forget that?" It seemed hypocritical to care about being underage when she'd already broken the law, but what bothered her more was that Natalie didn't seem to care.

"You might change your mind after I tell you the rest."

Del wasn't sure what Natalie could say that would make things any worse than they were, but a dread filled her.

"Your father." Natalie blinked. Del wanted to grab that bottle and toss it over the railing, but at the same time she was glad the alcohol was making her talk. She wasn't sure what they were supposed to do in the morning when Natalie had a hangover.

Did she want to hear who he was? She was tempted to dive back under the covers with Callie and Utah and pretend she was five years old and didn't have a care in the world. She didn't want to hear Natalie talk about a biological father out there somewhere, and yet she couldn't move either. This was her reality. She had to hear it, or she might miss the chance to know the truth for the rest of her life.

"Grant," Natalie said.

If the revelation that Grant Hudson had paid her mother to steal from a famous museum hadn't been enough, this was a gut punch. She had to ask Natalie to say it again.

"You heard me," Natalie responded.

Del did stand up then, the flimsy hotel bedspread still wrapped around her shivering back. "Grant Hudson is my *father?*"

"Surprise." Natalie raised her glass.

It was the way she said it. Del knew the wine was doing the talking now for Natalie, but she felt like smacking her. Instead, she snatched up the bottle and retreated into the hotel room. As quietly as she could, she crossed the floor to the bathroom, shut the door, flicked on the light, and dumped the liquid down the sink.

She clung to the counter with both hands, the bedspread falling to the floor at her feet.

45

Del stared at herself in the bathroom mirror. She felt dizzy, as if she really had indulged in the wine. Her pulse was pounding in her ears, and she had to squeeze the counter to ground herself to what was real. Had Mom and Dad known who her father was? Somehow she didn't think so. This revelation seemed to be something Natalie had kept to herself all these years, not even telling Grant about having his child.

Grant Hudson.

She pictured his chiseled, handsome face with the trademark, Hudson five o'clock shadow. Smiling and waving at a press conference, jogging down the steps of one of his family's private jets, or grabbing a cup of coffee at a street vendor's cart in New York City. If you lived in America, you knew Grant Hudson.

You did not wake up one morning and find out he was your father.

Del turned on the faucet and splashed warm water on her face. How could Natalie have kept this secret all these years? If the press got wind of Del she'd never be able to walk the street unnoticed again.

A faint knock came at the door. Del jumped. It would be Callie. Somehow she'd woken the girl despite her efforts. Had she heard them talking on the balcony?

Del turned off the light, instantly blinded but not wanting Callie's sleepy eyes to waken any more than they already were. A faint orange glow from the surge-protected plug was the only way she could even tell where the door was.

She opened it and, sure enough, Callie stood in the doorway. Del gave her shoulder a squeeze as they passed each other and Callie went to the toilet.

Del left the balcony door open and returned to her bed, tossing Natalie's blanket onto hers, which was still empty. She climbed in next to Utah, who thumped his tail when her hand brushed his side. Callie returned, bumping around in the dark, still half asleep.

Del lifted the covers for her sister, and Callie curled up beside her again, resting her head in the crook of Del's arm before Del could get comfortable. Not that she would be getting any sleep tonight anyway.

She held in a groan as Callie's arm brushed against her bandage. Sleep was what they both desperately needed, and the thought of not being able to enjoy the first real bed she'd had in days didn't help. Feeling Callie snuggled close to her and drifting back to sleep only increased her anxiety.

They had to get away from all this.

Del closed her eyes and tried to press the sense of urgency from her mind. But the urge wouldn't leave.

She heard the balcony's sliding door slam shut, Natalie making no effort to be quiet. Her steps were uneven, and Del heard a thud as if she'd walked into something.

Del lifted her head to watch Natalie's form make it to her bed where she fell onto the mattress, barely pulling the covers over herself. She was snoring before the clock hit three. By then, Del knew what she had to do.

≈

"Callie?" Del whispered in the little girl's ear.

She didn't stir, but Utah's tail thumped again.

"Kid, wake up." She gently shook Callie's shoulder.

"Wh . . . at?"

"Shh. Don't say anything, but I need you to get up really quietly." Del kept her face near Callie's, her voice low. She was glad Natalie had passed out.

"What's . . . going on?"

"I need you to trust me more than you ever have before." Del held the girl's hand in both of hers. "Because we have to leave."

Even in the darkness she saw the confusion on Callie's face.

"Why?" Callie sat up.

She would not lie. She had promised herself never to do that again to her sister, even if it hurt. But she knew if she told Callie what was going on the girl would either talk her out of it or make enough noise to wake Natalie. And Del didn't want Callie to see her mother drunk.

"I don't think we're safe here," Del said.

"But Mom said—"

"I know, but she's wrong."

"Does . . ." Callie's voice cracked. "Does she know we're leaving?"

Del paused for the longest second. "No."

For eight years old, Callie was a sharp kid. She seemed to sense Del's desperation, her fear even, because she didn't throw a fit about leaving the mother she'd longed for and had only just been reunited with.

257

"She told me things while you were asleep." Del hated to talk for fear of disturbing Natalie, but it was the only way she was going to convince Callie. "Things I can't repeat right now. I just have to . . . it needs to be just us."

"But will we ever see her again?"

"I don't know."

The seconds ticked by. Callie stared at Natalie's still form on the other bed.

"I think we might though," Del finally said. Even if it was only on the news.

That seemed to be all Callie needed. She slipped off the bed, pulling Utah with her.

Del handed the girl his leash. "I have everything ready. We'll just walk out as quietly as we can, okay?"

Callie gave a little nod as Del guided her around the bed and toward the door. Del gave one more glance back at Natalie herself, a pang hitting her in the stomach that had nothing to do with the fact that she was hungry.

Undoing the chain and dead bolt, Del shouldered the duffel bag and prayed the light from the hallway didn't hit Natalie's face.

She shut the door behind them as slowly as possible, but as soon as it latched, she urged a squinting Callie toward the elevator. Utah's ears perked up, and he looked at Callie in excitement as if wondering why he was being walked in the middle of the night.

The elevator ride down felt like an eternity, and that's when Del noticed Callie's feet were bare. She'd stuffed her Converse sneakers in the duffel bag but didn't have time to dig them out now.

"Where are we going?" Callie asked, staring up at her with those green eyes that made Del's throat tighten.

"Home," Del said.

It was the first time she'd thought of Elk Valley in that

way. Maybe it was being torn away from it that had changed things. But she knew they had to be there where they belonged. There was just one problem. Elk Valley was the first place Natalie would come looking for them.

Del tapped the toe of her sneaker on the elevator floor. She'd have to deal with that later. People had let her down there, but a few, like Christy and that bald-headed pastor, had also given her hope. Being with Natalie had taught Del one thing for sure. She didn't want to spend her life running. She would face the music in Elk Valley and pray the pieces fell into place in her favor.

Del led them straight across the lobby, being careful not to meet eyes with the clerk at the desk, who luckily was a different girl than the one who'd checked them in. Outside, Del took them straight to Natalie's SUV.

"Now would be a good time to do some of that praying." Del pulled Natalie's keys from her pocket and clicked the unlock button on the key remote. The SUV's lights blinked. They could deal with getting it back to Natalie later. She'd left a terse note back in the room telling her not to follow them.

"I'm not stealing it," Del made sure to explain to Callie as they climbed in. "Just borrowing."

"But how will she get by?"

Del thought of the American Express card and the wad of cash she'd found in Natalie's purse when she swiped the keys. She'd been tempted to take the money too, but she'd done enough stealing and would have to find another way to provide for Callie. She hoped Christy Williams had been serious about her offer of help, because she was the only person Del could imagine trusting at this point.

"She'll be okay," Del said. The statement was relative and dependent on so many choices Natalie would make in the coming days, but Del felt certain she could at least say this to Callie for now.

If there really was someone after Natalie, Del wanted to get as far away from her as possible. And she intended to talk to someone, a lawyer maybe, in Elk Valley about what she could do for their protection. Too bad the sheriff had creeped her out.

"Climb in the back so you can sleep." Del jumped into the driver's seat.

The little girl obeyed, and Del pulled out of the parking lot. She barely breathed until they got on the freeway. Had Natalie heard them leave? Del could only hope she still lay in her drunken stupor, because she couldn't think about what her bio mother would do when she woke up to find them gone.

46

I-25 South
Near Colorado Springs, Colorado

Del's eyelids drooped as they passed through Colorado Springs, and she had to concentrate to stay awake. The SUV handled a lot differently than her small sedan, and she found herself judging distances wrong.

It would be light soon. She wanted to be pulling into Elk Valley before sunrise, but she wasn't sure exactly where to go first. Maybe the church. They could sleep in the parking lot undetected for a few hours. She could still sell her car if the Lopezes hadn't impounded it already.

Callie slept soundly, Utah by her side. Del hadn't heard a peep out of either of them for miles, and for that at least she was grateful. Callie was the most resilient kid she'd ever met. Had she herself been like that as a girl? Del couldn't remember, and she wished more than anything Mom and Dad were around to ask. They would've liked Callie.

Del yawned and tried to focus on the road. Natalie's words reverberated in her mind over and over as she drove, and by the time they neared Pueblo she was a wreck, wondering if she'd just made the stupidest decision of her life. But what other choice did she have? Natalie's intentions felt murky, too gray. She understood the woman wanting to know her children, but Del wasn't sure if she wanted to know Natalie or allow Callie to. At least not until she was old enough to make up her own mind and not be unduly influenced by her drinking and her shady ideas.

Was she being selfish? Had she done all this because she wanted Callie to herself and felt jealous of her mother? Del shook her head. No. This was not about her. Natalie was the one who'd messed things up twenty years ago and dragged them into her problems here and now.

They turned onto U.S. 160 in Walsenburg, and she didn't realize she was speeding until she glanced at the speedometer and saw it pushing eighty-five. Del lifted her foot off the gas just as she saw the dark cruiser gaining on her bumper.

Oh, please, no. She was only miles from her destination. They'd almost made it.

Lights spun.

The siren came on.

Del nearly drove off the road. If she tried to get away, she'd be in even more trouble. But if she stopped, it would all be over. They'd run the plates. Natalie might've already reported the car stolen, and for all she knew this cop had a warrant for her arrest.

She had no option but to let the SUV drift to the shoulder. Unless Natalie kept her registration and insurance in the glove compartment, she didn't have those either. Her name wouldn't match anything. Nail in the coffin.

Callie stirred, lifting her head from the back seat where she'd hunkered down with her seat belt loosened.

"Where are we?"

"There's a cop behind us, and I'm screwed." She was so tired she didn't have the energy to watch her language around Callie.

"Can't you just tell them the truth?"

"I don't know." Del reached over to open the glove compartment.

A shrill ring at her elbow made her nearly jump out of her skin. She glanced down to see Natalie's cell phone light up in the cup holder. She hadn't meant to take it.

The screen lit up with the name *Abby Dawson.*

Del intended to ignore it. But before she could stop her, Callie scooped it up and answered with a quiet "Hello?"

"What are you—" she dove toward Callie, trying to grab the phone from her, but the little girl slipped into the back seat again.

"Who is this?" Callie whispered.

Del spun around in her seat. "Give me the phone."

"I'm Callie. Mom's not here," Callie said then paused. "Del is, but we just got pulled over by a cop."

She tried to grab the phone again, but a sharp pain jolted through her side.

Callie climbed up onto the back seat, looking out at the cruiser. "Near Elk Valley, I think."

The cop was walking toward them, backlit by the headlights.

Del lowered her window and tried to appear calmer than she was.

Abby turned down the police scanner on her dash. Except for some routine chatter, it had been pretty quiet for the past twenty minutes. She'd pulled out of the bed and breakfast before dawn in the hopes of making it up to Longmont by nine. As much as she wanted to stay in Elk Valley she still had a business to run, and there was a book sale she needed to attend.

She'd been trying Natalie's cell phone all night and finally got through. But it wasn't Natalie who answered, and everything changed when the child said the name *Del*.

"Are you still there, Callie?"

"Yeah."

"What's he doing now?"

"He's coming over."

"Is he wearing a uniform?"

"Not really."

"Where are you exactly?"

"I'm not sure. I think almost in Elk Valley."

"Look around. Is there any sort of sign?"

"It's dark."

"Try to see." Abby's fingers tightened around her phone. Natalie had held out on her, she knew, but two things the woman had unveiled: someone wanted her dead and she was desperate to find her kids. Why did Natalie's daughters have her cell phone?

She could hear the girl breathing in and out faster than normal. "Junction Route 12," she finally whispered, then sucked in a breath. "He's at the window."

"How you doing, miss?"

He wore a starched black shirt with a shield pinned to the pocket and a shoulder holster pulled tightly across his pecs. He looked more like The Rock than a cop.

"I've been better," Del said.

"Turn the car off."

She'd read somewhere this was procedure and obeyed him, glancing at Callie with what she hoped was a signal to hang up the phone. She had no idea who the girl was talking to. The last thing they needed was for someone to clue in their mother as to where they were. There was the sliver of a chance they'd get through this if she just played it cool.

"I'll need you to get out." The cop didn't even try to look amused. He touched the gun in his holster.

She glanced up into his square face, unable to see details in the poor light. A door slammed, and she realized there was a second cop coming over to the other side of the SUV.

"Was I speeding?"

"Yes. Now get out."

"Ask to see his I.D.," Callie whispered.

The second cop's shadow hovered near the passenger door, and she instantly regretted turning off the car. Was she being as paranoid as Natalie, or was something off here? She glanced at Callie, whose eyes looked as large as an anime character. She still held the phone to her ear, and Del thought she heard a tinny voice talking to her. Maybe it wasn't a bad idea to make sure these cops were real.

"Uh, I'm really nervous, Officer. Could I see your I.D.?"

Three seconds. She bet she could have the SUV started again in less than that. Flip it into Drive, release the brake, and they'd be gone.

"Am I going to have to drag you?" The cop nearly growled.

He was either having a really bad night and she'd end up charged with evading arrest, or her instinct was right and they were in deep trouble. Unmarked car. No uniform. Refusing to show I.D. *Oh, dear God, please help us.*

"Wait a minute, Officer. I'm not even—"

She dove for the ignition.

The cop's arm shot inside the car so fast Del didn't have time to react. His fingers crunched around her forearm, shoving it against her chest and pinning it there. He had the doors unlocked before she could get in a punch.

"Get out, Callie! Run!"

But there was no time. The second man opened Callie's door.

Run? Had Abby heard that right?

Her mind raced almost as fast as her car as she sped toward the freeway. "Callie?" That was the girl's name, right?

She glanced down at the cell phone screen. She hadn't lost the call, but the girl wasn't answering, and a sick feeling squeezed Abby's insides. If they were near Elk Valley, the only junction with Route 12, the road she was currently on, was where it intersected Route 160. That was less than a minute from her location. Could she make it in time to find out what was going on?

"Callie, can you hear me?"

Nothing.

Abby jammed her cell to her ear, straining to hear what was going on. Had Callie dropped the phone? Was it really a cop pulling them over?

Still nothing on the scanner.

She thought she heard a man's voice, and then someone screamed.

Pressing the gas pedal to the floor, she sped down the road leading to the freeway.

Del reached down and sunk her teeth as hard as she could into the arm holding her against the seat.

She tasted blood and the man made a guttural sound, but his grip didn't loosen. Instead he shoved her own arm up

266

against her throat, causing sharp pain to jolt through her wrist and elbow. She could barely breathe.

"Don't. Do that. Again," he said.

But he'd have to release her to open the door, right?

"Let me go!" Callie screamed.

Del twisted her neck, trying to see what was happening to her sister. She was startled to see the man who yanked Callie from the car was the same guy who had tried to take her from the apartment.

Callie was screaming bloody murder and Utah was barking. "I said let me go! Let me go! Let me—"

"Will you shut her up?" Del's captor ordered.

Skull Cap shook Callie. He tore the leash from her hands, but that transformed Callie into a kicking, screaming, scratching, biting machine. The flurry seemed to take Skull Cap aback, and Del thought for a moment it would be enough for Callie to get away.

It wasn't. He shook her again, but she kept screaming.

Please let someone hear us!

"I'll shut up if you give me my dog!"

But there was nothing out here except barren fields and the occasional ranch set way back from the road.

Del thought she heard Utah growl.

The man holding Del leaned forward, looking in the SUV. He pushed her arm harder. "Where is Natalie McGuire?"

Del glared at him.

Skull Cap cursed. "She was supposed to be here!"

"Get the kid in the car."

"Please let her go. Just take me," Del tried to speak. "I'll go willingly, but . . . please just . . . let her and the dog go."

"You're both coming." The fake cop pulled her door open. If she attacked him at this close range he'd probably pull his gun. She didn't want Callie to watch her die. But if they went with these men she wasn't sure if they'd live to see another day. She had to do something.

"Out," he ordered, nodding his head toward the sedan she'd thought was a police cruiser. A wave of guilt washed over her at her stupidity. She'd gotten them into this mess. If something terrible happened it would be her fault.

Somewhere in the back of her mind Del had thought they'd make it. Even if she'd had to give Callie up to Laura or social services for awhile, there would still be hope they would reunite and have a relationship. But when this bull of a man yanked her out of the SUV and she could see Callie being dragged toward the sedan too, Del's hope flickered out.

Natalie had been right.

"I'll give you one more chance." The Rock look-alike bore into her with his dark eyes. "Where is Natalie McGuire?"

Del kicked at the guy's crotch as hard as she could. How he anticipated the move she had no idea, but instead of landing a solid, you'll-never-have-children blow, he blocked her foot with his hand and spun her around so fast she didn't realize what was happening until she slammed up against the side of the SUV face-first.

"Nice try." He attempted to pull her arm behind her back, but Del flipped herself around to face him again. She threw a punch at the bridge of his nose, but he blocked this too, and her hand slammed into his fist with a bone-crunching jolt.

Then he sent his own punch into her side, and she was down. If he'd known of her wound he couldn't have planted a more painful hit. Del fell to her knees, doubled over.

"Sorry, but you asked for that," he said, pulling her to her feet and practically carrying her to the sedan. She could barely see much less resist.

"Get someone back to that hotel," she heard one of the men say.

And before Del knew what was happening, she was tossed

onto the back seat, the door slammed behind her, and the car was soon barreling down the highway, leaving their hope for a new life in Elk Valley behind.

∽

Abby hadn't done much praying in her life, but as she approached the Route 12 junction a plea to God fell from her lips.

What was she going to find?

She slowed the Acura. There. Beside the road. Was that their car?

She checked in her rearview for approaching traffic and crept by the white SUV. One glance at the license plate and she knew it was Natalie's. Where were the kids?

For twenty years Abby had fought for law and order, and putting a bad guy behind bars had given her purpose even through her messy divorce. But somehow she knew that tonight would define her. She had to find those kids.

Where? Was she too late?

God, please help me find them. Help them.

Abby pulled over to check the vehicle and make sure it had been abandoned, but then she stopped. She'd *just* heard the little girl on the phone. They couldn't have gone far.

Glancing down the highway, she saw nothing behind her, but ahead were the faint red tail lights of a vehicle maybe a half mile away.

She wasn't sure if it was intuition, or maybe even divine inspiration, but Abby pressed the accelerator.

47

Del felt Utah's tongue bathing her cheek. She must've passed out. Callie's face hung down over her, and she gradually realized her head was in Callie's lap. They were in the back of the car.

Why hadn't they been tied up?

She blinked and saw Skull Cap leering at her from the passenger seat. When their eyes met, he clicked something in his other hand. A flash went off, making her squint. She realized he was punching buttons on a smartphone.

"Where are you taking us?" She tried to sit up. Her side burned and felt wet. She guessed fresh blood was seeping through her shirt, but it was too dark to see.

She managed to pull herself up to a sitting position and wrapped her arm around Callie. She almost said "It's okay" to the girl like she'd said so many times in the past few days, but it wasn't true and they both knew it.

No use pretending. Callie was a smart kid. She'd probably see through any attempt she made at appearing strong anyway. Utah slithered onto Callie's lap and rested his head on her leg.

"We should pray," Callie whispered.

Was she expecting God to get them out of this mess?

Del swallowed hard, nodding. She reached for Callie's hand. Maybe they'd attached a tracking device to Natalie's car. How else could they have found them so close to Elk Valley? These men had thought Natalie was in the car with them.

Callie slipped the small Bible Christy had given her from her waistband.

"Hey, what're you doing?" Skull Cap snapped.

Callie held the book out to him. "Reading. It's a Bible."

His lip curled, like he smelled something bad. He glanced at the driver, the fake cop who'd punched Del, but he didn't seem to care and just kept his eyes on the road. The horizon was turning gray, and Del could make out the silhouettes of a few trees and hills. They seemed to be going up in elevation, the road winding around curves.

Callie flipped the Bible open, and holding it up to her face to read in the pre-dawn light, she paged through until she found something she liked.

"Come with great power, O God, and rescue me!" she read in a voice louder than Del would've preferred. "Defend me with Your might. Listen to my prayer, O God. Pay attention to my plea."

The girl seemed to gain confidence with each word she spoke. Del leaned back in the seat, trying to will the pain away. Would she ever have the chance to really get to know Callie, or would both their lives be cut short?

"For strangers are attacking me," Callie read even louder. "Violent people are trying to kill me. They care nothing for God."

"Shut up, brat," Skull Cap said yet didn't do anything to stop her. Callie wouldn't shut up. She sat up straighter. "But God is my helper," she read. "The Lord keeps me alive! May the evil plans of my enemies be turned against them. Do as You promised and put an end to them."

"I said shut up!"

Del reached out and touched Callie's arm, a silent plea not to provoke these men. She seemed to understand and settled down, still holding the book.

A proud, sisterly feeling came over her at Callie's boldness. After a few minutes, Callie closed the Bible and cuddled up against Del.

"We'll be okay," Callie whispered.

It wasn't a question, and Del envied the little girl's faith. If they got out of this alive, she might have to take a look at that book herself.

⌒

Woodmore Hill Hotel
Monument, Colorado

Natalie pried open her eyes, but they felt taped shut. With a groan she pushed up onto an elbow and glanced over at Del and Callie's bed. When she saw the rumpled covers, she jumped up even as a wave of nausea threatened to send her to the toilet.

She frantically checked the hotel room.

Balcony empty. Bathroom empty.

Their duffel bag and even the dog gone.

Natalie fumbled for her shoes and car keys, only then seeing the note. Written in a messy scrawl, the short paragraph was a dagger to her heart.

We had to leave. Please don't look for us. I'll leave your car somewhere safe. -Del

"No, no, no . . ." Natalie covered her face with her hands, regretting ever opening that bottle last night. It had loosened her tongue far more than she'd ever intended, and now Del would hate her forever.

Panic threatened to overwhelm her as she remembered the look of disgust on her oldest daughter's face. Natalie had hoped somehow she could make amends, that Del would believe her and maybe, eventually, understand she'd given her up out of love and left Callie with West for the same reason.

But once again, her selfishness had gotten in the way.

There was a knock on the hotel room door, and Natalie rushed to it. Had they come back? Were they—

The door flew open.

Natalie gasped.

Two men rushed inside.

She would've fought, maybe even tried to take them down, but before she could, one of the men held up a cell phone. The photo on the screen stopped her cold.

"We have your children," he said.

48

They drove higher into the mountains, and Del lost track of the road's twists and turns. It was light now, and with the morning came renewed terror as to what was going to happen to them. She thought about jumping from the car, but these men would surely follow. What chance would they have on foot?

So Del waited.

"Where are we going?" she asked the men again. They opened a bag of Cheetos and were passing it back and forth between them. Even if she reached up and tried to strangle Skull Cap, the driver would stop and pull her off.

"You'll find out soon enough," the driver grumbled.

"Are you going to kill us?"

"Why don't you just shut up like I said before?"

"Or you'll kill me? 'Cuz I figure whoever hired you probably wants to do that, or else you would've done it already."

She was bluffing, but she couldn't stand the silence anymore.

Callie's eyes drooped. She'd drifted off a few times as she

leaned against Del. She started mumbling something under her breath, and Del realized she was praying again.

Good. They needed it.

The men ignored her, and Del concentrated on the surrounding woods, trying to memorize the road. The sedan pulled off onto a gravel lane and climbed even higher into the mountains.

Apprehension gripped her like a pit bull. Isolated. No population. The perfect place to dump their bodies.

Del held Callie close and reached over and stroked Utah. She carefully undid his leash. Maybe one of them could survive.

They wound through Ponderosa pines, and even with the windows closed Del thought she could smell the spicy needles. The smell reminded her of the horses back home. She closed her eyes and tried to picture each one running free, their manes and tails flowing behind them.

Suddenly the sedan stopped at a black, cast-iron gate crossing their path. It was taller than the car and looked like it belonged in the English countryside, not in a Colorado forest.

Del sat up straighter. What in the world was a gate like that doing out here?

The gate opened, and their captor drove through. The gate immediately closed behind them. The forest opened to a clearing, and Del realized the reason for the gate. Before them was a cabin, if it could even be called that, unlike any she'd ever seen. Three stories high with a giant A-frame that looked like one huge window. The porch was larger than the Lopezes entire house, and a green lawn—unheard of this time of year—sloped up toward it. Was that a helicopter sitting on the grass?

The car pulled up in front of the cabin, and the driver got out. This was it. Their only chance for escape. She elbowed Callie.

"Ground rules," Skull Cap said. "No screaming, running, or fighting."

She and Callie stared at him.

The door opened beside Del, and The Rock look-alike grabbed her by the arm. She knew there would be no escape. Not now, at least. These men weren't stupid, and there was nowhere to go. She glanced out Callie's window and saw a squirrel hopping across the fire break between the cabin and the woods.

"Let Utah go," she whispered to Callie.

"But . . ."

"We'll come back for him."

Tears welled in Callie's eyes, but she seemed to understand that her four-legged best friend had a better chance running free than stuck with them.

Callie opened the door. Utah took one look at the squirrel and bolted.

"Hey!" Skull Cap reached inside his coat.

"It's just the dog!" Del said. "We're staying right here."

And then Del was pulled from the car and Callie followed. The men flanked them, marching them up the huge steps leading to the massive, double doors.

Could this log mansion belong to Grant Hudson?

He would have the money for a cabin like this. But had he really paid these men to abduct them? What would've happened if Natalie had been with them in the car?

Callie was crying and glancing over her shoulder, but Utah had disappeared. Del kept telling herself someone would find him and take care of him. It was better this way. They needed to worry about themselves now, and she knew Callie wouldn't take risks if she felt she had to keep the dog safe.

Skull Cap flung the thick doors open, shoving them into a massive entry room that made her gasp. She stared up at the ceiling far above them with its huge wooden beams and a giant antler chandelier hanging above them. She wondered if her voice would echo, but she didn't dare speak.

"Walk," Rock ordered, pointing them down a long hallway toward a closed door.

Their feet clicked on the wood floors, and Del thought she smelled some sort of lemon oil or air freshener. A place like this would employ at least one person full-time just to clean it, and she wondered if it was worth screaming for help. Could there be a maid around to hear?

She decided not to risk it.

Rock opened a door, and when Del saw the narrow stairs leading straight down into darkness she balked, planting her feet and shaking her head. This would be where they killed them.

"Move it," Rock said, giving her back a shove.

Was this her last stand? Did she want to die knowing she hadn't fought tooth and nail for Callie?

Callie put her tiny hand in Del's. Her tears had left tracks on her cheeks, and her eyes were pink. An understanding passed between them. Whatever they faced, they would face it together.

The men turned on the lights and herded them down into the cabin's basement, walking them first through an area that looked like a sports bar with a pool table, four flat screen TVs, and circular tables with chess boards painted on their surfaces. They came to another door, this one metallic and guarded with a keypad lock. Rock punched in a set of numbers—Del only got the five and two—and the lock made a slight click. The door seemed to whoosh a little as he flung it open and pushed them inside.

Instead of a cold, utilitarian bunker like she expected, the room was filled with soft light coming from the recessed fixtures in the ceiling. Along one side of the room, which seemed to stretch the whole length of the cabin, were floor-to-ceiling bookshelves holding hundreds of volumes, most leather, with some sections covered by glass doors. There was a bar with racks full of wine and a collection of pristine glasses.

But it was what was displayed on the wall right in front of

them that caused Del's eyes to widen. The paintings. She couldn't help taking a step toward them. She was no art collector, but even she recognized the bold strokes of the oil masterpieces her mother had stolen twenty years ago. What else could they be?

Each one was prominently displayed on the wall with its own light illuminating every brush mark. The aura of the room felt like an exhibit.

Hardly giving the paintings a second glance, the men pushed Del and Callie toward the center of the room to a cluster of dark leather chairs.

"We're here," Rock said.

One of the chairs swiveled around, and a man turned to face them.

Del could only stare.

"Please leave us," Grant Hudson said.

49

Hudson Chalet
Westcliffe, Colorado

Del wrapped her arm around Callie and backed them toward the door. She couldn't bring any words to her lips. If Natalie was to be believed, this man was her father. The shock of that revelation hadn't worn off, and now here she was standing before him.

He stood, looking like a suave George Clooney. "I'm sorry to have put you through all that," he said. "But I didn't think you'd come willingly."

To Del the words sounded as practiced as any campaign speech. She took another step toward the door. Those thugs had let them think they were going to die, and the man before her had hired them.

"Do you know who I am?" Grant asked.

Callie glanced up at Del, and she realized the girl might not recognize him.

"You look better on TV," Del said.

The twitch of a smile hit Grant's lips.

"What do you want with us?" The question made her

sound calmer than she felt, but she needed to stay as focused as possible or they'd never get out of here.

"That's the big question, isn't it?" Grant said. He wore a crisp, white shirt tucked into dark corduroys. She saw a leather sports coat tossed across the back of one of the chairs. Grant gestured toward them.

She shook her head.

"What did your mother tell you?"

The edges of her mind frayed, Del tried desperately to keep panic at bay.

"Where is she?" Del demanded.

He held up his hand, gold cuff links sparkling. "I suggest you sit down."

"Where *is* she?"

Callie tugged on her sleeve. "Is Mom okay?"

She couldn't answer the girl. Instead she balled up her hand and glared at Grant Hudson. Natalie had been right all along, hadn't she? This man really did mean her harm.

"Where's Natalie?" Del asked.

Grant glanced at his watch. "She was supposed to be with you. But no matter. She should be joining us shortly."

Del's mind raced. She didn't quite trust her mother, but that fear in Natalie's eyes had been real. She had a reason to be afraid, and Del now understood why.

As much as she hated the idea, Del knew they were stuck here. At least it sounded like Natalie was still alive. She was surprised at how much of a relief that was.

"Please have a seat," Grant said, pulling back one of the leather chairs.

"I'd rather stand."

"Del."

The way he said it, like a father scolding his child, stoked the fire in her. It took everything she had to keep from lashing out with the full force of what she felt toward this man, but she knew she had to rein herself in if she expected to get away.

Natalie had said he didn't know about her, but was that still true? Del wasn't sure if it would help or hurt them if Grant realized she was his daughter. She raised both hands in surrender. "What my mom did . . . it can stay in the past, as far as I'm concerned. We just want to go home."

Grant sat down again. "First, we need to talk."

First? Did that mean he intended to let them go?

Del squeezed Callie's shoulder, hoping to reassure her that she had things under control even if she felt like their plane was in a nose dive. She lifted her chin. He'd had them kidnapped. That's all she needed to know. A man who would do that was not someone she could trust.

"We want to leave now."

"Not until we talk."

He said it as if that was all the explanation they needed. Was that the way a man born into power controlled people, by simply ordering them around? Was she supposed to jump if he said jump just because he was a Hudson?

"Talk about what?" Del tried to sound confident, but one of the most powerful men in America staring her down was unnerving.

Grant gestured toward the chairs again, and Del slowly steered Callie toward them, whispering in her ear, "Be ready to run."

"Who is he?" Callie tried to whisper back, but her words came out loud and clear in the acoustics of the room.

Grant came over and reached out his hand. "I'm Grant. Nice to meet you, Callie."

Callie hesitated then put her hand in his. "How do you know my name?"

"Because I'm smart, Callie. I know a lot of things. I bet you do too."

Del couldn't resist any longer. Not when he was trying to manipulate a little girl. She placed herself between Callie and Grant and shoved him in the chest with both hands. "Get away from her."

He stumbled back two steps and she flinched, expecting him to strike her. Instead he just laughed. "Feisty. Just like your mother."

"I swear, I will—"

"Do what?" Grant shook his head. "There's nothing for you to do, Del. I need you here, and that's where you're staying until I say so."

"But why do you need us?" She could feel Callie pressed close behind her.

"How much did your mother tell you?"

She instinctively glanced at the paintings displayed on the walls. If they played dumb, would it help? Somehow she didn't think so, but it might be best to zip up and let him do the talking.

"Did she tell you how we met?" Grant asked.

Del pulled Callie over to the chairs and they both sat down. The leather that had appeared soft was deceivingly hard. And cold. Grant sat across from them.

"In the college cafeteria," Grant continued. "I saw this beautiful girl sitting alone at a table. From that moment, I was smitten."

"Then why do you want her dead?"

There. It was out in the open. Del was tired of beating around the bush. She was going to shoot straight and hope she'd gotten the trait from her biological father.

Grant acted as if he hadn't heard her. "I'm a driven man," he said. "How else could I have gotten where I am? Over the years, I've made many mistakes, and losing Natalie was one of them."

"How 'bout abducting us?"

Grant's expression didn't change. "For her own good I had to find her. She would never come if I asked, but if I had her children . . ."

"So the end justifies the means and all that crap." If only Callie didn't have to hear this conversation.

"I'm not a monster, Del."

She hated how he kept using her name as if they were two chums chatting over a cup of coffee. "Then let us go."

"There's a lot more at stake here than you realize."

"I know what's at stake."

"Do you?" Grant leaned forward, and Del resisted the urge to recoil. He held their lives in his hands, and she wouldn't needlessly put Callie in any more danger, but Del also thought there was the chance Grant might respect her show of confidence.

"Her friends are dead," Del said. "And she thinks she's next."

Grant seemed to wince ever so slightly. "I know."

"Did you have them killed?"

He sighed and tapped his finger on the table.

Callie's eyes widened. She'd only heard half of Natalie's story, and Del wished it had stayed that way.

"No," Grant finally said.

She started to fire off another accusation, but he held up both of his hands. "Just stop there," he said. "I'm not a murderer."

"But you knew about it?"

"Not in the way you think." Grant abruptly stood. He crossed his arms and his eyes met hers. It felt like she was staring into a mirror.

"I'm gonna be straight with you, Del," Grant said. "Did I try to intimidate your mother? Yes. Did I try to bribe her? Yes. And when she made it perfectly clear she couldn't be bought, I hired people to scare her. I did not intend for her to run away."

"What about her friends?"

"They *could* be bought."

"Then why are they dead?"

"It was never my intention for anyone die."

"Your men made us think we were going to die!"

"I told them not to hurt you." Grant paced over to the wall of paintings then came back to the table. "Have you watched the news lately? This country is a mess. The economy's in shambles, unemployment's through the roof, and trust in the government's at an all-time low. America needs a leader."

He stared off into space, and Del saw something change on his features. A resolve firmed his jaw. He glanced back at Del with fire in his eyes, but it wasn't directed at her. She imagined this is how he looked when he delivered a speech, except she and Callie were the only ones to hear.

"I can change this country. I can be that man who unites and transforms things for better. I can revive the American dream." He waved his hand around as if emphasizing the point. "But if the press ruins me, that much-needed change will never happen, and by the time another leader rises up it might be too late. Do you understand?"

She was starting to. "Are you even listening to yourself?"

Grant shook his head. "Confidence is the lifeblood of any leader. I cannot allow everything I've worked for crumble because of a mistake I made twenty years ago."

She glanced at the paintings.

Grant followed her gaze. "I've kept them to remind me how quickly the mighty can fall."

You're a coward, she wanted to say but held her tongue. She sensed she could only push so far.

Callie was the one who spoke up. "You're using us to get to our mother," the girl said softly.

"That was never my intention either," Grant said. "But I had to find her. She needs to understand what's at stake."

"You hired the PI, didn't you?" Del narrowed her eyes at Grant.

"Natalie didn't make things easy for me."

Callie and Del glanced at each other.

Pulling a cell phone from his pocket, Grant punched a button and said, "What's your ETA?"

Pause.

Grant gave a nod then ended the call. "Looks like the elusive Natalie McGuire is about to make an appearance."

50

Hudson Chalet
Westcliffe, Colorado

Natalie managed to stay quiet through the long drive into the mountains. But when they pulled up to the Hudson chalet dread nearly paralyzed her. Everything she'd endured to protect her daughters—the years of loneliness, the constant shuttling from rental to rental to cover her tracks, obsessively following Grant's career and whereabouts—all of it had been for nothing. It was happening. Her worst fears were coming true.

The men practically dragged her through the cabin, and Natalie wondered if she'd ever come back out. They descended a flight of stairs and came to a door that looked like it belonged in a bunker.

The taller of the men punched in a combination and flung open the door. He stepped back and gestured for her to enter. Natalie took a deep breath. It didn't surprise her to see Grant Hudson waiting for her. He hadn't changed much since she'd run into him at the fundraiser eight years ago, but she hadn't noticed then how the crinkles fanned out from his eyes. Smile lines. What had he been smiling about while she'd been watching her back?

"Mom!"

Little Callie jumped up from one of the leather chairs. Everything in Natalie wanted to run to her daughter and hold her so tightly nothing could separate them again. But Grant hadn't brought her here for a reunion with her children. He stood erect, hands in his pockets, the ultimate personification of everything she'd feared for the past twenty years. She should hate him.

"Natalie," he whispered then cleared his throat. "I'm sorry for all this, but—"

She held up her hand. "Don't even."

Grant didn't seem bothered by her bluntness. "You're a difficult woman to find."

"That was the idea, Grant."

Natalie met Del's beautiful eyes. The nurses had called them green marbles when they'd placed her wriggling body in her arms for the first and last time. Natalie had given her up to give her a better life, but now that Del's adoptive parents were gone, who was going to look out for her as she grew into womanhood? She was just a kid, really, with the weight of the world on her shoulders.

Natalie tried to convey her sorrow for what was happening, but Del just stared at her. Natalie felt the knife slice her heart. She had dreamed this would be different, that somehow her children would forgive her and allow her back into their lives. But that was the pipe dream of a woman who'd run from her maternal responsibility, wasn't it? Were they going to die here together?

Natalie stepped in front of Del and Callie like a human shield, hoping they'd feel how much she wanted to protect them.

"You have me," Natalie said. "Let them go."

Grant closed the space between them. "What did you tell them?"

"How dare you bring them into this." She hoped her voice conveyed her disgust over Grant's misuse of power.

His lips tightened. The same way they had when she'd slapped him the day he dumped her.

Grant spun on his heels and walked over to the paintings she'd helped steal for him. How could he display them like this?

"Do you know how many reporters are salivating to ruin me?"

Natalie felt Del move nearer to her, and she took brief comfort in it.

"I am the man this country needs in the White House." Grant pointed at Del and Callie. "Their future is at stake."

Had he locked the door? What would he do if she gathered her kids together and just walked out of the room? The guards were probably waiting outside, but would they really harm them?

Natalie walked closer to Grant so she alone faced him. Eye to eye. It was as if all the years of running and wishing she could undo the past culminated in this very moment. She would stand up to the man who broke her heart and threatened her children. He was not the same boy who'd gently kissed her that night when they'd delivered the paintings.

"Do you regret it?" she asked him in a lowered tone.

"Yes."

"Then make it right."

"I'm trying to."

She stared deep into his eyes searching for genuine warmth. There was a flicker.

"I have to win that nomination," Grant said. "But I don't want you to get hurt. You have to believe that."

"My friends are *dead*, Grant. And you dare stand in front of me and pretend you didn't have anything to do with it."

"Nat, I—"

"And you kidnapped my *kids!*" She shook her finger in his

face. "I know what kind of man you think you are, but what you've done—"

"I know Javier and Adam are dead," Grant said. "And when I found out, I knew I had to find you. Warn you and protect you."

She wasn't buying it. "And save your own hide along the way."

Grant laughed. "You haven't changed, Nat."

He was wrong. Having children changed everything.

"My offer still stands. I will make sure you are comfortable, that your children are too, but I can't have my past exposed."

So it was all about him. Maybe it always had been.

"Despite what you might think," Grant took a step toward her, "I actually do still care about you."

She held up her hand. "Don't."

"I don't want you to get hurt."

She had a feeling she knew what he was implying. He might not order her dead himself, but his family might. Let someone else get blood on their hands. Grant Hudson would never get his dirty. And he was trying to bribe her again. Natalie placed her hands on her hips and faced Grant down, but the move felt as fake as it probably looked. She didn't have the strength anymore to say no. Especially not if her kids' lives were at stake.

"Tell me what I need to do to get out of here with my children, and I promise to keep your secret. They will too. Just let us go. You'll never hear from us again."

Grant started to respond, but then he crossed his arms, a cocky smirk pulling up his lips. He was in control, and he knew it. Natalie didn't care. She'd do what he wanted to get Del and Callie out of here.

"That's more like it," he said.

Goose bumps popped up on her neck.

Spinning on his heels, Grant faced the wall of paintings. They'd been arranged evenly on the wall, only a few inches apart.

"Why did you even do it?" she whispered. She hadn't asked him twenty years ago, but it was important now.

"Because I could," Grant responded back just as softly. "It was one thing my aunt couldn't control. But I also did it to take care of you. You would never have accepted my help voluntarily, but I knew you couldn't resist pulling off a heist like that. You'd been dreaming of it for years."

"Does anyone know the truth?"

"Only my aunt." Grant turned toward her, his face somber. "Everyone else thinks they're copies, but I can't keep them here anymore. Too much risk."

Out of the corner of her eye she saw Del pull Callie close, and she was glad they had each other. If she didn't make it out of here, she knew Del would do her best for Callie. West had been wise to put them together.

"Help me get rid of them," Grant said.

"What?"

"You're the perfect woman for the job."

She wasn't sure if her shock reached her face, but she hoped it did.

He pulled a piece of paper from his pocket. "Mexico. It's all arranged. The buyer's waiting, and they'll never connect it to me."

Natalie eyed the paintings, masterpieces that deserved to be appreciated. Perhaps there was a way to right the wrong of her past.

"Grant." She said his name as gently as she could, hoping he wouldn't lash out.

"You can have the money for them. You'll be able to start over."

"That's not what—"

"You asked me what you could do." He cocked his head. "This is it. I need you one more time, Nat."

"I could return them to the museum."

"Are you out of your mind?"

"Anonymously. They would just be happy to have them back."

"And the FBI wouldn't be able to figure that out?"

"This is our chance to make it right."

"Too late."

"It's not too late, Grant."

"No."

Natalie tried to gauge how far she could push, but his face was a political mask he'd perfected over the years. She could not find the Grant she used to know.

They were just paintings. Her kids mattered far more.

"Where in Mexico?" Natalie asked.

Near Westcliffe, Colorado

Abby had followed the beige four-door up to Walsenburg where she'd managed to catch sight of two men in the front, but the back windows were blacked out. Those girls had to be in there. Then she spent an hour straining to keep the vehicle in her sight without being obvious as it headed toward Westcliffe. The car just kept climbing up into the mountains. A few times she'd had to draw back and let them almost disappear for fear of discovery. But if they'd guessed she was tailing them, she couldn't tell.

Then the car seemed to disappear around a tight bend. Abby slowed to a crawl and scanned the evergreens for hidden driveways. She found three gravel turnoffs, but which one should she take? If she picked the wrong one she could spend a half hour twisting through the forest only to end up at a dead end. Natalie's kids would be gone.

Abby pulled onto the shoulder. Why hadn't she called the police on the freeway when she still had reception? If she'd told them she suspected a kidnapping they would've responded. But she hadn't been completely sure the girls were even in this car.

She rubbed her eyes. Once again, she'd taken matters into her own hands without thinking things through. Was it because she still had doubts about Natalie's story?

Abby let her car idle and stared out the windshield. *God, I know I haven't exactly been great about talking to You, but I could really use some help here.*

51

Hudson Chalet
Westcliffe, Colorado

Callie sniffled and buried her face in Del's chest. All Del could do was hold her and stroke her hair.

"I have a van ready," Grant Hudson said.

Del watched Natalie's face carefully, hoping to catch her eyes. But her mother was focused on Grant. If Natalie left for Mexico, what would happen to them?

Natalie went over to the paintings, her hands on her hips. "How long have you been planning this?"

He'd called in some of his hired thugs, the same men who'd brought Natalie, and they were already pulling the art down. Soon all of the paintings were leaning up against the wall in their frames.

Del and Callie remained huddled together.

It took an hour for the men to pack the art into the van, and only then did Grant allow Natalie to bring Del and Callie up the steps and out to a four-car garage where the black utility van was parked.

"Get in," Natalie finally said to Del and Callie

"What about you?"

"Just get in."

Del helped Callie up onto the front bench seat and climbed in behind her.

Grant hovered by the door, and Del turned for one last look at his face. Did he know she was his daughter? He'd shown no indication either way.

Natalie slammed the door behind them, and it echoed in the cavern of the garage. Blood pounding in her ears, Del tried to hear what Natalie and Grant were saying beside the van but could only catch their low tones.

"We have to find Utah." Callie's voice caught in her throat.

"He's fine," Del said.

"What if a wild animal—"

"Callie." She tried to sound firm. "We have to get out of here ourselves first."

Callie's hair was a frizzy mess, and the tip of her nose was red. "Is he letting us go? Why are we taking the paintings?"

She wasn't sure how much to tell her. "I think these are the ones Mom stole from the museum."

"And she's returning them?"

"I'm not sure."

Callie leaned forward, trying to watch Natalie and Grant out the window. "She'll do the right thing."

If only Del believed that.

Finally Natalie climbed into the driver's seat, and the garage bay door opened for them. She started the engine and slowly backed the van out.

"He's really letting us go?" Del asked.

"Apparently."

"And the paintings?"

"Let's get out of here first," Natalie said.

"Does he know who I am?"

298

Natalie turned the van onto the narrow dirt lane that only hours before Del had thought would be the last road she ever saw.

"I never told him," Natalie said.

Callie wiped her face with her fingers. "Told him what?"

It might be better to keep Callie in the dark on that one.

"Just something Del and I were talking about last night," Natalie said, giving Callie's leg a pat. "Grown-up stuff."

The van dipped into a rut, throwing Del against the door. She thought about the paintings stowed in the back, covered with blankets protecting each corner and frame.

"I don't get it." Del held onto the door handle. "He kidnaps Callie and me, uses us as bait to bring you here, and then just lets you go with million-dollar paintings on the promise you'll take them to Mexico?"

"I gave him my word."

"No offense, but how much is that worth?"

Natalie hesitated. "It got us out of there alive, Del."

"For now."

"That's all I care about."

The van rocked again as the cabin dropped farther and farther behind them, and they finally reached the iron gate. This time it was open, and Del held her breath as they drove through it, one step closer to freedom. When they'd arrived at the compound, the lane had felt like it was ten miles long. It seemed even longer now. Del half expected men with machine guns to burst from the trees and pelt them with bullets.

"When I woke up this morning, I thought I'd lost you." Natalie's voice was low and throaty. "I vowed that if I got to see you again I would tell you both what I've longed to say for twenty years."

Del thought she heard the deep thumps of a helicopter's blades churning the air. Was Grant leaving, or was someone else arriving?

"I love you, Del. I gave you up because I knew I couldn't be what you needed, but I never stopped loving you."

It seemed surreal to hear this as they traveled inside a van loaded with the evidence of her crimes. But she was trying to make amends, and Del had to admit that took guts. She had endured a pregnancy knowing she would never see her child grow up, never hear her laugh, never watch her take her first wobbly step.

Could she ever love this woman? Del's mother would always be Kelly Mangini, but that didn't mean Natalie McGuire couldn't have a place too, and for the first time Del realized that not having Natalie in her life would hurt.

Natalie let go of the wheel with one hand to tenderly touch Callie's tear-blotched cheek. "And I'm so sorry I left you, sweetheart. I was afraid you would get hurt again because of me. I knew your daddy would take care of you, but that's no excuse. I love you more than you can possibly know. Can you ever forgive me?"

"Stop!"

The little girl's scream made Del jump, and Natalie jerked her hand away. Callie's eyes were focused out the windshield. She pointed, and Del saw the dog bolt across the road at the same time Callie lunged for the door.

Del's reflexes were too slow to grab the girl before she flung the van's door open and leapt over Del and off the running board. Natalie slammed on the brakes.

Callie fell to the ground with a thud. She caught herself with her hands and was on her feet tearing into the woods before Del could stop her. "Utah! Utah!" she called.

"Callie, no!"

Del shot out the door herself, flinging a quick "I'll get her" over her shoulder at Natalie. They couldn't lose their chance at freedom over a lost dog.

Already a stone's throw away, Callie's legs pumped

through the pine needles, and Del tore after her as fast as she could, pulses of agony zapping through her body.

"We'll come back to get him," she called as loud as she dared.

"I'm not leaving him behind!"

Utah had stopped when she called, and Callie fell to her knees, sobbing into his neck.

Del was gasping for breath when she reached the pair, but she quickly grabbed the leash Callie had pulled from her pocket and reattached to his collar, her other hand clutching the back of Callie's shirt. She guided them both toward the van. "Come on. We have to go!"

They zig-zagged around the trees while Del scanned the forest. Almost there. She could see the van shining through the trees like a beacon of safety. Natalie stood outside the driver's door, waving them in.

That's when the van exploded.

52

Hudson Chalet

Grant poured himself a brandy and sunk with relief into his recliner by the fire. Step one finished. Now he had to trust Natalie would keep her end of the bargain.

He took a sip of the liquor. She would. That part of the woman hadn't changed. He could tell simply by looking into her eyes. But even though he'd long ago reconciled himself to a life without her, he couldn't watch her leave.

Holding the tumbler upward in a mock toast, Grant smiled. "To Natalie."

Then he heard the boom outside his window.

Del yanked Callie to the ground and threw herself on top of her.

"Mom!" Callie screamed.

Inwardly, Del screamed too. She'd clearly seen Natalie's body thrown into the air like a rag doll, and the heat of the flames shooting from the van's blown-out windows hit them seconds later.

Del thrust Utah's leash into Callie's hand and propelled herself toward the mass of writhing fire, scrambling for her footing on the forest floor.

They'd been set up.

Someone really wanted them dead.

Flames engulfed the vehicle and clawed dangerously close to the overhanging tree limbs along the narrow drive. Natalie lay in a crumpled heap, face down. One pant leg of her jeans was on fire, and Del heard herself yelling as she frantically patted it out with handfuls of dirt and her bare hands. The back of Natalie's head glistened with dark blood.

She wasn't moving.

"Stay where you are, Callie!"

Heat roared at her back, and Del grabbed Natalie's shoulders and dragged her away from the burning wreckage.

Another explosion blew the van apart, sending sparks stinging across Del's face and arms.

No longer thinking about her side or her burned hands or even escaping, Del pulled Natalie to safety beside the tree where Callie sat hugging her knees and rocking herself back and forth, clinging to her dog.

"Is she alive?"

Del turned Natalie onto her back and felt her neck for a pulse. It was so faint she could barely detect it, but it was there.

"I think so," Del said, huffing in breaths. Had Grant planted explosives in the van himself, or had someone else? Had everything he said been a lie?

The flames blazed behind them. She had to get her sister and Natalie away from this place! Did she have the strength to carry her mother? She wasn't a large woman, but Del wasn't even sure if she could carry Callie much less an adult in her weakened condition.

She had to try. She knelt down and pushed her arms under Natalie's torso and legs, then tried to stand up. But she couldn't get her legs underneath herself. Natalie was limp and slipping out of her arms.

A quick glance down the driveway, and she saw movement. A car? If someone had planned this, they wouldn't be coming to offer assistance. They'd come to finish the job.

Callie clutched her small hands together. "Please, God, please help us!"

Pushing as hard as she could with her legs, Del felt like her muscles would rip. Could she somehow get Natalie onto her own back and carry her that way? Should they just drag her, or would that worsen her injuries?

Blood dripped from a gash on Natalie's pale forehead. Part of her sleeve was shredded and revealed charred skin. Suddenly Natalie's eyes fluttered open. For a moment she didn't seem to realize where she was, but then her eyes rested first on Callie, then on Del.

Del set her back down and twined her bloody fingers with Natalie's. "Stay with us, please. We need you." She'd only just met this woman and hadn't treated her with anything close to kindness.

"Thank you," Del managed. "For what you did for me, for having me. I'll never forget you."

Natalie's eyes closed as her features went slack.

"No." Del frantically felt for Natalie's pulse. It was like a tremor under her fingertips, not a steady beat, and she knew they were losing her.

Just then a vehicle came bumping and jerking down the driveway from the direction of the main road. Self-preservation told her to take Callie and run—what Natalie would no doubt want her to do—but Del couldn't leave her. She wouldn't abandon her now.

The vehicle stopped in a flurry of dust and spraying gravel, and a dark-haired woman in a leather jacket jumped out.

"Callie!" She ran over to the wreckage. "Del!"

How did she know their names?

Shielding her eyes, the woman tried to get close to the van. Then she caught sight of them before Del could pull Callie out of view.

"Over here!" Callie called.

The woman ran over. She took one look and dropped to the ground beside Natalie, checking her injuries like she knew what she was doing.

"Natalie, can you hear me?"

"Please help her." Tears streamed down Callie's cheeks. Natalie didn't respond.

Grant jumped to his feet, sloshing brandy onto his trousers. What was that sound?

He rushed over to the window and could barely see smoke rising through the evergreens. A fire of any kind was a danger up here, but especially at this time of year when the forest was a tinderbox. Grant ran out into the hallway, cell phone in hand, a nagging fear nipping at him like a wolf.

He almost ran into Aunt April.

"What are you doing here?" She wasn't supposed to arrive until tomorrow.

"I'm early," she said.

Grant started to push past her down the hallway, but she stepped into his path.

"Wait," she said.

"I heard an explosion, saw smoke."

"It's being taken care of." April's spindly fingers squeezed his arm. Age hadn't stolen her strength.

There was something about her tone. Grant pulled away.

"Remember, Grant. She wasn't good for you."

"What are you talking about?"

"Nothing will stop you now."

Grant clenched his jaw. "What have you done?"

"What you couldn't."

53

Mercy Hospital
Cañon City, Colorado

Callie lay asleep beside Del on a hospital waiting room chair. Del yearned for rest too, but there was no way she was lying down. Not until she knew Natalie's condition.

Pacing across the room with a cell phone to her ear, their rescuer Abby Dawson was gesticulating with her free hand. When she ended her call, Abby came over to Del and sat down with a sigh. "No news?"

She shook her head. They'd taken Natalie into surgery, but that was all she knew. On the frantic drive here, Del had cradled her in the back seat desperate to see sparks of life, but Natalie barely breathed. Then the ER team took her away and descended on her gurney like vultures. She knew they were there to help, that they'd try to save her at all cost, but it still felt wrong to watch Natalie's body probed and prodded and to hear the nurses and doctors stating her vitals and barking out orders like they were ordering a latte.

It was Abby who'd pulled Del and Callie away from the scene and sat them down here in the waiting room.

"Does she even have a chance?" Del asked softly. Abby

had told them she used to work in law enforcement. Surely she'd seen accidents like this before and would know Natalie's odds.

Her elbows resting on her knees, Abby kept her eyes on the nurse's station. "I knew a guy who got shot four times in the chest and somehow survived. Doctors can do amazing things these days."

But a head injury alone could kill someone. Del slumped in her chair, replaying every second before and after the explosion. Why had Natalie stayed with the van instead of running after Callie too?

"I didn't know your mother long or very well," Abby said. "But she's a fighter. If anyone can make it, she can."

Tears pooled in Del's eyes. She gently touched Callie's arm, wanting to hug her but not wanting to pry her from much-needed sleep. The police would be here soon, and she'd have to decide how much to tell them. If she accused Grant Hudson of a crime, she knew the media maelstrom would probably ruin their lives. And that was before they found out she was his daughter.

Del stared down at Callie's face, so peaceful in sleep, and she caught a glimpse of why Natalie had spent twenty years in silence. Some things were more important than justice.

She rearranged her aching arms and tried to pull her thoughts together. Grant had to know by now they'd escaped the explosion, but it was possible he didn't know where they'd gone. Abby had been careful to make sure they weren't followed. Was there a chance Grant hadn't planted the explosives and someone else was to blame? Yet how convenient it would have been to destroy the paintings and the only people left who could testify against him all in the same awful moment.

"I don't want the police to take my sister away."

Abby nodded and pulled out her phone again. "Just talk to them. I'll stay with you."

C. J. DARLINGTON

A few minutes later a gray-haired doctor approached. Del jumped to her feet. There was blood spatter on his green scrubs, and a mask hung loosely from his neck.

"Are you Natalie's family?"

"I'm her daughter," Del said.

He cleared his throat.

One look into his eyes, and she knew.

"We did everything we could," he said.

With Abby standing beside her and Callie still dozing in the hospital chair, Del listened to the doctor explain in a monotone voice that her biological mother was gone. She understood perfectly what he was saying, but the part of her that had quietly begun to hope for a relationship with Natalie McGuire hovered above it all, unable to process the news.

It wasn't like when her adoptive parents died. Del didn't burst into tears or pepper the doctor with questions in disbelief like she had then. She just asked Abby to watch Callie and then walked out of the hospital.

Sitting on a cement bench outside, she rested her elbows on her knees and closed her eyes. For the past six days Del had been so absorbed with the news that she was adopted and had a sister, there'd been little time to imagine a future with Natalie McGuire. Now that she didn't have the chance for one, she yearned for it.

How was she going to tell Callie? The kid had just lost her father and had seen things a child should never have to see. She might be scarred for a long time. The image of Natalie being thrown through the air was something she herself would never forget.

Del wasn't sure how much time passed before someone sat down beside her. She looked up, surprised to see the bookstore owner, Christy Williams.

"Abby told me," Christy said. "I'm so sorry."

"I didn't realize you knew each other."

311

"Friends for a long time. I came as soon as I could."

They sat for a moment in silence. As the sun slowly sunk below the horizon, Del couldn't hold her grief in any longer. She buried her face in her hands and sobbed.

Christy quickly pulled her into a hug and held her like a mother would if Del still had a mother. But she'd never have one again. Mom and Dad were gone. Natalie was gone, and Del's hope with her. Why had she left Natalie in that hotel room? If she'd stayed, this might never have happened. How could she be dead?

"I never told her I loved her," Del sobbed into Christy's shoulder.

Christy just patted her back and let her cry.

Soon numbness replaced her tears, and Del pulled away. She'd been too busy being angry with Natalie to realize she'd begun to long for a mother's love again. What would it feel like for Callie?

Del swallowed back the clamp around her throat, not wanting to lose it in front of Christy a second time. "She was bleeding internally. They tried to save her, but she didn't wake up."

Christy wiped at her own eyes with the tips of her fingers then looked away as if she didn't want Del to see. That almost made Del cry again. She didn't know why Christy cared since she knew so little about Del, but it touched her that she did.

"Callie looks up to me," Del said. "And she'll ask a million questions I don't know how to answer."

Christy gave her a gentle smile. "Maybe she just needs you."

"But what if the police take her away?"

"Why would they? You're her sister."

"Because I haven't exactly taken good care of her."

"Anyone can see you need each other right now."

"I don't even have a place to live. How can I possibly give her a decent life?"

She pictured Callie's emerald eyes and quirky smile. The way she giggled when Utah licked her face and how she thought everything was an adventure. Callie needed to have a real childhood with a real family. Not the fragmented, hand-to-mouth existence Del had given her. But thinking about living her life alone again was more than Del could bear. She stood up, needing to move or run or do something to keep herself from crying again.

"Del, it's going to be okay."

She shook her head. "No it isn't."

Rising from the bench, Christy got right in front of her and rested her hands on Del's shoulders. "I know it's hard for you to see right now, but it will get easier. Trust me. I know what it's like to lose someone you care about. It hurts like you-know-what, and you can't see the light at end of the tunnel. But it's there." Christy's eyes met hers. "And it's okay to ask for help. You don't have to do everything by yourself."

Del sniffed and wiped her face with the sleeve of her sweatshirt. "I'm sorry I didn't tell you the truth."

"Would you like to now?"

She nodded and told Christy about her parents, being adopted, Callie showing up on her doorstep, and even how she'd broken into the house. She expected some sort of disapproval when she mentioned that, but Christy only hugged her again, and Del didn't mind.

"I just don't know what to do," she said.

Christy let her go and crossed her arms. She gazed out at the parking lot for a moment, and Del remembered she'd need to check on Utah. He was safe in Abby's car but probably had to be walked.

"Tonight you're staying with me," Christy said. "And sleeping in a real bed."

She tried to smile. "That sounds nice."

"After that we'll take it a day at a time, okay?"

"But why would you help us like that?"

"Let's just say I know what it's like to be desperate." Christy nodded toward the glass hospital doors. "I'll tell you about it sometime, but right now you have a little sister who's probably wondering where you are."

Del straightened her shoulders and wiped her eyes again. With Christy beside her, she walked back into the hospital.

"What do I tell her?"

"Kids need the truth just as much as we do."

She found Callie still in the waiting room chair. Abby sat beside her, gesturing in the air like she was telling a story. But the second Callie saw Del she leapt to her feet.

"What's going on?"

Del knelt down in front of her and opened her arms. Callie fell into them.

"She didn't make it," Del whispered into her hair.

She wasn't sure if Callie heard at first, but then she felt the girl's body shaking. Del held her until Callie let go and stood sniffling and trying so hard to be strong and brave.

"She's in Heaven with Daddy, right?"

Del glanced at Christy who gave her an encouraging nod and handed Callie a tissue.

"Of course she is," Del said.

"How do you know?"

"Because I just—"

"Did she know Jesus?"

Del sighed and sat down in one of the chairs, patting her lap. Callie climbed up without hesitation. "Here's what I do know," Del said. "Our mother loved us very much, and she tried to do the right thing, even when it was hard."

Callie blew her nose.

"And she wouldn't want you to be sad."

"But I am."

Del stared at the floor and pulled Callie into another hug. "Me too, kid."

It was dark by the time they left the hospital emotionally broken and battered. Callie stayed glued to Del's side, and she kept a protective arm wrapped around her as they walked across the parking lot to Christy's car.

Callie started crying again when Utah eagerly greeted them, but she couldn't resist his frantic licks to her tear stained cheeks.

"Someone missed you," Del said, trying to lighten the moment.

Callie looked up at her. "He saved our lives."

"I guess he did."

"Thank you, boy," Callie whispered.

On the ride back to Elk Valley Del and Callie sat together in the back seat with Utah curled up beside them. Callie rested her head on Del's shoulder, and she felt the girl get heavier.

"Do your hands hurt?" Callie mumbled in the darkness.

Half her right palm and several fingers of her left had suffered second-degree burns. They'd sent her home with a bag full of antibiotics, medicated cream, and gauze. Christy had the doctor check her side too, and a nurse properly washed the wound and re-bandaged it with clean dressing.

"A little," Del said, closing her eyes.

"Will they take me away from you?"

So far the police hadn't questioned her custody. She'd told them about the explosion but left out any information about the paintings and her relationship to Grant Hudson. She also begged them to keep their names out of the press.

"Not if I can help it," Del said.

"But they could?"

Del squeezed Callie tight and glanced at Christy in the

rearview mirror. Even with her and Abby's promised help, she knew what her case would look like to a judge if it came to that.

"I won't let them," Del said.

54

Christy's Apartment
Elk Valley, Colorado

A small hand shook Del from a dreamless sleep.
"Del, wake up."

She opened her eyes. Callie's face was inches from hers.
Del jumped. "Kid, why do you do that? Go back to sleep."

"I'm hungry."

"For crying out loud. You ate before bed."

"It's almost noon."

"What?" Del slowly sat up. Daylight glowed yellow around
the curtains in Christy's bedroom above The Book Corral. Last
night she had insisted she was happy to take the sofa so they
could get some real sleep.

Tossing off her blankets, Del saw Callie was already fully
dressed in her wrinkled jeans and pony t-shirt. "How long have
you been awake?"

The girl shrugged. "Can we have peanut butter sandwiches?"

Del pulled on her own clothes with a tired laugh. She
never wanted to see a peanut butter sandwich again.

In Christy's kitchen, Del read a short note from their host
telling them to eat whatever they wanted and come down into

the bookstore when they were done. They were just sitting down to bowls of cereal when they heard footsteps coming up the stairs. Abby walked into the apartment without knocking.

"How'd you guys sleep?" she asked, pushing her sunglasses to the top of her head.

"Fine," Callie said through a mouthful of Cheerios.

Abby came over and placed a ring of keys on the table. "I think these are yours now."

Del set down her spoon, instantly recognizing them as Natalie's. She'd left them in the ignition switch of the SUV when those men kidnapped her and Callie. "How did you—"

"Christy and I drove up early this morning. The car was still there."

"Our stuff?"

"Untouched." Abby glanced at Callie then focused again on Del.

She recognized the subtle reminder that Callie's young ears didn't need to hear whatever Abby wanted to say. Del pushed away her bowl and scooped up the keys. "I'll be right back," she told Callie and followed Abby downstairs and outside.

Natalie's SUV was parked next to Christy's Honda.

"Won't the police want to confiscate it?" Del asked.

"If they knew about it I'm sure they would."

She punched the unlock button, and the SUV chirped its response.

"I checked it for any tracking devices," Abby said. "It's clean."

"Then how did they find us?"

"I've been thinking about that." Abby leaned up against the SUV, looking as stern as any of the cops Del had met last night. If she hadn't seen her softer side she might've been intimidated. But even though Abby didn't know her any better than Christy did, last night she'd offered to pay for Natalie's funeral and help get Callie enrolled in school again. Del didn't know how she'd ever make it up to her or Christy. They'd been a lifeline when Del felt like she was drowning.

Abby reached into her pocket and pulled out a smartphone. She handed it to Del. "If they had her number, an experienced hacker could find her through her phone's GPS."

Del eyed the device as if it was a ticking bomb. "What do I do with it?"

"Copy the contacts and anything else you want, and then give it to me. I'll make sure it's destroyed just in case."

She almost handed it off to Abby right then, but what if there was information about her mother on here she needed to see?

"Do you know where she lived?" Abby asked.

"Alamosa, I think."

"We'll have to figure out if she had a will or any other assets, but I don't see why you shouldn't have her car for now."

It made her uncomfortable to take anything of her biological mother's so soon after her death. Daughter or not, Del had known her for such a short time.

"Do you think she'd mind?"

"She'd want you to have it."

Then Del remembered something she knew Abby needed to hear. "She had a gun."

Abby straightened. "Where?"

"I don't know. She had me hold it at my apartment, but I gave it back to her. Maybe the glove compartment?"

"Nothing there but maps and the car manual."

So Abby had already searched the vehicle. Somehow that didn't surprise Del. "Maybe she had it in her suitcase. But that's probably still back at the hotel."

"And we better leave it there."

"But what if—"

"When they realize you and Callie made it out alive—and they no doubt have by now—the first place they'll go is the last place she was." Abby waved toward the mountains. "You need to stay as far away from anything to do with Grant Hudson as you can."

"Tell me something I don't know."

"He held a press conference this morning," Abby pulled out her cell phone and swiped her finger across the screen.

A cloud of dread hit Del. "What did he say?"

"You need to see it."

Abby turned the phone toward her and clicked Play on a YouTube video. The camera zoomed in on a solemn Grant Hudson standing in front of an American flag.

"As many of you are already aware," Grant began, "yesterday my vacation home in Colorado was the site of a terrorist attack."

"What?" Del glared at the screen. "How can he—"

"Just listen," Abby said.

"I was not present at the time of the attack, so I have very few details at this time, but I am deeply saddened to hear a life was lost in the explosion." Grant paused, seemingly searching the crowd of reporters. "The cowards who orchestrated this act of terror will not go unpunished. We are working closely with the Department of Homeland Security and will leave no stone unturned in our search for them."

Reporters immediately began firing off questions, but Grant raised his hand. The din of voices stilled, and he glared directly into the camera. It felt like he was staring at Del.

"Whoever you are, wherever you are, we will find you," he said. "You may think you scared us, but the American people are stronger and braver than you can imagine." He turned and faced the reporters again. "We will not cower in fear. This will not break us. The enemy may have thought bringing terror to my back door would deter me, but he or she made a big mistake. I am more determined than ever to run for president of the United States.

"This very act only reinforces why we *must* have change in our country," Grant continued. "The terrorists who would steal our freedom, our very God-given liberty, are now among us. We must stand strong and fight against this evil. I will continue my campaign so an attack like this will never darken *your* door. As president, I will make our country safe, but I need your help to do it. Thank you."

Questions flew through the air, but Grant strode away from the podium leaving them unanswered.

The video cut out. Abby clicked out of the screen and pocketed her phone.

"But we told the police what happened," Del said. "This is all a lie."

"And he's a smart politician," Abby responded. "He has to spin this in his favor. He probably knows you won't want to come forward either."

"Should I?"

Abby crossed her arms again. "Only you can decide, Del. But I'd think long and hard before you do anything."

Del felt shell-shocked as she opened the SUV's hatchback and found her suitcase exactly where she'd thrown it in her mad dash. Unzipping it, Del pushed her hand inside until she touched plastic and pulled out the bag she'd stowed under her clothes. Just seeing Mom and Dad's memorial flags brought her grief to the surface.

"My parents died fighting a fire," she said. "They were heroes. But for a long time I was angry they left me. They chose to risk their lives for a stranger rather than make sure I'd have a mom and dad." Del slowly tore a hole in the corner of the plastic bag she'd kept wrapped around the flags. Blue fabric stared back. "Does that sound selfish?"

Abby gave her a sympathetic smile. "It sounds like you loved them very much."

She opened the hole wider and showed Abby. "Their

casket flags. I never wanted to see these things again, but I couldn't bring myself to get rid of them either."

"They'd be proud of you, Del."

"Would they?" She stared down at the flags. Then she buried the bag back under the clothes and shut the hatchback. She turned around to face Abby. "Would you help me with one more thing? There's something I need to do."

55

Neighborhood Outside Elk Valley

Abby pulled up to the small, adobe-themed house. "Sure you don't want me to come with you?"

Del nodded. She'd set the worst example possible for Callie, and she had to make this right. It's what her parents would've wanted her to do.

Stepping from the car, she stared at the simple home which looked so different in the light of day. The well-kept flower beds full of cactus and lava mulch showed care and attention. Planters hung from the gutter, and colorful blooms contrasted with the adobe and Spanish tile roof. She hadn't seen any of this in the darkness. Desperation had won only a few nights ago, but today her conscience would be the victor. She could only hope the consequences of her stupidity wouldn't defeat her.

Del walked up to the front door and lifted the brass knocker before she could second-guess herself. She tapped it three times, then stepped back to wait. Maybe no one would answer.

The door opened, and a gray-haired woman wearing pressed khakis and a white cardigan greeted her like she was a kid selling candles. "Can I help you?"

Her mouth was suddenly unable to form words. Did she really need to do this? Couldn't she just live a good life and never do something like this again? Getting arrested surely wouldn't help Callie. The little girl needed her to be there for her, not locked up awaiting arraignment.

"I . . . I heard you had a break-in the other night," Del finally said. Perfect. That sounded intelligent.

The old woman's eyes widened. Her smile vanished.

"I'm glad you're okay," Del added.

"Who told you we had a break-in?"

Okay, this was a really, really bad idea. She'd promised Callie they'd stay together, and now she was opening the door for them to be ripped apart. She wanted to run and let the old woman think she was just some nosy neighbor. But Del knew she could never look Callie in the eye again if she didn't tell the truth. Natalie had regretted not doing the right thing when it mattered, and Del didn't want to make the same mistake.

The woman started to close the door.

"Please wait. There's something important I need to tell you."

"Thomas!" the woman called over her shoulder.

Del glanced back at Abby waiting in the driveway. The ex-cop was watching her every move, but it didn't make this any easier.

"I know who broke into your house," Del said.

The woman yelled for Thomas again, and Del's pulse spiked when she saw the man who'd confronted her come to the older woman's side. She guessed they were husband and wife.

"What's the matter?" He was wiping his hands in a dish towel but froze when he saw Del. By the way he stared she knew he recognized her, and for a second she thought she saw fear spark in his eyes. He looked older than she remembered. "You better come inside," he said to Del, gently guiding his wife away from the door.

"But Thomas—"

"It's okay." He gently touched his wife's arm.

Del reluctantly followed the couple into the living room where a crucifix hung on the mantel and a TV played a muted news broadcast. She couldn't see the back door from here but wondered if they'd had the shattered glass repaired.

"My name's Thomas," the man said. "This is my wife Helen." He eyed her for a moment then gestured toward an upholstered sofa near the television. "Why don't we sit down?"

Helen pursed her lips, clearly unhappy with her husband's decision, but she sat down beside him on the sofa facing Del who took the wooden chair by the bay window. If he knew who she was, why was he being so hospitable?

"It was me," Del said, her voice cracking.

Neither Thomas nor Helen responded. Del could hear the clock on the end table ticking away the seconds. Maybe they didn't understand.

"I broke into your house."

Helen and Thomas exchanged glances.

"I know," Thomas said softly. "I remember your face."

"I came to make things right. If I can."

Thomas twisted the dishrag he still held in his hands. His Adam's apple dipped. "I fired two shots."

She lifted the edge of her T-shirt to reveal the bottom of her bandage. "You didn't miss."

He scooted to the edge of the sofa. "Are you okay?"

"It just grazed me," she said. "I—"

"We didn't report what happened," Helen said.

"What?"

Thomas draped the rag onto the arm of the sofa, then

took off his glasses and rubbed his eyes. "I was so worried the neighbors heard."

"I don't understand," Del said.

"You were running away, but I still shot at you."

"I deserved it."

"But you were no longer a threat." He set his glasses on the table with the clock. "I was scared, but I shouldn't have shot at you. I'm sorry. I didn't tell the police because I thought they'd arrest me."

"Arrest *you*?" If that had happened she would never have forgiven herself. "I'm the one who should get in trouble. Not you."

Helen threaded her fingers through her husband's. "What's your name, dear?"

She told them and explained a little of her story. "But I'm not trying to get out of anything. I was wrong, and if you want to call the police I'll tell them I did it and that you didn't do anything wrong."

The couple conferred with their eyes again, and Helen patted Thomas's hand. "I don't think that will be necessary."

She sunk into the chair.

"It was brave of you to come back," Thomas said, reaching for his glasses again. "Most kids these days wouldn't have."

"I'll pay you back somehow." She had no idea where that money would come from, but it was a debt she needed to erase.

Thomas climbed to his feet. "You know, I'd been meaning to replace that back door. The lock isn't what it used to be."

"That's a good idea," his wife agreed.

Were they being serious?

"I think we all learned a lesson, don't you?" Thomas said.

Del let out the breath she felt like she'd been holding.

You have no idea.

56

Christy's Apartment
Elk Valley, Colorado

Christy made spaghetti and meatballs for dinner that night, and Del couldn't remember the last time she'd tasted something so good. She reached for her fourth piece of garlic bread. The butter dripped from the soft slice, and she stuffed a generous chunk in her mouth.

"This is delicious," Del said.

The pain of losing Natalie was still raw, but it made all the difference in the world to know she had people like Christy and Abby on her side. After visiting Thomas and Helen, a huge weight had lifted from her shoulders. She was starting to believe she wasn't going to end up in jail after all.

"Want some more?" Christy held up the pasta fork.

"Yes, please," Callie said.

Del elbowed her. "Don't overdo it."

"I'm still hungry."

"Right, I forgot. You've got a bottomless pit for a stomach."

Callie didn't respond to the joke. She'd been quiet through the whole meal, and even when Christy asked her questions about Utah she answered with monosyllables.

After dinner Del offered to help Christy clean up while Callie watched TV in the living room.

"I don't know how to thank you," Del said quietly while wrapping the remaining pieces of bread in tin foil.

"I'm just glad I can help," Christy said.

"I promise we won't overstay. I'll work hard and earn my keep."

Christy handed her a Pyrex bowl for the leftovers. "Speaking of jobs, Callie mentioned you've worked around horses and that got me thinking. My younger sister owns a cattle ranch outside of town and trains horses on the side. I talked to her this afternoon, and she's actually looking for some part-time help. It would probably only be a couple hundred a month plus room and board, but if you're interested, you could start any time."

Del dumped the leftover pasta into the dish. She didn't deserve help like this.

"That would be really great," she finally said.

When the kitchen was clean Del suggested she and Callie take Utah on a walk through the streets of Elk Valley, and Callie reluctantly agreed. In the quiet stillness of the evening, the greyhound padded silently beside them, sniffing the air and only pulling on his leash when an errant candy wrapper blew across the sidewalk.

Normally Callie would've giggled at the big dog, but tonight she was quiet.

Del wrapped her arm around the girl. "How you doing?"

"Okay."

"Talk to me, kid."

Callie shrugged.

A few businesses were still open, and their shop windows glowed invitingly as they passed. Del caught a whiff of cocoa as they approached the Perfect Blend coffee shop where people crowded around the outdoor tables laughing and sipping warm drinks. As if life was good, and a brave woman named Natalie hadn't just died.

"You were right, you know. I should've trusted Christy sooner."

Callie pulled away and kicked at a tree root that disfigured a section of sidewalk.

Maybe the girl just needed time. Del understood that. After Mom and Dad died it hadn't really sunk in until days later.

"I might get a job on a ranch," Del said. "Wouldn't that be neat?"

"I guess."

"We could live there for awhile. You'd be around cows and horses, and maybe even more dogs. Utah would make a lot of friends."

"He doesn't like cats."

"A lot of dogs don't," Del said holding back a chuckle. "And once you get back in school you'll make lots of friends too."

"Kids don't like me."

"The ones who count will like you." Del blew out a breath and tried not to think about how much she had to learn about raising a little girl, especially one as precocious as Callie.

"They think I'm weird." Callie suddenly stopped in the middle of the sidewalk. A café sign blinked above the next storefront, bathing the little girl's face in a light blue. Her lower lip trembled.

"Hey." Del crouched so they could see eye-to-eye. "It's gonna be okay."

"That's what you said before." Callie's voice cracked. "But Mom died."

"I know, but you and I are still here, and we're okay."

"Everyone always leaves me."

A deep pang hit Del at the girl's words. She reached for

Callie's hand, which was still sticky from the brownies they'd had for dessert. "I will not leave you, kid."

"But I always end up alone," Callie said.

Del knelt on the hard cement. How could she make this little girl understand she wasn't like her dad's girlfriend or even Natalie? Gently Del pulled the greyhound closer and rubbed his ears. He sat down and gave her hand a single lick.

"Remember when we let Utah chase that squirrel at the cabin?"

Callie's lip still puckered, but she nodded. "I was so scared I'd never see him again."

"But you didn't abandon him. You didn't leave without him."

"I couldn't."

"Why is that?"

Callie eyed the dog, then without hesitation said, "Because I love him."

"And that's why I'm never leaving you." Del reached up and cupped Callie's cheek, stroking it with her thumb. "Kid, I was missing so much in my life, and I didn't realize it until you came knocking on my door. The same way Utah needs you in his life, I need a little girl named Callie."

Without warning Callie threw her arms around Del and squeezed her so hard she could barely breathe. When she finally let go, they looked at each other for the longest time, tears streaming down both their faces. Del wasn't sure if she'd gotten through, but then that beautiful, goofy smile appeared on Callie's face.

"And I need a big sister named Delaware."

57

One week later

Triple Cross Ranch
Elk Valley, Colorado

Y ou look nervous."

Del glanced over at Callie, surprised she was picking it up. They were almost at the Triple Cross, the ranch Christy's sister May Williams owned.

"I'm sure it'll be great," Del said for Callie's benefit.

They drove under the ranch sign and followed Christy's car down the long driveway. Callie took off her seat belt and hung out the window.

"I see horses!" Callie pointed to a pasture.

"Get back in the car, kid."

Soon the ranch house came into view, and Del pulled Natalie's SUV beside a pickup that looked like it had seen better days.

"Well, here we go." Del gave Callie a high-five. With Utah in tow Callie skipped over to Christy who waved them to the back door of the house.

"I'll get our stuff and meet you inside," Del said.

She really shouldn't be nervous. Christy had been nothing but kind, and Del was sure her sister May would be the same.

Del walked around the car and leaned against it for a

minute, out of view from the house. She could hear Callie chattering to Christy about keeping Utah on a leash, and it made her smile. She couldn't imagine life without the kid anymore, who was back to thinking every new experience was an adventure.

Staring up at the Spanish Peaks, Del wondered what the future held. Despite the help of their new friends, their problems hadn't disappeared. She'd need to have more money than this part time job would provide if she was going to buy Callie new clothes and school supplies, not to mention pay back her debt to the Lopezes, something she was determined to do. And what would happen when the police interviewed her again about the explosion?

"Beautiful, isn't it?"

Del startled at the man's voice. A familiar cowboy walked toward her from around the car, and she did a double take. The handlebar moustache, felt hat. It was him, the guy who'd caught her trespassing near the horses, the man she'd run from in the coffee shop.

He took off his hat and wiped his brow with the back of his arm. "I wondered if it was you kids coming."

Del found herself squirming for words. "I don't understand. How did you . . ."

The cowboy chuckled. "This is where I work."

"But those horses were miles from here."

"It's a big ranch. And we lease some of the BLM land."

Del glanced out at the pastures. *Her* horses. Could they really be part of this ranch?

"That herd is mostly retired and living the good life," the cowboy said as if reading her thoughts. "We just moved 'em back here from the summer pasture where you saw them."

"So May Williams is your—"

"Boss." Reaching out his hand, the cowboy shook hers, and this time she returned it.

"Del," she said.

"And I'm Jim, in case you forgot."

Jim didn't seem nearly as intimidating now. But she still needed to explain herself.

"I'm sorry for trespassing. I just loved visiting them."

Jim replaced his hat. "We've had some kids messing around on the property, and I jumped to conclusions. Anyone with eyes could see you weren't doing anything but lovin' on those horses."

Turning to the car, Del reached for her suitcase and Callie's duffel bag, but Jim quickly shooed her away and took the luggage himself. "It'll be good to have you two around. We've got plenty of work this time of year. Haying, chopping wood, fixing fences, you name it. "

Del laughed. "I'm tired already."

"May's got lunch almost ready, but I think maybe you've got somewhere to go first."

She studied him for a second, trying to figure out what he meant. Jim tilted his head toward the corral by the barn, and Del caught a flash of black and white. Even from where she stood she heard the horse nicker.

"Yeah, I think I do." Del felt a grin spread across her face, and she almost ran to the corral. She climbed in without hesitation and stared for a moment at the horse she thought she'd never see again. "Hey there, girl."

Del reached Queen and scratched her neck under her mane. The rest of the herd quickly closed in on her, nuzzling her clothes and sniffing for treats. Only Ghost hung back like she always did.

Then Del wrapped her arms around Queen's neck, resting her cheek on the horse's shoulder. She might not know what would happen next week, but she knew one thing for sure. It was time to stop running.

ABOUT THE AUTHOR

C. J. has loved to read since she was a kid dragging home bags of books from the library. When she was twelve she started dreaming about becoming a published author. That dream came true when her first novel *Thicker than Blood* won the 2008 Jerry B. Jenkins Christian Writers Guild Operation First Novel contest. It became the first book in the Thicker than Blood series, which also includes *Bound by Guilt*, *Ties that Bind*, and now *Running on Empty*. She has also written *Jupiter Winds*, the first book in a teen space adventure series. C. J. lives in Pennsylvania with her family and their menagerie of dogs and a Paint mare named Sky.

Visit her Web site at www.cjdarlington.com

Visit the Mountainview Books, LLC website for news on all our books:

www.mountainviewbooks.com

CPSIA information can be obtained at www.ICGtesting.com
Printed in the USA
BVOW05s0821121215

430055BV00003B/40/P